THE WHITE HORSE TRICK

D1332069

Kate Thompson

RED FOX

THE WHITE HORSE TRICK
A RED FOX BOOK 978 1 862 30941 8

First published in Great Britain by The Bodley Head,
an imprint of Random House Children's Books
A Random House Group company

Bodley Head edition published 2009
This editon published 2010

1 3 5 7 9 10 8 6 4 2

Copyright © Kate Thompson, 2009

The Random House Group Limited supports the Forest Stewardship Council (FSC),
the leading international forest certification organization. All our titles that are printed on
Greenpeace-approved FSC-certified paper carry the FSC logo. Our paper procurement
policy can be found at www.rbooks.co.uk/environment.

Set in Bembo

RANDOM HOUSE CHILDREN'S BOOKS
61–63 Uxbridge Road, London W5 5SA

www.**kids**at**random**house.co.uk
www.**rbooks**.co.uk

Addresses for companies within The Random House Group Limited
can be found at: www.randomhouse.co.uk/offices.htm

THE RANDOM HOUSE GROUP Limited Reg. No. 954009

A CIP catalogue record for this book is available from the British Library.

Printed int he UK by CPI Bookmarque, Croydon, CR0 4TD

THE WHITE HORSE TRICK

Also by Kate Thompson:

The Switchers Trilogy
Switchers
Midnight's Choice
Wild Blood
The Switchers Trilogy
(3 in 1)

The Missing Link Trilogy
The Missing Link
Only Human
Origins

The Beguilers
(CBI Bisto Award 2002)

The Alchemist's Apprentice
(CBI Bisto Award 2003)

Annan Water
(CBI Bisto Award 2005)

The New Policeman Trilogy
The New Policeman
(Guardian Fiction Prize 2005,
Whitbread Children's Book Award 2005,
CBI Bisto Award 2006
and Dublin Airport Authority Children's Book Award 2005)
The Last of the High Kings
The White Horse Trick

The Fourth Horseman

Creature of the Night

For younger readers:
Highway Robbery

For Mother Earth and all her children

The idea for this book arose out of my research into climate change during a three-month residence in Bristol. This was initiated and supported by the RSA Arts and Ecology Centre (www.RSAartsandecology.org.uk), working with Situations, a Bristol-based research and commissioning organization (www.situations.org.uk). The residency was generously funded by the Calouste Gulbenkian Foundation. It was a wonderful opportunity to spend time learning at my own speed and in my own style, and I would like to acknowledge the financial and practical help I received. Particular thanks to Claire Doherty and Katharine Daly for facilitating the somewhat unpredictable directions of my research.

Kate Thompson, 2009

PART ONE

THE END

1

They came in the dead of night when the family was sleeping. If there had been any dogs left they might have heard the men approaching, but there weren't. There hadn't been dogs there for years. Who could afford to feed dogs? So the people had to listen for themselves in the night, and even though they all slept lightly, with one ear open, the violence of the wind and the rattling, gurgling torrents of rain engulfed the house in noise, and the sound of approaching footsteps was lost in the din.

The first things the family heard were the crash of the front door breaking down and the yelling of dangerous men as they burst in. It was a small house. There was no back door and nowhere to hide. The mother and her two children jumped out of their beds just as a heavy boot smashed through the door of the bedroom. A powerful beam of light blinded them all and made the children, who had never seen a working torch before, reverse into the corner, wailing in terror.

'Take whatever you want!' the woman said. 'There's

apples in the larder. Potatoes. Take everything, we won't stop you. Just leave us in peace!'

'We don't want your apples,' said a man's voice, deep and powerful, as though it came from an enormous chest. 'We only want the boy. Hand him over and there won't be any more trouble.'

'No.' The mother clung to her children, one arm around each of them. They gripped her hands and stared like night creatures into the light. When the torch beam dropped for a moment, they could see dark figures gathered behind it, huge ones, all of them slick and shiny from the rain.

'Don't be a fool,' the same man said.

'Get out of here!' the mother yelled. 'Leave us alone!' She pushed the children behind her into the corner and stood between them and the advancing men, as though her thin, frail body could possibly deter them from taking whatever they wanted. But she had to try. She had already lost too much.

'Just the boy.' The torch came closer, the dark, hulking figures of the men behind it.

'No. You're not having him.' Her husband had set out to search for firewood on a winter's morning three years ago. She had begged him not to go and she had been right to. He had never returned. He was dead in a ditch somewhere – killed for the firewood he had found or perhaps for nothing, just because he was in the wrong place at the wrong time. A year later, her elder son had slipped away in the night and joined the army. She couldn't bear to lose his brother as well.

'Hand him over,' said the man. 'Commander's orders.' He was right in front of her. She could smell his breath, but because of the torch beam in her eyes she still couldn't see his face.

'But why? What do you want with him? You've already got my other boy.'

They took them young into the castle army, she knew that, but not this young. Billy had just turned seven. There was only one reason for taking him that she could think of, and that was to put him to work on the terraces. The idea filled her with horror. She would die before she would allow that to happen to him.

But the argument was over, and she was suddenly struggling with slippery waterproofs and the heavy men inside them. It was entirely useless. They pushed her aside, dragged Billy out of the desperate grip of his sister and took him, flailing and screaming, away with them. She tried to follow, but one of the men stayed behind to delay them. He stood in the doorway, as big and heavy as a boulder, and just as immovable. When the mother grew tired of fighting him, she went to the kitchen and picked up a heavy frying pan, but by the time she got back to the door he had gone out and closed it behind him, and was holding it to prevent her getting out.

She changed tactics and sneaked away to climb through a window, but the windows were small and it took too long, and already it was far too late. The door-blocker had outwitted her and vanished into the darkness, and there was no way of knowing which way he had gone.

2

The other men, taking it in turns to carry Billy, were already far away, striding through the storm across the uneven surface of the Burren. From time to time one of them would slip or stumble and curse the rocky ground and the darkness, but they didn't turn on their torch, so Billy had no idea where he was being taken.

He was tucked under strong arms and draped over massive shoulders. He squirmed and kicked and punched, but he was wasting his energy. These men were too strong and too determined for him, and eventually he exhausted himself and submitted to captivity. For a long, long time the men walked on, neither ascending nor descending but keeping on fairly level ground and skirting sinister black lakes that glistened in the darkness like windows into hell. Gusts of wind rocked the men so hard that sometimes they lost their balance and their footing, and had to hang on to one another to stay upright. And sometimes, when the wind dropped for a minute, Billy would shout out, 'Where are you taking me?' or 'What are you going to do with me?'

But although the men mumbled and grumbled

to each other, none of them bothered to answer him.

The front door and the bedroom door were both broken, and the best Billy's mother could do in the darkness was to prop furniture against them to keep them closed. It wasn't enough to stop the wind from blowing in, though, and for most of the night the storm tore through the house, drenching everything it touched, and rattling and rocking and shaking and breaking anything that moved. There was no more sleep to be had for mother or daughter that night. They huddled together beneath a couple of damp blankets, reassuring each other as well as they could. Finally, in the early hours of the morning, the wind dropped quite suddenly, and left them feeling frightened and alone, listening to the silence.

Sometimes Billy's ribs hurt from lying over a brawny shoulder, and sometimes his back hurt because he was under someone's arm and his legs were dangling at the wrong angle, but none of the men ever carried him for very long, and every few minutes he was passed from one to another, so he could exchange one kind of cramp or pain for a different one. It felt to him as if his fear and discomfort would never end, but eventually he sensed that they had begun to go downhill, and a short time after that the storm gave one last violent heave, which almost knocked them all off their feet, and then decided to call it a day. The rain came at them from above instead of from the sides. Then it, too, stopped, and the darkness all around them was suddenly silent and, just as suddenly, warm.

The man who was carrying Billy gave a great sigh and slapped him on the back in a way that was almost friendly.

'Nearly there now,' he said.

'Where?' said Billy. 'Nearly where now?'

But he got no answer, and no one spoke to him again. Their pace slowed as the terrain underfoot became more difficult, with bigger rocks and loose stones, and then the torch went on again, blinding Billy with its sudden brilliance. There was a lot of scuffling and grunting among the men, as though they were trying to manoeuvre something heavy, but he couldn't see what it was. He was pushed quickly through a narrow gap and on to some kind of floor; then he heard a door closing and more grunting, and then the sound of the men's footsteps departing.

'Hey!' he called out after them. 'What about me?'

There was no answer. Billy listened. He could hear the irregular dripping of rainwater from the roof, and something else as well. Someone breathing. His blood ran cold.

'Hello?' His voice was tight with fear.

'Hello,' said a voice. Another child, like him. It didn't sound nervous, or threatening either.

Billy let out his breath. 'What's happening?' he said. 'Where is this place?'

'We don't know,' said the child. 'All we know is that we're locked in here and we can't get out.'

3

At first light, the woman and her daughter set out for the castle to find out what had become of Billy. Their journey was a slow and cautious one. The storm might have ended but its aftermath still affected their progress. During the woman's lifetime the rainfall had increased so much that new lakes had developed. Some of them were temporary, and came and went depending on the rainfall, but others were more permanent and only dried up when, once every three or four years, there was a prolonged drought. These new lakes had changed the landscape, filling up every hollow and flooding the low points in the valleys. It meant that a lot of the old roads and paths had become blocked and new ways had to be found. So mother and daughter made for the high ground and followed the ridges of the hills wherever they could, staying just beneath the horizon so as not to be seen, because it was dangerous to be out and about in the wild places, by day as well as by night.

There were no trees or bushes to give cover, but the Burren was full of boulders and crevices, and as they approached castle territory they slowed down and stayed low, and managed to creep from one hiding place to the next without being seen. When the notorious terraces came into view, they concealed themselves behind an outcrop of limestone and settled in to observe the scene. The mother knew what went on here and she wished she could prevent her daughter from seeing it, but it was too dangerous now for them to be separated and they had to find out whether Billy was there or not.

The castle stood on a broad shoulder of Sliabh Carran. To its west was a series of shallow cliffs known as the stony steps. To the north, the windowless face of the castle looked out over the sea, and on its opposite side, facing south, the hillside sloped gently down towards a shallow lake which had once been the meadows and woods at the foot of the great cliff called Eagle's Rock. It was on this slope that the terraces were being built.

The weather patterns had changed. Ireland had always had a wet and windy climate, but over the past few decades the storms had increased in frequency and severity, and now, throughout the whole region, the soil was being washed away; swept into streams and rivers and carried out to sea. The woman and her family were, in that respect, among the luckier ones. Their garden lay on a gentle slope, which was sheltered on two sides by high crags, and the lie of the land meant that most of the rainfall was channelled down one side of it. Even so, the rain washed the nutrients out of the soil faster than they could be replaced, and every year the vegetables were smaller and harder to grow.

But at least they still had something. They were looking down now on the ones who had nothing; the poor souls whose farms and gardens had failed completely and who had been rounded up by the commander's army and brought here to work. The 'Social Welfare Project' is what the soldiers called it, but everyone knew that it was a labour camp, pure and simple, and that there was no prospect of any kind of life beyond it. People worked on it until they died. They were out there now, the old and the young, lugging rocks or baskets of soil, building walls, grinding stones for mortar. Almost everyone these days was thin, but these people were more than thin. They were just skin and bone; so emaciated that it was amazing they could still stand, let alone labour all day in the sun and the storms.

Indeed, it soon became clear that not all of them could. An old man staggered and sat down, resting the rock he was carrying in his lap as though it were too precious to drop. One of the soldiers on guard watched him, but he said and did nothing. The woman tore her eyes away from the scene and examined the children instead. They were working among the adults, doing the same jobs and wearing the same hopeless expressions. Their bodies were thin and stiff, with none of the grace and energy that children ought to have.

'Do you see him?' she whispered to her daughter.

'No. He's not there.'

'Right. I want you to wait here and stay out of sight. I won't be long.'

'Why? Where are you going?'

'To the barracks. I'm going to try and find out what's going on.'

But she paused a moment longer. The old man lay down on his back, the rock on his belly. He struggled to get up, but failed. The soldier prodded him with his boot, then bent down and pushed the rock off him. Still he didn't get up.

The worst of it was that all these suffering people were fighting a losing battle. What they were attempting to do was build a series of walls across the hill to hold in the soil and stop it from being washed away, but it was clear that they were failing. The storm of the previous night had left its mark on the works. There was a clear trail made by one of the raging streams that appeared all across the land whenever that kind of torrential rain fell. It had broken through walls and washed stones, even quite big ones, down the hillside. It had poured across the vegetable plots, uprooted plants and gouged out precious topsoil in long gaping gashes. There were still some crops remaining, mostly beans and beetroot and cabbage, but the plants were small and weedy and their leaves were yellow from the lack of goodness in the ground.

4

Billy slept, and when he woke up it was broad daylight. There were two other children in there – a girl of about his age and a boy who was a bit younger. Both of them were still asleep, so Billy set about examining the surroundings.

They were in a funny little house which seemed to be made out of plastic and tin. It had two rooms, one with beds in and another with sofas and a table, and a little old cooker and a sink, neither of which worked. Beside the bedroom was a tiny bathroom with a smelly toilet bucket and a basin of water. There were windows everywhere, but they were made of plastic and they were all scratched and cloudy. In any case, it seemed to Billy that they all looked out on to high stone walls, so there was nothing to be seen outside them anyway.

'What are we doing here?' he asked the others when they woke up. Neither of them knew. They just shrugged and yawned and scratched themselves.

'Well, I'm getting out,' Billy said.

The door was narrow and had more of that plastic

glass in the top half. Billy put his face up against it, but it was scratched like the others and he could see nothing outside except for vague grey shapes in a misty white gloom. The handle moved when Billy turned it, but there must have been some kind of lock on the outside, because the door wouldn't open. He pushed it with his shoulder and thumped on it with all his strength, but it wouldn't budge. He tried the windows next, tugging and hammering on the old fastenings, but they were rock-solid as well, as if they had rusted into place.

'It's no good,' said the girl. 'We've tried all that already. There's no way to get out.'

She didn't seem to be very upset about it, and nor did the young boy. 'It's not so bad,' he said. 'We don't have to work in the garden like we did at home.'

'And no housework or cooking,' said the girl. 'We get more food here, too.' She pointed to a large pot beside the sink. Billy opened it. It was full of stew – barley and beans from the look of it. 'They bring it every night.'

'I don't care,' said Billy. 'I hate them. I'm not going to eat their food.'

'That's what I said to begin with,' said the boy, 'but you'll eat it when you get hungry enough. There's nothing else to do.'

He took a worn and bent spoon out of his pocket and began to tuck in.

5

The commander-in-chief had his feet up and was watching a DVD and having a cup of tea. A knock came at the door. One of his private guards put his head round it.

'Message from the general, sir,' he said.

'At this time of night?' The commander hit the pause button on the remote. 'It better be important.'

The guard stood aside and a soldier came into the room. He was very small. His camouflage fatigues and his boots were several sizes too big for him. He didn't look much more than ten or eleven years old, but his eyes were hard and clear, and there was nothing youthful or innocent about them.

'Out with it,' said the commander. 'What's the message?'

'Where's my brother?' said the boy.

'You what?' said the commander, so astonished by the child's effrontery that he couldn't come up with a more forceful way to respond.

'My brother,' said the soldier. 'Your men kidnapped him last night. What have you done with him?'

The guard, realizing that he had been tricked, stepped forward to get hold of the boy and throw him out, but he was too slow. The little soldier was already halfway across the room and was launching himself at the commander-in-chief. As he hit him, hot sugary tea erupted from the commander's mug and sloshed all over both of them.

The guard grabbed the boy by the collar and hauled him off the commander, but he could do nothing to stop his wildly kicking feet landing several bruising blows. 'Where is he?' the boy was yelling. 'What have you done with him, you fat, evil toad? It was your people who took him! Your goons in their waterproofs. I know it was them. What do you want with him? Where is he?'

The boy continued to struggle and swear, but the guard had a better grip on him now and his flailing feet couldn't connect with their target. Slowly, menacingly, the commander stood up. His face was broad and fleshy, and it was flushed with rage. With the edge of a feather duvet he wiped at the sticky tea.

'You'll pay for that, you little worm,' he said.

More guards appeared in the room, alerted by the noise. The commander stopped the first of them in his tracks.

'Fetch the general,' he said. 'Right now!'

The guard didn't even pause to turn up his collar, but plunged straight out into the rain. While he waited for him to return, the commander paced up and down the room, struggling to control his temper, casting the occasional vicious glance at the boy soldier. Then running footsteps crossed the inner courtyard and the guard returned, breathless. Behind him, more measured footsteps could be heard approaching, and the general calmly opened the door and came in. His eye fell on the soldier and he shook his head disapprovingly.

'What's been happening here?' he said.

'I'll tell you what's been happening,' said the commander. 'This young gutter rat has lied his way in and accused me of kidnapping his brother.'

'He did kidnap him,' said Pup, still struggling to get free from the guard. 'His men took him away last night.'

'I want him punished,' said the commander. 'I can't have this kind of thing going on in my armed forces.'

'Quite right,' said the general. 'I'll make sure he doesn't do it again.'

'Oh, he won't do it again,' said the commander. 'There will be no fear of that. I want to see him court-martialled at eight o'clock tomorrow morning, and then I want the entire army gathered outside the castle at nine. There's only one way to stop this kind of mutinous behaviour. I want him shot by firing squad in front of all your men.'

The general paled, and for a moment he seemed at a loss for words. Then he regained his composure and turned to the guard, who was still holding on to the squirming boy.

'Put him in the lock-up,' he said. 'The rest of you leave

us alone for a few minutes. I want to talk to the commander-in-chief in private.'

The guards glanced at their boss. He thought long and hard, and finally nodded. Reluctantly, taking the boy soldier with them, the guards left.

'Well?' said the commander. 'This better be good.'

'What's this about kidnapping children?' said the general. 'What are you up to this time?'

'I'm working on a plan, as it happens,' said the commander. 'I'll let you in on it if and when you need to know. Until then it's none of your business.'

'It's my business when it causes problems in the army,' said the general. 'You can't just go shooting my soldiers. I'll have a mutiny on my hands.'

The commander-in-chief stepped up close and pushed a finger into the other man's chest. 'If you have problems with control, then maybe I'll have to find someone who doesn't,' he said.

Quietly but firmly, the general pushed the finger aside. 'You could do that,' he said. 'Or for once in your life you could try thinking outside the box.'

'Oh?' said the commander, with heavy sarcasm. 'Please enlighten me.'

'I have a much, much better idea of what to do with that soldier,' said the general. 'In fact, I've come up with an idea that could solve all our problems in one fell swoop.'

'All our problems?' said the commander, grinning in disbelief.

'Most of them anyway,' said the general. 'We have too many mouths to feed and not enough to put in them. I've thought of a way we can make the old and the sick productive. We'll all benefit from it. It'll be all winners and no losers. And best of all, no more bony old corpses to dispose of.'

'Really?' said the commander-in-chief. 'Sounds way too good to be true. You'd better sit down and tell me all about it.'

So the general did, and the commander listened carefully, uncharacteristically quiet. His silence continued long after the general had finished, and when he finally did speak, his voice was full of disdain.

'Ridiculous,' he said. 'It's a childish fantasy.'

'I don't agree,' said the general.

'Well, even if worked, which I don't think it will, how do you intend to pay for it? Didn't you ever discover that there's no such thing as a free lunch?'

'Indeed,' said the general. 'And I don't expect to get anything for nothing. I have it all worked out, and I know exactly what I'm going to offer in exchange.'

6

It was not unknown for people to stumble across the time skin into Tír na n'Óg, but Jenny had never heard of so many people coming in at once. There were seven of them altogether, and they stood looking around them in the middle of the main street.

All of them were wet through and covered in mud, as if they had just crawled up out of a ditch. Six of them were old, or if not old, then exhausted and worn out. They were emaciated. Their clothes were drab, mud-coloured, patched and re-patched. They stared around with disbelieving eyes, entirely lost and bewildered. But the seventh was quite different. He was young, just a boy, and very small. He was dressed in camouflage fatigues and enormous brown boots. And across his shoulder, the business end pointing skywards, was a very serious piece of weaponry.

It made Jenny nervous, and when the boy walked towards her, she had to work hard to control her in-clination to turn him into something less harmful. There was, she realized, no immediate danger. She would have plenty of time to act if things got rough.

'Where's the stuff?' he said.

'Stuff?' said Jenny. 'What stuff?'

'Stuff,' he said. 'We're here to get supplies. We can pay for anything we take. We brought—' He stopped, as if he wasn't entirely sure what they had brought. Then he went on, 'Where are the shops and the pubs?'

Jenny gestured towards the low, dark building beside them. It wasn't exactly a shop, but in the other Kinvara, where Jenny had once lived, it had been Fallons' supermarket. All seven of the newcomers looked through the glassless windows at the gloomy interior, where dusty, rickety old shelves held nothing but a few sprouting potatoes and wilted cabbages. A furious roar came from within and made everyone jump, including Jenny. The boy got a grip on his gun and turned it round, but he still kept the muzzle pointing towards the sky. There was another yell from inside the shop.

'What the hell is happening over there?'

Aengus Óg appeared in the doorway. He, too, was soaked to the skin but, unlike the others, he wasn't muddy.

'And who the hell are you lot?' he bellowed at the strangers.

They reversed rapidly towards the other side of the street, all except the boy, who stood his ground. Jenny noticed his fingers tightening around the stock of the rifle.

'Calm down, Daddy,' she said.

Aengus turned his wild gaze on Jenny, and it was as well that she was his favourite daughter, because he was angry enough to cause some serious havoc.

'How did you get so wet?' she asked him.

'High tide on the other side.' He looked back into the dark interior of the shop. 'Very, very high tide.'

'Ah,' said Jenny smugly. 'It's really happening, then. I told you it would.'

'What?' said Aengus. 'What did you tell me would happen?'

'Global warming,' she said. 'I read it in the winds of change before I came over.' She had also read about it in the newspapers and heard everyone around her talking about it, but she saw no reason to tell Aengus that. 'I told you all about it. The Greenland ice melting. Sea levels rising. Remember?'

'Oh, that stuff,' said Aengus sourly. 'End of ploddy existence and all that. It's all very well, but where am I supposed to go to get my tobacco now that Fallons' is gone?'

Jenny shrugged. 'Try Gort,' she said.

'Gort?' said Aengus Óg. 'Gort!?'

Jenny remembered the stories she had heard about how Aengus had been stationed in Gort when he was a policeman, long before she was born. It clearly didn't fill him with happy memories.

'Have you got a better idea?' she said.

If he had, Aengus Óg didn't share it. He turned his

attention back to the newcomers. 'Who are these people? What do they think they're doing here?'

No one answered. Aengus looked at the boy soldier. 'Is that thing a gun?' he said.

'Don't worry about it, Daddy,' said Jenny. 'I'll take care of things here.'

There was an explosion of salt water and black feathers, and Aengus Óg, in the form of a raven, flew up above the rooftops and set off in the direction of Gort.

In the main street of Kinvara there was a long, long silence. The boy watched the raven until it was out of sight. The others watched Jenny fearfully, as though they expected that she, too, might turn into something nasty. She toyed with the idea briefly, but these people were too pathetic to play games with. She found she almost felt sorry for them.

One of the old women turned to the others and spoke for the first time. 'I told you. We've died and gone to hell.'

It was the boy soldier who answered her. 'It doesn't look like hell to me,' he said. 'It looks more like heaven.'

'How would you know?' said the old woman. 'What would you know of heaven or hell at your age? People don't turn into ravens in heaven, I can tell you that much.'

'But look around you,' the boy said. 'The sun is shining. Everyone is healthy and happy. It feels peaceful and safe, doesn't it?'

'But none of this can be here,' she said. 'I told you that

already. This place is like Kinvara was in the old days, but we all know Kinvara isn't there any more.'

'Well, it is here,' said Jenny, deciding it was time to get involved. 'It always has been and it always will be. The only new and surprising thing here is you people. So why don't you start at the beginning and tell me how you got here?'

'We met a man with a beard,' said the boy soldier. 'He was out on the hillside looking for a goat. He told us to come this way and we'd find the stuff.'

'That'd be Devaney,' said Jenny. 'But how did you get into Tír na n'Óg in the first place?'

'Tír na n'Óg?' said the boy. 'Is that where we are?'

'It is,' said Jenny. 'So what are you doing here?'

'We were sent,' said the boy. 'We're running out of everything. If we don't get new supplies soon, we'll all be finished.'

7

The general looked over his gathered army. It seemed to him that every day the men were more dispirited, but when he called them to attention, they made some kind of an effort at least, standing a bit straighter, pulling their heels together, shouldering weapons.

He walked along the rows. The soldiers were in desperately bad shape. Many of them were ill: coughing or sneezing or running temperatures. Their uniforms were rotting on their backs, their boots letting in water, and there was only one waterproof jacket for every three men. None of it was their fault. It wasn't his, either.

'Present arms!'

They did. The general retraced his steps, checking the rifles for cleanliness and safety. Some of them were worn out or broken, and others were useless because there was no ammunition left to fit them, but all the soldiers carried them anyway, because the people they aimed them at were unlikely to know which ones were working and which ones weren't.

When he had completed his inspection and arrived

back where he started, the general stood up on a concrete block and addressed the army.

'A-Troop on terrace duty.'

There was a moan so faint that it could barely be heard, and it certainly couldn't be identified as coming from any one individual. The general ignored it.

'C-Troop to Tubber for tax collection. D-Troop on castle guard. B-Troop to Carron under the command of Colonel Crowley, to bring back any remaining people from the settlement there. And I'm going to want four volunteers to accompany those people on a raiding party through the old fort when they get here.'

There was a sudden and total silence. All the coughs and the running noses and itching heads and feet were suddenly forgotten, and not one soldier moved a muscle.

'Come on,' said the general. 'Four volunteers.'

The men were so quiet that everyone could clearly hear the rats on the rubbish tip, rummaging among the empty cans.

'Right, then,' he went on. 'Since there are no volunteers I will pick the men.'

He began to walk along the lines again. The youngest or the oldest? The fittest or the frailest? He had been bothered by the same problem the last time and the time before. He knew he hadn't planned his campaign well. He ought to have sent the raiding parties through much closer together, instead of leaving so much time between them, before the men began to realize that the first lot might not be coming back. So should he pick the most reliable men or the least reliable? The ones he liked best or the ones he liked least? It was going to be a hard decision, but there was no one who could make it except him.

There was a whipping noise in the air above and he looked up. A massive raven flew low over their heads, quite clearly looking down at the men gathered there below it. The general held his breath. There were plenty of ravens up there in the mountains – they were one of the few species that were doing well out of the changing weather patterns. But there was something disturbingly different about this one.

'Dismissed,' he said to the army. 'Get ready for your operations. We'll sort out the volunteers later.'

The men ambled off through the rain towards their quarters, but the general stayed where he was. The raven had circled and was coming in again, right over his head. It had a knowing look, and he was struck by a powerful sense of recognition that he couldn't quite bring himself to accept. A raven was a raven, after all. Just a bird.

Under normal circumstances it was, anyway.

8

Aengus Óg was pondering over a sense of recognition as well. He had seen that tall old man somewhere before, but he couldn't for the life of him remember when or where. That was one of the problems with ploddies. They didn't stay the same. One day they were young and full of future, and the next time you saw them they had one foot in the grave.

But the mystery ploddy was of little interest compared to the other things Aengus was seeing as he flew overhead. This world always changed between his visits, but he had never before seen changes as drastic as these. The most astonishing one was the complete disappearance of Kinvara. It had vanished beneath the waves, along with the outlying townlands of Aughinish, Doorus, Mountscribe, Croshua, Moy and Funshin. The sea now covered the plain all the way up to the hills, and it was as though the little town and its surrounding farms had never been.

And the sea itself looked different, too. It had carved a new coastline for itself at the foot of Sliabh Carran; new cliffs, a whole set of small rocky islands, where miserable seabirds crouched. The remains of boats and fishing nets were strewn about all over the place, and there was no sign of any new ones out on the sea. It gave Aengus the impression that the love-hate relationship between the ocean and the fishermen who lived their lives upon it was over, once and for all, and that the sea had definitively won. And although it was calm just then, the water had a dark and brooding aspect, which made him think that it wouldn't be calm for long.

There were changes on the land as well. JJ Liddy's house, which Aengus had been visiting for generations, was abandoned and roofless, nothing remaining but the shells of a few of the old rooms, all filled with ivy and brambles. Some of the other houses in the foothills were still standing, but only just. Ropes and sandbags held their roofs on. Hay sheds and barns had lost their corrugated iron and all that remained were the girders, rapidly being eaten away by rust. There were no trees anywhere. Even the hazel scrub was gone, as if grazed to the ground by some huge and voracious ruminant. The Carron road was washed to rubble and there wasn't a motor vehicle to be seen.

And then, in the middle of it all, there was this extraordinary thing. Aengus flew over the castle and the barracks again, uncertain of what it was he was seeing. It looked like something made out of building blocks by a child, except that the blocks were massive, each one of them big enough for four sets to dance in. Somehow they had been piled up on top of each other and made into walls. But how? And why?

He circled the complex again, flew close to the tall ploddy for one last look, then went on his way towards Gort. But the whole thing with the sea and the boats and the tumbledown houses gave him a very bad feeling. It gave him a feeling of dread that weighed down his glossy black wings, because it didn't look at all like the kind of world where he would be likely to find a packet of his favourite tobacco.

9

The conversation with the wet people had turned out to be very unsettling. Or, if Jenny were to be completely honest with herself, not so much unsettling as intriguing and delicious. The rise in sea levels had been predicted, and so had the storms and the heavy rainfall and the occasional ferocious droughts. What hadn't been so well predicted, at least by the time Jenny had finished growing and come to live in Tír na n'Óg, was the social consequences of the changing climate.

From what the wet people said, they were devastating. As the rising sea drove them from their homes, the people of Kinvara and the surrounding townlands made for the hills. Some of them were lucky and moved into old houses or were given a piece of land by a good-hearted farmer, where they managed to construct some kind of rough habitation for themselves. Others, mainly the late-comers, were not so lucky. They had to find what shelter they could among the rocks and the scrubland. Very few of these people survived.

It wasn't only small places like Kinvara that were

affected. Dublin was deluged as well, and countless major cities around the world. International trade had collapsed, supermarkets had closed, governments had lost control and dissolved. Looting and gang warfare took over in the cities, and in the country areas, new warlords arose and introduced their own violent forms of government. But now there was nothing left to loot or raid, and that was why the muddy people had been sent through the souterrain to collect supplies. They needed them desperately, not just for the castle, but for the hundreds of people who were dependent upon it.

'What kind of supplies are you looking for?' Jenny asked the boy soldier.

'All kinds,' he said. 'Anything you can eat or drink. Livestock. Firewood. All the basic necessities.'

'I see,' said Jenny. 'Well, why don't you people just relax here in the sunshine for a while and I'll go and talk to my father about it.'

'Your father?' said the old woman. 'I thought he had just turned himself into a raven and flown away.'

'Oh, he has,' said Jenny. 'But I have another father as well, and he may be more use to you. I won't be long.'

The wretched little raiding party watched her as she ambled away down the main street, clearly not in any hurry at all. Nothing here made any sense to them, but unaccountably they found that they were not worried about it. In fact, when they thought about it, they found that they were no longer worried about anything at all.

10

As Aengus Óg had feared, Gort did not look promising. It was a long way inland and the sea hadn't reached it, but parts of it were flooded all the same. The river that ran through the centre of the town had burst its banks and, judging by the ruinous state of the inundated buildings on either side, it was a regular, if not permanent, condition.

On the outskirts of the town there was another kind of flood, caused by saturation of the land by heavy rain. When Aengus had last been there, hundreds of new houses were being built around the town. They were all in ruins now, some of them undermined by floods and others just fallen down. The only part of the town that appeared to be intact was the higher end of the main street. Everything else – including, he was delighted to see, the Garda station where he had once been stationed – was either derelict or submerged.

Even the bit that had survived did not look good. The cheerful shop-fronts that Aengus remembered, with their bright signs and colourful window displays, had disappeared. All he could see from above was a tiny group

of dingy market stalls in the middle of the road. He v
the point of descending to get a better look wh
sudden powerful squall hit him side on. He beat his w
furiously and regained his balance in the air, but he v
out of danger yet. Another gust hit him and
knocked him out of the sky. He flapped desperatel
turned his back to the wind, which caught him up and
drove him ahead of it at a hundred miles an hour across
the ruined town and in the direction of Loughrea.

Aengus now saw the weakness in his plan. He had
often become a raven — it was the best way of covering
distance at speed — but he had never flown in storm
conditions before. The weather in Tír na n'Óg was perpet-
ually perfect and on this side he had, he supposed, always
been lucky. The trouble was, he only knew the basics of
flying and none of the advanced stuff. Like, was it safer to
fly against the wind, at the risk of exhausting himself, or
to let its unpredictable currents carry him along, at the risk
of being dashed into a tree or a hillside? Luckily for him,
he didn't have to work it out. He had a third option, un-
available to the average raven. He took it, and burst
through the time skin into the bright calm of Tír na
n'Óg's eternal sunshine.

11

JJ was sitting on a beer barrel. He had his fiddle out but
there were no tunes, because Devaney had not come back
with the goat. Jenny perched on the edge of the table
between JJ and her ploddy mother, Aisling. Her fairy
mother, Drowsy Maggie, was sitting at the other side of
the table, dozing over her fiddle.

'Some people have arrived,' Jenny said.

'What kind of people?' said JJ.

Jenny thought for a moment, then said, 'Wet people.
And a soldier boy.'

JJ scratched his head. 'A soldier boy?'

Jenny watched him thinking, amazed by his white
hair and the way he and Aisling had got smaller since she
used to live with them. Well, not smaller exactly, but
slighter. For the first eleven years of her life she had
believed that JJ was her father and Aisling was her mother.
And even when she discovered the truth – that she was a
fairy changeling sent to the ploddy world to grow up –
she had decided to stay on with the Liddys until she was
old enough to come and live in Tír na n'Óg. That time had

come when she was nearly seventeen, and the parting with the Liddys had been a sorrowful one. But they had all known, even then, that they would probably meet again.

No time passed in Tír na n'Óg, so Jenny was still sixteen, going on seventeen, and that's the way she would stay, unless and until she decided to return to the other side of the time skin for a spell. But over there JJ and Aisling had continued to grow older, and the demands of family and other worldly preoccupations had kept them busy until they were both nearly seventy. By then the effects of climate change were already well under way and there was nothing anyone could do to stop it happening. The best thing for all concerned was for them to get out and leave the farm and the house to the next generation.

It wasn't a sudden decision. Jenny had known that JJ and Aisling planned to retire to Tír na n'Óg. But even so, nothing had prepared her for the shock of seeing how much they had both aged, and she was still having trouble getting used to it.

'So what are they doing here, these wet people?' said Aisling.

'Well, that's the thing,' said Jenny. 'They're looking for stuff.'

'Stuff? What kind of stuff?'

'Provisions,' said Jenny. 'They're running out of things to eat on the other side. And firewood, and clothes. Everything, apparently. So they've been sent over to get all that kind of stuff and take it back with them.'

.

'The nerve of them,' said JJ.

'Well,' said Jenny, 'it's not quite as simple as that.'

'How come?' said JJ.

'It wasn't their idea, you see. They were sent, under strict orders. That's why the soldier boy is with them, to make sure they do what they're told.'

'So who sent them?' said Aisling, and there was something in the tone of her voice that told Jenny she wasn't too keen on hearing the answer.

'General Liddy did,' she said.

'General Liddy?' said JJ. 'Oh, no. It has to be Aidan, doesn't it? Calling himself a general now, is he?'

'Afraid not, Dad,' said Jenny. 'That's what I thought, too. But the soldier boy is quite certain about it. General Liddy's first name isn't Aidan. It's Donal.'

12

Never in his wildest dreams had Donal Liddy imagined he would become a military officer. But then, never in his wildest dreams had he imagined the world he now found himself living in. Much as he disliked his brother Aidan, he had to give him credit for his foresight. Because Aidan had imagined this world, and he had set himself up to be its most powerful man. He had started early, when most people were still in denial about what was happening, and he had done it in the most ingenious of ways. He had spotted opportunities where no one else had, and he had invested and gambled his way into a small fortune by the time he was twenty-five. And then he had set out to spend it.

One of the first things he had done was to buy dozens of road-transport containers when the scarcity of oil made them too expensive to cart around the roads any longer. His castle, up on the hillside above the farm, was made from them. They were stacked four high in an unbroken circular wall, practically impenetrable to anyone who wasn't invited inside. The army barracks, just a couple of hundred metres from the castle, was built from them as well. Some of the containers had been converted into living quarters and others into storage rooms. They were inelegant heaps of rust by now but they continued to serve their purpose.

In a partitioned corner of one of them, Donal Liddy was huddled over a tiny pot-bellied stove. His second-in-command was huddled there, too, wheezing and coughing and, from time to time, spitting dark phlegm into the fire-box. Donal was worried about the colonel's health, which had recently begun to deteriorate rapidly. There were no medicines for the kind of illness he had, and if he followed the usual pattern, he would not last much more than a few months.

Donal wasn't sure that he could do without Curly Crowley. He had been the first officer Donal appointed when Aidan put him in charge of the army twenty-five years ago. Crowley had been a young man then, in his early twenties, but his abilities had already been evident. Within a very short time Donal had come to depend upon him to keep discipline, especially when, as sometimes happened, he himself ran out of conviction and his authority failed.

But it wasn't just that. Despite the horrors and hardships he had seen, Curly Crowley had retained his humanity. There were many others in the army who, unfortunately, had not, and if a time ever came when those men took command, the miserable survivors in Aidan's region were in for an even harder time than they were having now. So Donal worried about Crowley, and gave him as little to do as he could get away with. It made no difference, though. It was the conditions that were killing him, not the work.

The storm rising around them sucked hard at the chimney and hammered the steel walls.

'You can hardly blame them for not wanting to volunteer,' said Crowley. 'If anyone had come back, it would be different. But they have no idea what will happen to them when they go down into that hole. Nor do I, when it comes to it.'

Donal shook water from his woollen hat and drew his chair closer to the stove. Above their heads, rain thundered on the steel roof. From the adjoining containers they could hear soldiers grumbling as they got themselves ready to go out, and arguing about whose turn it was to wear the waterproofs. Aidan had stockpiles of new ones somewhere in his warehouse containers and had promised to release supplies to the army, but he was becoming increasingly miserly as time went on, and there was still no sign of them.

'We're soldiers, Crowley,' said Donal. 'It's not our place to question orders that come down from above.'

'I know that,' said Crowley, 'but—'

'But there are no buts. We're soldiers and there are no buts.'

He reached for some sticks to add to the fire, then

hesitated. It hurt him to burn them. There was almost nothing left now of the hazel scrub that had once occupied all the forgotten corners of the Burren. Since the End of Imports there had been no oil or coal or gas, and firewood had become the main source of fuel. There was still turf, further inland, but those areas were under the control of other warlords. In the past, Donal and his army had made several successful raids and transported good loads of it back to the castle. But those days were gone. The gruelling effects of bad weather and poor nutrition had taken their toll, and the army was no longer capable of any missions as ambitious as that.

And nor, he had to admit, was he. He was sixty-seven last time he remembered to check what year it was. In his father's time sixty-seven was still young, and a man might expect to live for another ten or even twenty years. But in these hard days sixty-seven was old. Few people reached such an age. And with every year that passed Donal felt the cold and damp drilling further into his bones and sapping his remaining strength. He looked at the hazel sticks in his hand and was amazed at how strongly their colour and texture reminded him of his younger days and his visits to the peaceful, magical hazel woods. Reluctantly he surrendered them to the fire.

'No buts, then,' Curly was saying. 'I think your brother has lost his marbles.'

Donal looked up, deeply shocked. For any soldier to speak of his commander-in-chief like that was mutinous. But for anyone at all to speak of Aidan Liddy like that indicated a powerful death wish. Donal cleared his throat.

'Did I hear you correctly, Colonel?'

'Oh, come on, Donal,' said Crowley. 'Let's stop playing these ridiculous games for once. We go back much too far for that.'

It was true. No one knew better than Crowley how Donal ran things and why he operated in the way he did. He knew him through and through. If he hadn't, he would never have dared to speak to him the way he did.

'Look what he's doing,' he went on. 'Sending people down into a hole in the ground and telling them to come back loaded with loot. I could understand it if he was just trying to get rid of a few superfluous old folk, but why does he want to send our men with them?'

Donal had to admit that, from his perspective, Crowley had a point. He wanted to tell him that the whole scheme had been his idea, and not his brother's. And he wanted to tell him how much he longed to go down into that hole himself and never come back. But the time wasn't right, not yet. There were still things to be done. And in any case, he was sure Crowley wouldn't believe him.

He was saved from having to reply by a knock at the door.

'Enter!' he said.

A waterproofed corporal put his head round the door.

'B-Troop all present and correct, sir,' he said. 'Waiting on Colonel Crowley and ready to proceed.'

Crowley gave Donal a long, significant look.

'Dismissed, Colonel,' said Donal. 'Your orders are perfectly clear.'

13

If there had been anyone watching from the ground, they would have been astonished to see the speeding raven vanish from the sky mid-wingbeat. But the land that lay between Gort and Loughrea had been turned from productive farmland into sour, impenetrable bog by the relentless rainfall which fell year round, three years out of four. Nothing lived there now except for marsh birds and frogs, and the occasional gaunt feral dog.

A lot of the west country and the midlands had gone the same way, but Aengus didn't know that. He was back in his own world again, where no winds blew unless ordered to do so by his father, the Dagda, and where the land was just as it had always been and always would be.

He flew back the way he had come until he reached the place that, on the other side of the time skin, was the remains of Gort town. It was a place he disliked intensely, populated as it was by leprechauns, clurichauns and their creepy distant relations, the little red mischief-makers, fír dearg. In the normal course of events Aengus never went near the place, but he was going to have to brave it now if he wanted his tobacco.

He stayed aloft for a while, examining the layout of the town and looking for a good place to land. There was some kind of a market happening down there, and he could see the dogs and sheep of the clurichauns all saddled and bridled and tethered in the market square. If he flew low enough, he could make out the high-pitched, angry bickering of the leprechauns and the drunken ranting of the clurichauns. It was probably a gold market, then. All of them loved gold. The clurichauns liked to exchange it for what they called goods and chattels but essentially amounted to alcoholic drink. The leprechauns loved it because ... well ... they were leprechauns, and leprechauns love gold. Everyone knew that. As for the fír dearg, they were a law unto themselves and no one ever knew what their motives for anything were, other than playing nasty tricks on people and having a great laugh about it.

Aengus circled one last time, as low as he dared. The arguments beneath him seemed to be increasing in intensity and he wondered what the point of these markets was. He couldn't imagine what the clurichauns could possibly possess that would induce the leprechauns to part with their gold, and he strongly suspected that, in fact, no gold changed hands at all. He was wondering whether the leprechauns set them up just for sport, to taunt their drunken cousins, when an accurately aimed boot – a red one, of course – hit him on the head and knocked any further wonderings out of his mind.

He plummeted down towards the heaving market-place. A thousand eyes peered up at him, all as small as shirt buttons. Among them he spotted the red man who, he was sure, had thrown the boot. He was dancing on the spot, laughing and cheering with delight. Aengus dreaded to think what might happen to him if he landed in the middle of that mob. He had always hated leprechauns and dreaded their little hammers. The clurichauns thought they were incredibly suave and witty, but would in fact bore you to death in the course of an evening. As for the fír dearg, there was just no knowing what they might do, and Aengus found he had no desire at all to find out. So once again he took the only escape route he could, and dived through the time skin into the other Gort, the ploddy one. It was a last-ditch effort, and he was only just in time. He landed, very painfully, on the crumbling tarmac remains of the high street, and the shock jolted him out of the bird shape and back into his human one.

He let out a string of furious curses. He was a god, and not at all used to being tossed around by gales and hit on the head by boots. That evil wind was still blowing and the rain was coming down as if there were water cannon up there in the sky instead of clouds. And as if all that wasn't bad enough, when he finally managed to get himself to his feet, he found that he was staring straight down the twin barrels of a shotgun.

14

Donal stayed where he was and listened to the men assembling in the parade ground. Troop by troop they moved off, until there was no sound remaining apart from the wind and rain. Still he didn't move. His bones hurt and his spirits were low. He hated being at odds with Curly Crowley, and wished he could make things right between them. Until he could do that, there was only one remedy for the way he was feeling now.

Mikey.

Donal still experienced a twinge of guilt when he thought about his friend. He knew now that he had not been responsible for Mikey's death, but at the time it happened he had been convinced that he was, and the emotional response to it had never entirely let him out of its grip. He had only been nine, and the old man had been his closest friend outside the family. So when Mikey had asked him for help getting to the top of Sliabh Carran, Donal had agreed. Mikey had said he wanted to stand on the beacon, the massive pile of stones that was up there, one last time before he died. To this day, Donal couldn't decide whether he would have done what he did if he had known Mikey's real reason for going up there. He wasn't like Jenny. Jenny was a fairy, and she didn't see things the same way ordinary people did.

Because she *had* known. She'd known about the ancient peace agreement between the púcas and humans which was symbolized by a hatchet buried deep beneath the stones, and she had known that the púca was trying to break it. She'd known about the ghost that lived up there as well, and that it was the only thing in the human world that could protect the beacon from the púca.

When he thought about the púca, Donal's feelings were mixed. He knew what would have happened if he had managed to get at that hatchet. He had seen the nature god in his warlike form, and his scalp still crawled when he remembered the sight. But seeing the state the world had got into, he couldn't help feeling a certain sympathy for him as well. After all, he had only been trying to save what he had created from the excesses of mankind.

Jenny had helped him take Mikey to the top, that day. The púca had tried to stop them, but she had called upon Aengus Óg, and between them all they had succeeded. Donal hadn't known that the boy ghost, who had been guarding the beacon for thousands of years, was weakening and preparing to leave, but he was the only one who hadn't. The púca knew, and so did Jenny. Most importantly, Mikey knew it. That was why he had gone to all that trouble to get himself to the beacon. That was why he had died up there, in Donal's arms. And that was why he was still there now, a vigilant ghost, keeping mankind safe.

Safe from the púca, anyway. It was still up there on the hill, watching the beacon from a distance. Donal had seen it nearly every day for more than fifty years. When Mikey died, he had willed his land to Donal, and Donal had been going up there ever since. And that, if only he could get his painful old joints to cooperate, was where he intended to go now.

15

Jenny walked up the main street with JJ. She was glad he was there, even if he was old and grey. When he saw them coming, the boy soldier got up from where he was relaxing on the ground and held his gun in a half-ready position; not exactly threatening but not particularly friendly, either. Jenny wondered whether it was time to do something about it. Maybe not quite yet. It was probably enough to keep a close eye on him for the time being.

When they got closer, the old woman stood up, and there was a look of delight and amazement on her face.

'JJ Liddy!' she said. 'It is, isn't it? Can it be?'

'It is,' said JJ, 'but I'm not sure . . .'

'Oh, no,' said the woman. 'You wouldn't know me. Eileen Canavan is my name. I came to your dances once or twice when I was a girl, but mostly I know you through your CDs. Back in the old days, that is. When we could still play them.'

'But he's been dead for years!' said the old man beside her.

'I know he has,' she said. 'Which just goes to prove

what I've been saying all along. We've died and gone to
. . . well . . . I don't know any more whether this is heaven
or hell.'

'No, no,' said JJ. 'I didn't die, no matter what anyone
said. And this isn't heaven or hell.'

'I told you,' said the boy soldier. 'You wouldn't listen
to me.'

'Well, where are we then?' said the old woman.

So JJ sat them all down in the street and told them
about the place they had come to, and how there was no
time here, and how it was that he was still alive and
unchanged despite all the years that had passed on the
other side since he left. He told them that coming and
going between Ireland and Tír na n'Óg had once been
commonplace, and that this was how the Irish myths of
fairies and gods had arisen, and how it had created the
misconception that Aengus Óg and his people were
immortal. And when he was finished with all this, he asked
them about the world they had just come from, and what
he heard made his heart very heavy.

His youngest son, Aidan, had been a law unto himself
from the day he was born. He had been a strong-willed
and belligerent toddler and, contrary to all expectations, he
had never grown out of it but had gone on to become a
greedy and selfish child and a truly impossible teenager.
Unlike the rest of the laid-back Liddys, he had always been
a go-getter, obsessed with money and possessions. He had
begun gambling when he was still in national school,

setting up crazes for poker and blackjack, then cleaning out all the other players. And that was only the beginning. Aidan, it seemed, had been born to be wealthy and powerful, so it came as no great surprise to JJ to hear, from the wet people, what he had become.

But Donal? Aidan's right-hand man and commander of his army? It made no sense. Donal had always been the most sensitive of all the children. He didn't have an ambitious bone in his body, and he had no more interest in power than the daft old dog, Belle, that he had inherited from Mikey when he was a child. Still, JJ couldn't ignore what he was hearing.

'Yes,' said the old woman. 'It was General Liddy's men that came every week to steal food from us.' She glanced at their young guard as she spoke, but he made no attempt to contradict anything she said. 'They called it taxes, and said it was to pay for our protection, but it's a long time since we got anything in return for what we handed out. And then the time came when we had nothing left to feed ourselves with, let alone give to them, so they rounded us up and took us all to the castle. The young people were put to work on the commander-in-chief's building works, and us old folks were sent into a hole in the ground.'

JJ shook his head slowly and took a deep breath. 'I'm sorry about all this,' he said.

'It's not your fault,' said the old woman. 'No one's blaming you.'

'But they're my sons. I feel responsible for what they're doing.'

'Can you stop them, do you think?' she said.

'I don't think so,' said JJ. 'I can't go back, you see. But maybe Jenny could go over and see what's going on. Could you, Jen?'

'Oh, thanks,' said Jenny. 'Just what I need. A trip into a war zone. A chance to be kidnapped and get shot at.'

'But they're your brothers,' said JJ. 'They won't shoot at you.'

'They're not really my brothers,' said Jenny, 'any more than you're really my dad.'

'Well, thanks a lot,' said JJ. 'That's gratitude for you. And where was your real father for all those years when you were—'

Abruptly the boy cut across them. 'Can you two save this for later?' he said. 'I need to get these people going. Just tell us where the stuff is and we'll leave you to it.'

'What stuff are you talking about?' said JJ.

'Anything,' said the boy. 'Anything we can eat or drink or burn. We have payment for it. We left it up beside where we came in.'

JJ shook his head. 'I think you've got a wire crossed somewhere. There's nothing like that here.'

'What do you mean, nothing like that?' said the boy. 'How can you not have food and firewood and stuff?'

'We don't need it,' said JJ. 'There's no time so we don't get hungry. The sun never goes down so it never gets cold.

We don't have any use for money because we have everything we need. And I don't know what you've brought along to try and pay for it with, but whatever it is, we don't want it.'

'That's ridiculous,' said the boy. 'You're just making it up to try and get rid of us.'

'He's not,' said Jenny. 'It's true. And listen, why don't you just forget about going back? It isn't as simple as you think, and by the sound of it you're far better off here than you were over there. Eternal sunshine. Great music when that fella with the beard catches the goat. No cares. No worries. Why would you want to go back?'

The wet people exchanged bewildered glances.

'I'd like to stay,' said Eileen Canavan, and the others cautiously nodded their heads in agreement. All except for the boy. He thought about it for a while, looking at the odd, crooked houses that lined the street. When he finally spoke, he sounded regretful.

'I can't,' he said. 'I'd like to, but I can't.'

'Why not?' said JJ.

'I have to report back to the general,' he said. 'And I have to find my brother. I heard all that you people said about my army, but you don't know the whole story. We aren't half as bad as the commander-in-chief's private guard. They're the ones who kidnapped my brother and took him away.'

'Kidnapped your brother?' said Jenny. 'Why?'

The boy shrugged. 'Nobody knows. The goons just

arrived one night a few days ago and took him away. I have to go back and try to find out what happened to him.'

Jenny was impressed. Tír na n'Óg tended to have a narcotic effect on everyone who entered it. The peace and the sunshine and the absence of time relaxed people and took away their anxieties, and a lot of their memories as well. This boy must have really cared for his brother to be concerned about him even here. It made her mind up for her.

'All right,' she said to him. 'I'll go if you will. But you might not be able to. We'll have to see when we get back to where you came in. I'll explain it all on the way.'

'Thanks, Jenny,' said JJ. 'I knew you wouldn't let me down.'

16

Aengus looked up from the muzzle of the gun and into the eyes of the man who was holding it. He was young and he looked more frightened than dangerous, but even so Aengus was taking no chances.

'I don't like guns,' he said, and he turned the man into a . . . into a . . .

'Oops . . .' said Aengus Óg. He wasn't at all sure what it was that he had turned the man into. In the heat of the moment, and with the blow to the head and the hard landing, he must have got muddled. What was it he had been thinking of?

He looked up. There were half a dozen people standing there; one woman and the rest of them men. The woman had a few pathetic bundles of sticks laid out on the ground in front of her. Two of the men were behind makeshift market stalls. One of the others had a gun, but the minute he saw Aengus looking at it he put it down, very carefully, on the ground.

'That's the idea,' said Aengus.

Beside him, the terrible beast was snuffling around in

the road. It was rare for Aengus Óg and his kinsfolk to get their creatures mixed up, but it wasn't unknown. When it happened, the fairies were inclined to forget it immediately, but the ploddies never did, and they hung on with absurd tenacity to their stories of mermaids and griffins and centaurs and minotaurs.

'What did you do to him?' the woman asked.

Aengus wasn't entirely sure. The beast he had created was fantastically ugly, but he made himself examine it. There was a bit of sheep, certainly, and a bit of pig, but there were some other things he could see, too. A chicken's beak. A goat's horns. And very definitely something dog-like in its manner.

'I turned him into a . . . a shpigengog,' said Aengus.

'What's a shpigengog?' said the woman.

'That is,' said Aengus. 'And I'll do the same to the rest of you if anyone tries any funny business.'

Each and every one of them nodded solemnly. The man with the gun stepped further away from it, as though it were a nasty smell in the road and nothing to do with him.

'All I want is some tobacco,' Aengus went on. 'Then I'll leave you to carry on with whatever it is you're doing.' He looked at the two stalls, but nothing he saw made him hopeful. One of them had a pile of small turnips and a few blighted potatoes. The other had a gruesome collection of unidentifiable bits of animals, and a very old enamelled sign saying MEAT TO PLEASE YOU!

'Tobacco?' said the turnip man.

'Tobacco?' said the butcher.

'Where have you been hiding this past twenty years?' said the woman. Then she added hastily, 'With respect, sir. With respect.'

'We haven't seen tobacco since the old world went down the plughole,' said the butcher.

'More's the pity,' said the turnip man.

It was just as Aengus had feared. The ploddy world appeared to have been knocked back into the Middle Ages. He looked gloomily from face to face, then down at the shpigengog, which was licking his shoe.

'Get off,' he said, but the ugly creature just wagged its bald tail and raised a friendly paw. Or was it a claw? Too much dog in it, anyway. He pushed it away with his knee, then bent and picked up the shotgun. The movement made his head spin. He didn't feel very well at all, and wondered whether the bang on the head and the fall might actually have done him some damage.

'Surely there must be some tobacco somewhere in this godforsaken world?' he said.

'I doubt it,' said the turnip man. 'They stopped growing it years ago. Droughts and floods in the places it did best. And even if there still were places where it could grow, who's going to waste good land growing tobacco when they could be growing food?'

'And how would they get it here anyway?' the butcher chimed in. 'There's no shipping or aeroplanes or nothing any more. Not since the End of Imports.'

'All right, all right,' said Aengus impatiently. 'But surely there must be some left over. Someone must have kept some.'

His words were met with silence, and he got the impression that something was being hidden from him. He raised the shotgun experimentally, but it didn't create the reaction he expected.

'That thing isn't loaded, by the way,' said the butcher.

'What's the point in having it then?' said Aengus.

'Well, you didn't know, did you? There are a lot of very hungry and dangerous people around these days, which is why we need protection. And luckily most of them don't know, either.'

Aengus threw the gun away from him in disgust. It clattered on to the cracked and crumbling pavement and the shpigengog lumbered happily off in pursuit.

'You're hiding something from me,' he said. 'Someone, somewhere, has some tobacco, don't they?'

There was another long silence, during which the beast dropped the shotgun, now covered in drool, at Aengus's feet. Way, way too much dog. He did his best to ignore it.

'Come on,' he said. 'Out with it. Or do the rest of you want to have a go at being one of these things?'

He trusted that no one would say yes. He was pretty sure he couldn't do it again even if he tried. But everyone looked at the shpigengog and there was a general anxious clearing of throats before they all began speaking at once.

'There's only himself.'

'But you would have thought of that.'

'I doubt he'd still have any after all this time.'

'Who?' said Aengus.

'He might – you never know.'

'He'd never part with it, though.'

'He might, if you had something good to barter against it.'

'What?' said Aengus.

'I wouldn't go up there, no matter what I was after.'

'Nor me. I wouldn't go within a mile of the place.'

'Stop!' said Aengus. 'What are you all talking about?'

'Himself,' said the butcher. 'The container man.'

'Container man?' said Aengus. 'What container man?'

The shpigengog picked up the shotgun in its beak and dropped it on Aengus's foot. It did nothing to improve his mood.

'All right,' he said. 'Let's start again, shall we? Let's all pretend I've been away in fairyland for fifty years and I haven't a clue what's going on here. You tell me there is someone who might, just might, have some tobacco. Now, who is he and where is he to be found?'

The shpigengog picked up the gun again and this time swung it around, clouting Aengus hard on the shin. Before he could react the woman blurted out, 'Commander Liddy. It's Commander Liddy that might have some.'

'Liddy?' said Aengus. 'And which Liddy would that be?'

'Aidan,' said the woman. 'Commander Aidan Liddy. He's the only person left in the county that has any kind of stuff left from the old days, but it won't be easy to get anything off him.'

'Aidan?' said Aengus. 'JJ's son Aidan?' He laughed. 'Sure he's only a little fella.'

He put out a hand at the level of his thigh to demonstrate the height Aidan had been when he had last seen him. The shpigengog licked it.

Aengus was, he knew, approaching a state of apoplectic rage. The only cure for it was tobacco. What he needed to do was to find out how to get some before he visited some painful and permanent revenge upon these idiot ploddies. So he took several long, deep breaths, then he turned the shpigengog back into a man. There was a cheer from the rest of the gathering, but Aengus was slightly concerned. Something wasn't quite right.

'What happened?' said the man.

'I visited a rare privilege upon you,' said Aengus. 'No one in the history of the world has ever seen the inner workings of a shpigengog's mind.' He inspected him closely as he spoke. Had his ears always been that shape? he wondered. And had they always been there, so close to the top of his head?

'A what?' said the man.

His fingers looked very peculiar as well. Aengus decided to keep talking.

'And no one ever will again, if I can help it. But listen to me now. This Aidan Liddy. I know what you're going to tell me. He's all grown up while my back was turned, isn't that it?'

He was met with six blank stares.

'Never mind,' he said. 'Just tell me where the little creep lives.'

17

Over the years, Donal's feet had worn a track between the barracks and the beacon at the top of Sliabh Carran. It was a long time since he had kept any cattle up there – the last of those skinny beasts had been eaten long ago – but he still came up nearly every day to talk to Mikey.

By the time he was halfway up the stony steps his clothes were waterlogged, so he was carrying nearly a stone of extra weight. It happened to him most days and he was well used to it, but that didn't mean it ever got any easier.

His health was not good. He suffered terribly from rheumatism and arthritis, and the constant damp conditions meant he never got any relief from the pain. Occasionally he managed to wheedle some aspirins out of his brother, but these days Aidan was less and less inclined to be generous, even though he had plenty left in storage. So Donal just had to put up with it, and waged a constant battle against pain and exhaustion. It was wearing him out. He would have to go soon – follow his parents into retirement in Tír na n'Óg, but the trouble was, his work on this side was nowhere near completed yet. It was one aspect of that work, a private dream he had, that kept him bound in with his brother and made him an unwilling accomplice in his despotic schemes. Because not all of those old lorry bodies were filled with Aidan's stockpiles. One of them, in the special 'dry' wall of the castle, belonged to him. And although he had made a start in sorting it out, he still had a very long way to go.

18

The turnip man told Aengus that Commander Liddy lived in the steel castle underneath the stony steps on Sliabh Carran. Aengus remembered the enormous circular thing he had flown over. So that was what it was. The head-quarters of a tyrant.

He fingered the empty pipe in his pocket. 'And you're sure he'll have some tobacco?'

'No,' said the turnip man. 'But if anyone does, he does. He has practically everything up there, stashed away in his storehouses.'

'So people say, anyway,' said the butcher sourly.

The shpigengog man was examining his fingers, and an expression of alarm was rapidly spreading across his face. It was definitely time for Aengus to make himself scarce, but as he turned to leave, the woman called out after him.

'Excuse me. Do you mind if I ask your name?'

Aengus stopped. Why hadn't he thought of that before? He did not, on his visits to this world, go by his own name. Like most gods he was vain and lived under the impression that everyone would recognize him the instant they heard his name. He preferred to travel incognito and keep his powers a secret. So each time he came he invented a new name for himself. But this time he hadn't. He'd only planned to nip over for some tobacco, after all. He'd had no idea his shopping trip was going to turn into such an ordeal.

He searched his mind for a suitable name, but he couldn't even remember what he had called himself last time, when he had been a policeman. It was useless. The shpigengog man was showing the butcher his misshapen hands. Aengus turned back to the woman, met her gaze forcefully and said, 'Yes. As a matter of fact I do.'

He walked rapidly away through the rain, down the wet high street. He was soaked to the skin, still in the shirt-sleeves that were all he ever needed in Tír na n'Óg. Everything about this place made him nervous. The expanse of foaming water where the bridge used to be. The dark windows of the dilapidated houses, behind which shadows occasionally moved. He itched to duck into a doorway and turn back into a raven again, but he was afraid of what might happen if he did. His head was still spinning from the red man's well-aimed boot, and the episode with the shpigengog had given him a bad fright. What if he got it wrong and turned himself into something as dreadful as that? And what if he turned himself back and came out all wrong, the way the man had?

Nor could he get home. If he crossed the time skin here, he would land in the bedlam of the leprechauns' insane market. So he was left with no alternative but to walk out of Gort just the way he was. When he got clear of the town boundaries, he could decide what to do next.

The swollen river was a frothing torrent surging across the road, but the citizens of Gort had constructed a pontoon of blue plastic barrels, tethered to the buildings on either side. It juddered continuously as Aengus went across, and the water slopped up over his feet, but when he reached the other side he had to give a moment's grudging respect to ploddy ingenuity.

At the town square he turned left. The sun came out abruptly, sending up a blinding glare from the wet road and creating spectacular rainbows over the rooftops. It was suddenly incredibly hot, and within minutes the rainbows were lost in a fug of steam which rose from everything that was wet, including himself. His skin crawled as he walked on between ruined buildings that loomed like ghosts of themselves through the white mist.

He hated this town. Always had, always would.

19

The driving rain was so dense that Donal was quite close to the beacon before he was able to see it, and as soon as he got his first glimpse of the top of it, he could tell that there was something terribly wrong. There was a white shape that had never been there before. It was a thing that shouldn't be up there, that couldn't be up there, but that was, beyond a shadow of a doubt, up there now. It was the púca.

Donal stopped in his tracks. In a habit born of long practice, he turned his head to one side to observe the huge pile of stones out of the corner of his eye. Mikey was there, his ghostly outline clear and strong against the sodden sky. But it was impossible. He and the púca were immortal enemies. How could they be sitting together like that as if they were the best of friends? Donal was still trying to decide whether it was safe to go on or not when his presence was noticed. The púca came bounding down the steep side of the beacon and danced over to him, tossing his horns like a kid in spring sunshine.

There was nowhere for Donal to run to. He stood his

ground, the wind whipping at his coat and fluttering the end of his scarf. He braced himself for the impact of the púca's horns, but it didn't come. Instead the huge white goat skidded to a halt in front of him and said, 'How delightful!'

He was soaked to the skin, his heavy white coat flattened against his bony frame, but he didn't seem to care.

'Come on up and join us,' he went on. 'Mikey has been expecting you.'

He turned and scaled the heap of rocks in four powerful leaps. It took Donal a lot longer, and he was in considerable pain and discomfort by the time he got there. But Mikey was the same as always, whole and unharmed and cheerful; the only soul that Donal knew who was entirely immune to the weather.

The púca stretched out into his long, humanoid form. His jaw shortened and his knees and hocks reversed their angles of operation. The cloven hooves on his forelegs receded and he grew hairy white fingers and thumbs. Donal stared in amazement. This was a thing he had heard about but hadn't seen before.

'I don't understand,' he said. 'How can you be here? How come you allowed it, Mikey?'

Mikey, like most ghosts, had no voice, but over the course of a lifetime Donal had become adept at interpreting the images Mikey sent to his mind. The púca put the same information into words.

'It's all over,' he said. 'There's nothing left for us to fight about.'

'All over?' said Donal. 'What's all over?'

'It's all over for the human race,' said the púca, sitting down on a rock and crossing his legs. 'It's only a matter of time now.'

'Does that mean the agreement is broken, then?' said Donal. 'Are you going to dig up the hatchet? Go back to the old ways and kill us all off?'

'No need,' said the púca, and Mikey silently agreed with him. 'All we have to do is wait. And not for much longer, either.'

'How do you know?' said Donal.

'It's not rocket science,' said the púca. 'I would have thought that even a birdbrain like you could see it coming.'

Donal pulled his wet coat tighter around him and turned his back to the wind. It was true. He could see it coming, and that was why he was trying so hard to get everyone out. But somehow this truce between the púca and the ghost made it all so much more final and terrifying.

'How long?' he asked.

The púca shrugged. 'How long do you think? What's left to eat? What's left to burn?'

'We're getting somewhere with the terraces,' said Donal. 'They should produce a crop soon, and an even better one next year.'

The púca shook his head. 'You might get a year or two more, if you're very clever and very lucky. But there are storms around the corner that you can't even begin to imagine. And behind them are more storms and more droughts, and then, in another millennium or two – well – a new ice age. But you needn't concern yourself with that. None of you lot will be around to see that.'

Donal lowered himself carefully on to his favourite stone and listened gloomily.

'Great for the old global detox, ice ages are,' the púca went on. He was irritatingly cheerful about the end of the world, and Mikey didn't seem too bothered either, though he was doing his best to cheer Donal up with encouraging images. Like Donal gathering the sick and the hungry and sending them away to a life of warmth and comfort. There was still that kind of hope, at least.

'But I don't understand why you ever tried to stop us, if you could see all this coming,' he said to the púca. 'It was only sixty years ago, after all. Why did you go to all that trouble to try and unearth the hatchet and stuff if we were all heading towards extinction anyway?'

The púca laughed. 'That is just so typical of human arrogance. Do you think you're the only ones going down with your *Titanic*? You're taking the entire world with you, you know. All my beautiful creatures. And not just the big pin-up models like tigers and elephants and horses. Everything's on the way out now, even the lizards and beetles and worms and plankton. You might not care, but each one of my creations is as special to me as the next one. They all have their own job to do, their own place in the order of existence. But not any more. One by one those lovely things are being snuffed out, and all because you lot couldn't keep your appetites under control.'

'So if you had stopped us back then, you might have saved the rest?'

'Exactly,' said the púca. 'Not all of them, obviously, but enough to be going on with. The worst of it is that you could have stopped it yourselves if you'd only tried a bit harder.'

Donal nodded. He had lived through it, after all. The great hopes before each of those climate meetings, when representatives from all over the world came together to discuss how they could lower carbon emissions. The increasing despair as failure followed failure. The gradual realization that it had all been left until much, much too late.

'You'll forgive me for saying so,' he said to the púca, 'but you seem very cheerful for someone who's watching his life's work go down the spout.'

The púca laughed again. 'No point in crying over spilled milk, is there? Give it a million years or so and we can start all over again. I can't wait, actually. I've got loads of brilliant ideas for new kinds of birds and beasts. We'll do it even better next time around.'

'Meaning you'll leave us out, I suppose?' said Donal.

'You?' said the púca. 'Human beings, you mean? You don't think we created you, do you? No. You were never anything to do with us. You came from somewhere else entirely.'

'Really?' said Donal. 'Where?'

But the púca had clearly had enough of the conversation and was already reverting to his goat shape. He hopped down off the beacon and splashed away across the waterlogged ground, kicking his heels with joy.

Donal watched him go, then sat in silence for a while, trying to find a position where the wind couldn't penetrate his clothing, but failing. Finally he said to Mikey, 'No reason for you to stay any longer then, is there, my old friend? You might as well go on and see what happens next.'

Mikey had told him he had no idea where souls went after they left the Earth, and he wasn't in any hurry to find out. He still wasn't, apparently. He told Donal, through his picture-talk, that he was going nowhere as long as Donal was still here struggling with his plans. Their plans. For without Mikey's constant help and encouragement Donal would have found it hard to go on.

'Thanks, Mikey,' he said. 'I suppose you may as well stay until the end. It looks like it won't be long anyway.'

The ghost's outline nodded gravely.

'Will you be sad, Mikey?' Donal went on. 'You always had such a lot of time for people.'

But the images that the ghost put into Donal's mind were of suffering, because that was all the news Donal ever brought him now. And no one, not even Mikey, could be sorry to see that come to an end.

20

As Jenny walked out of the town with the boy soldier she noticed that he was limping.

'What's wrong with your leg?' she asked him.

'It's nothing much,' he said. 'I just got some blisters. My boots are too big, that's why.'

'That's a shame,' said Jenny.

'Not the first time it's happened,' he said. 'They'll get better in a couple of days.'

'Not here they won't,' said Jenny.

'Why not?'

'Because there's no such thing as a couple of days here. If you're ill you're ill. You won't get any worse but you won't get any better. Same with this.' She touched his sopping wet sleeve. 'You won't get dry, either.'

'You're making no sense,' the boy said. 'I'll dry off in an hour or two in this sunshine.'

'No you won't,' said Jenny. 'There are no hour or twos. There isn't any time at all.'

They walked on quietly, past the great rock edifice

that was the Dagda's home and on to the Moy road, which led across the plain towards the hills.

'What's your name?' Jenny said.

The boy paused, as if this were a question he had to think about. Then he said, 'Pup. It's not my real name, but it's what everyone calls me.'

Jenny looked at him again. He was only as tall as her shoulder, and in the oversized boots and baggy clothes he came across as almost comical; a child dressed as a soldier. But there was nothing remotely comical about the gun he carried. You wouldn't dream of laughing at someone who carried a thing like that.

'It's so weird,' he went on, looking around. 'All this is under the sea where I come from.'

'I guessed as much,' Jenny said, 'when Aengus came out of the shop that time.' She laughed, remembering. 'He just nipped across to get his tobacco and found himself taking a swim.'

'So he doesn't need to go through the crawl-hole and the wall like we did?' said Pup.

'No. Nor do I. We can go through anywhere. But you can't. You might not be able to go back at all, actually. Time keeps passing on the other side, you see, and your life keeps passing with it. If too much time has passed, you could find you're very old when you get back there. Or even dead.'

Pup shook his head. 'Not me,' he said. 'That could never happen to me.'

Jenny was irritated by his arrogance, and she might

77

have changed him into a donkey to teach him some respect if he hadn't suddenly turned to her with a charming smile.

'I like it here,' he said. 'I don't care what the general or anybody says. Once I've found my brother I'm going to come back, and I'm going to bring my whole family with me.'

Jenny smiled back. He wasn't bad looking at all, and there was something about him that she found mysterious and alluring. It was a shame he was so young.

'We'll see about that,' she said. 'One step at a time.'

21

Aengus walked on through the hot, steaming sunshine. It was not in the least bit pleasant and he began to suspect that he would never get dry at all, since any moisture his clothes released as steam was immediately replaced by his own sweat. There wasn't much to see as he walked through the outskirts of Gort. Here and there a rusting wire fence surrounded a patch of weeds that might once have been a vegetable garden, but there was little sign of current human habitation. Most of the houses were in ruins, and swarming with fearless rats, inside and out.

He wondered what he should call himself this time round. He remembered now that he had called himself Larry when he was a policeman, and Lad the time before that, when he had masqueraded as a farm labourer and courted JJ's grandmother. He quite fancied himself as a David, but there was always a danger that people would shorten it to Dave, which he couldn't stand, and there was no point in looking for trouble. He liked Michael, too, but his skin crawled at the thought of being called Mike or Mick. A lot of the good names had the same problem. He liked Patrick but hated Pat and Paddy, liked James but couldn't bear Jim. It appeared to be an intractable problem and he was quite glad when the sight of a person sitting at the roadside took his mind off it. And he was even more pleased to see, as he drew closer, that the person was a young woman. He was always ready for a bit of flirtation with the ploddy girls.

'Good morning to you,' he said as he drew level, although now that he came to think about it, he had no idea at all what time of the day it was.

'Just keep walking,' the woman said coldly. She had a deep basket on her lap. There was a grubby checked cloth thrown over it, and one of her hands was concealed underneath it.

'No need to be like that,' said Aengus Óg, flashing his most winning smile. 'Are you heading for the market?'

'Just keep walking,' she said again. 'I'm in no mood for small talk.'

'I know how you feel,' said Aengus, 'but I was just going to warn you that they're an odd lot there in Gort. There are a couple of fellas with guns, would you believe?'

'I would,' said the woman. 'Are they anything like this one?'

She pulled the cloth away to reveal the hidden hand. It had a pistol in it and it was aimed straight at him.

Aengus took a step backwards. 'Well, no, actually,' he said. 'Theirs were much bigger. But that's a very handy one, isn't it? Just right for a pretty little thing like you.'

The young woman wasn't exactly what you'd normally call a 'pretty little thing'. She had that gaunt look that Aengus remembered from a visit he had once made during the great famine in the nineteenth century. But she would probably have been pretty if she had been better nourished.

'Don't try and flatter me,' she said. 'Do you think I was born yesterday?'

'Would I?' said Aengus. His words sounded innocent but there was nothing he loved more than a challenge. He seldom, if ever, failed to get his way where ploddy women were concerned. He glanced around casually. There was room on the low wall beside her but it would be far too forward to try and sit there. The road was wet, but then so were his clothes, so he sat down just where he was and crossed his legs. The woman looked startled, but she didn't say anything.

'There isn't much to buy in the market,' he said. 'Not that I could see, anyway.'

'I'm not planning on buying anything,' she said, loosening up a little but keeping the pistol aimed steadily at his chest. She tilted the basket to show him the apples inside.

'Good for you,' he said. 'Excellent. I love apples, don't you?'

She stared at him blankly, and he was struck by inspiration. 'Tell you what. I don't think there are any buyers there anyway, and maybe I can save you a trip. What about this? If you can guess my name, I'll buy the whole basketful off you.'

The woman's expression didn't alter by a millimetre, but Aengus could clearly see a glimmer of interest coming into her eyes. 'Are you having me on?' she said.

'Nope,' said Aengus. 'A deal's a deal. If you can come up with the right name for me, I'll buy all your apples.'

The interest in her eyes hardened into suspicion. 'Buy them with what?' she said.

Aengus hadn't thought that far. 'What do you want for them?' he said.

She looked him over. It was clear that he had nothing on him to offer by way of barter. 'Silver or gold,' she said. 'I won't take anything less.'

Aengus thought quickly. He was leaning back against the road, and as he straightened up he surreptitiously scooped a few pieces of gravel into his right hand and stuck them into his trouser pocket. When he pulled his hand out again, the gravel had changed into shining coins, silver and gold. The woman's sullen expression vanished and her eyes were suddenly bright and eager.

'What'll you give me for them?' she asked.

'Oh, I don't know,' Aengus said. 'The lot, if you like. But you have to guess my name first, don't forget.'

The light went out of her eyes as quickly as it had come. 'Oh yes,' she said. 'How many tries do I get?'

'As many as you like. And I'll give you a clue to start off with. It's not Rumpelstiltskin. It's something nice and strong that can't be shortened to anything stupid like Mick or Paddy or Jim.'

The woman looked him full in the face, appraising him carefully and, so Aengus thought, liking what she saw. He noticed that her pistol hand had relaxed on her knee and the gun was no longer pointing at him.

'John,' she said.

'No,' he said. 'Too common.'

'Hmm,' she said, finally relaxing and warming to the game. 'A fine, handsome fella like yourself must have a fine, handsome name.'

'Exactly,' said Aengus. 'Now you have the right idea.'

'Lionel!' she said.

'Lionel? Where did you get Lionel from?'

'OK. Not Lionel. I know. Cormac.'

'Not bad,' said Aengus. 'Not bad at all.' He thought about that for a moment, but eventually he shook his head. 'No. It's not Cormac.'

'Finn, then,' said the woman. 'It has to be Finn.'

Finn was perfect. A good, strong Irish name. No way of shortening it.

'Spot on,' said Aengus. 'You're clever as well as beautiful. And might I ask what your own name is?'

'Maureen,' she said. 'Maureen Ryan.' She reached out her hand and Aengus went to shake it, but she pulled it away again. 'The money,' she said. 'The money for the apples.'

'Oh, yes.' He reached into his pocket and produced

the coins again, still shining, still silver and gold. He tipped them into her outstretched hand and she examined them closely before breaking into a broad smile and handing him the basket of apples. If gods could feel guilty, Aengus might have then. With the passage of time – maybe hours and maybe days – those coins would revert to what they were made from. A few bits of grit from a Gort road. But then, it turned out that the young woman was not above a bit of trickery herself. When Aengus inspected his purchase he saw that the apples on the top were beautifully round and fresh, but the ones underneath were misshapen and scabby.

Seeing him looking at them, Maureen Ryan stood up and said perkily, 'Perhaps you'd walk a bit of the road with me, since I don't have to go into town after all.'

Aengus looked up from the apples, from which a distinct smell of decay was beginning to rise. He had to remind himself that he didn't want them in the first place and that he had got himself an excellent name from the transaction. It would have taken him hours to come up with such a good one himself. And now she was offering him an opportunity for a bit more flirting.

'Why not?' he said.

22

Jenny and Pup walked on towards the hills.

'Is that thing loaded?' Jenny asked, nodding towards the rifle.

'Sometimes,' said Pup.

'Now?' she said.

He didn't answer. She decided it was time to broach the matter.

'You were lucky back there,' she said.

'Back where?'

'Back in the town. When my father saw you with that gun.'

'Why?' he said, and he had a smug expression on his face. 'What could he have done to me?'

'We have powers you know nothing about,' said Jenny. 'That thing would be useless to you if my father had stayed around much longer. You're lucky he needed a smoke.'

'Huh,' said Pup, and Jenny was very tempted to give him a demonstration of her abilities, but just then they turned a corner in the road and he spotted the white horse that lived there, forever grazing in a field beside the road.

It raised its head and watched them, a wistful look in its eye.

Pup stopped dead. 'What is that thing?' he said.

'It's a horse,' she said. 'Surely you've seen a horse before?'

'No,' he said. 'I've heard about them all right, but I've never seen one before.'

'Don't people use them over on your side? Now there are no cars any more?'

'They used to,' said Pup. 'But then they ran out of cows and pigs and sheep to eat, and they ate the horses.'

'That's crazy,' said Jenny. 'How could they eat their own horses?'

'They got stolen, mostly,' said Pup. 'But you should try being hungry some time. You'd eat anything if you were left with no choice.'

'Well, no one's eating this one,' said Jenny. She went over to the wall and the horse came up to talk to her. Pup was nervous, hanging back, but eventually he found the courage to come up beside her.

'Not just any old horse, this one,' she said.

'What's special about it?' said Pup.

'Remember the story of Oisín?'

'No. Who's Oisín?'

So Jenny told him the story, because it was one that every ploddy who came to Tír na n'Óg needed to know.

'Oisín married a fairy woman and went to live with her. After a while he decided he wanted to go back home and see his friends and neighbours again. His wife's people told him he could only go if he rode the white horse they gave him, and stayed on its back the whole time. So he set off, and when he arrived home he found that three hundred years had passed and he didn't know anyone there any longer. But he was OK as long as he stayed on the white horse.'

'Was it this white horse?' said Pup.

'Spot on,' said Jenny. 'The very same one.'

'So it worked, then. They got back OK?'

'Afraid not,' said Jenny. 'The horse did, but Oisín had a bit of an accident on the way. He passed some men who were trying to move a big rock in a field and they asked him for his help. So he leaned off the horse to help them move it and he lost his balance and fell.'

Pup studied the height of the horse. 'That must have been sore.'

'A bit worse than that,' said Jenny. 'He turned to dust. His life had all passed away in his own land while he was in Tír na n'Óg, you see. That's why it might not be possible for you to go back, Pup. There's no way of knowing on this side how much time is passing over there. It might be only hours since you left there or it might be a hundred years.'

'Huh,' said Pup, in the same dismissive tone he had used when Jenny mentioned the fairy powers.

'You'll see,' she said, setting out on the road again.

Around the next bend they saw another group of

thin, ragged people making their way towards them. This time there were two soldiers with them. Before Jenny had time to speak, Pup dived into the hedgerow and disappeared. Jenny waited where she was, but these new people were wandering towards her so slowly she decided to go ahead and meet them. Pup would have to look after himself.

All of them, even the soldiers, looked lost and bewildered.

'Welcome to Tír na n'Óg,' said Jenny. 'Make yourselves at home.'

'Where did you say we were?' said one of the soldiers.

'Tír na n'Óg,' said Jenny. 'The land of eternal youth.'

There were about eight of the wet, muddy people, and all of them gazed at her blankly. The soldiers did, too, and Jenny noticed that both of them looked nearly as thin and worn out as the people they were guarding. Her scrutiny clearly made them uncomfortable, because one of them made a visible effort to pull himself together, and said, 'Where will we find supplies?'

'Oh,' said Jenny. 'You're looking for stuff, too, are you?'

'Yeah,' he said. 'Have the others been along?'

'They have,' she said. 'And they're all getting on fine. The best thing you can do is carry on down this road until you come to the village. Then look for JJ. He'll tell you what to do.'

'JJ who?' said the soldier.

He had nasty sores around his mouth and Jenny tried

hard not to look at them. 'Just JJ,' she said. 'There's only one JJ.'

'And he'll tell us where the stuff is?'

'If there's stuff to be had, then JJ is the man to tell you where to find it,' said Jenny.

A flicker of something keen and greedy crossed the soldier's face, then melted away again, replaced by the familiar dazed expression. But it worried Jenny, and she began to wonder if she was taking all this soldier business less seriously than she ought to. She stood aside and let the weary group shuffle past her, and then, when the soldiers drew level, she turned them, one after the other, into sheepdogs.

She was disappointed by the reaction she got, or didn't get, to her magic. The people in the raiding party were all so dazed that they didn't turn round, even when the guns clattered noisily to the ground. And when Pup caught up with her, it was clear that he had been keeping himself hidden behind the hedge and had seen nothing. Jenny didn't bother to tell him. It would just sound like showing off, and he probably wouldn't believe her anyway.

23

Aengus and Maureen began walking along the road together, and Maureen chatted happily, clinking her coins together in her pocket like a primitive percussion instrument. But before they had covered a mile of the road her mood began to change.

'This will be a great help,' she said, jingling the coins one last time, 'but I can't see anything saving us in the long run. Not unless the weather gets better, and there's no sign of that happening, is there?'

'It's not too bad just now,' Aengus said. The sun was still out, the sticky, steamy mist had burned away and he was at last drying out quite rapidly.

'I don't mean today,' she said. 'I mean the rain and the storms and the droughts and the way you can hardly grow food any more. Do you know that we have some of the last apple trees in the whole area? Everybody else's have died or been cut down for firewood. But they won't be enough to keep us alive with things the way they are. Some people say we'll only last a few more years, if that.'

The change in her tone irritated Aengus. He liked

happy women, not miserable ones, and he had no intention of staying around and listening to a torrent of woes.

'You've only yourselves to blame,' he said.

'What?' she said. 'What do you mean by that?'

'Well, it's not as if you didn't see it coming, is it? You could have stopped it happening if you had put your heads together and come up with a plan. But you weren't prepared to give anything up, were you? Your cars and your central heating and your aeroplane trips around the world!'

'Aeroplane trips?' The young woman was practically shrieking now. 'What are you on about? I've never seen an aeroplane in my life. It wasn't me. My generation never had anything – how can you not know that? It was our grandparents that ruined everything, not us.'

The apple basket was growing heavy and Aengus was half inclined to give it back to her and make a run for it. He couldn't take much more of this ploddy hysteria, but there was no sign of the woman calming down.

'Don't you feel the same? Don't you hate your grand-parents for what they did to us? Using up everything in the world and ruining the climate and leaving us in this mess? How can you say we had it coming? We never did anything to deserve it!'

He hadn't meant her in person. He meant ploddies in general – her entire restless, ambitious, acquisitive race. But if he tried to explain all that, he would have to reveal who he was and why he and his people were different, and it was all far, far too complicated.

In any event, he was beginning to devise a better plan. His head was a lot clearer now and the coins he'd created had worked out fine. But he still wasn't ready to risk becoming a raven again. What he needed was a bit more practice first.

'How much further is it to your house?' he asked.

'Oh, not that far,' she said. 'A couple of miles perhaps.'

'Thing is,' he said, 'it's a bit further to where I'm going and I'm finding it quite tiring carrying all these apples.'

'I'm not giving you your money back,' she said. 'You bought them fair and square.'

'Oh, I did,' said Aengus. 'That wasn't what I had in mind at all. It just occurred to me that you might come with me to Liddy's castle.'

'Liddy's castle?' said Maureen. Her face paled, as though he had just asked her to accompany him to the gates of hell. 'What would I want to go there for?'

'Just for the ride,' he said. 'Because we'd both get there much quicker if you were a horse.'

24

As Donal returned to the barracks he was met by another of Aidan's guards. The man looked cold and bad-tempered, as though he had been waiting to deliver his message for quite some time.

'Boss wants you,' he said.

'I'll be in when I've dried off and had a cup of tea,' said Donal.

He predicted the response he would get to this and he wasn't wrong.

'Now, General. The boss wants you now.'

Donal sighed and followed the goon to the castle. He was tired and wet and depressed and he had no desire to know what new schemes his brother had come up with to make everyone's life more miserable. But there was no sense in trying to thwart him. It would only mean more trouble in the future.

Aidan Liddy's living quarters were like a museum displaying the final days of consumerism. His large sitting room had three leather sofas, their patches discreetly hidden beneath fat cushions. The floor was carpeted and the insulated walls were hung with beer adverts and posters of football teams. A polished sideboard held glass candlesticks and a bowl of shiny plastic fruit. In one corner was a television that still worked. It was more than fifteen years since there had been any broadcasts for it to receive, but there was a DVD player and discs stacked in twin piles that almost reached the ceiling. All the electrics, including the lights, ran from a small generator outside, powered by stockpiled diesel. It was in no danger of running out of fuel just yet, even though other things – more important things – were.

'Hello, Donal,' Aidan said. 'Make yourself at home.'

One of Aidan's guards moved hastily to slip a folded blanket on to the seat that Donal chose. It wouldn't do for his wet and dirty trousers to defile one of his brother's cushions.

'What's this about, Aidan?' said Donal.

'Where have you been?' said Aidan. 'I sent for you an hour ago.'

'I've been up the hill, that's all,' said Donal.

'Still going up the hill every day?' said Aidan. 'That's loyalty for you.'

Donal said nothing. An enamelled stove was kept lit in there day and night, and the place was so warm and dry that his clothes were already beginning to steam.

'Have a drink?' Aidan continued. It was a gesture of apparent generosity. Donal knew how fond his brother was of the poitín that his men made for him in the distillery behind the castle. He also knew how short his supplies of it were, and the response Aidan required to his offer.

'Bit early in the day for me,' he said.

'Pity,' said Aidan. 'But you won't mind if I do, will you?'

'Go ahead,' said Donal.

Aidan did, pouring a generous slosh of the clear liquor into a crystal sherry glass. 'So,' he said, 'I just wanted an update on our supply situation. Anything come through from the other side yet?'

'Not yet,' said Donal. 'We're organizing another party to go through today. This time we'll send four men over with them.'

Aidan shook his head, and Donal saw his expression harden. It was a sign of approaching danger, and all too familiar to Donal. He had been exposed to these tantrums since Aidan was a toddler.

'But it isn't working, is it?' he said.

'Give it time,' said Donal, hoping he sounded calmer than he felt.

'How much time?' said Aidan. 'The first lot were sent through a month ago. What's happened to them?'

'You know how it is,' said Donal. 'I don't have to explain to you about the way time works over there—'

Aidan's temper erupted. 'No. You don't have to explain it to me. I've been stuffed with the family stories of Tír na n'Óg since I was a toddler. And I've been brushing up on it as well.' He gestured towards a stack of books on the coffee table, and Donal saw that they were collections of Irish fairy stories. 'Doing a bit of research. And I'm still not sure I believe a single word of it.'

'You know it's true,' said Donal. 'You know as well as I do.'

'Well, where are the results, then? Where's the proof? Where are my raiding parties?'

'You just need to be patient,' said Donal. 'It could be a good while before—'

'A good while?' said Aidan. 'What is that supposed to mean, a good while? I don't know why I ever let you talk me into this ridiculous scheme. As far as I can tell, it might be ten years before those idiots come back with any loot. Or it might be fifty! We'll all be dead before we see anything coming out of that grimy hole!'

'Calm down, Aidan,' said Donal. The goons, sitting on guard in each of the four corners of the room, stirred in readiness for trouble. No one else in the world would be allowed to address the commander-in-chief in such a way. 'You know that people don't always think straight when they get into Tír na n'Óg. They might have forgotten what they went over for. But I told the last three lads to round up the other parties and bring them back, and I'll tell the next lot—'

Aidan shook his head. He emptied his glass and refilled it. 'The next lot is going to be different,' he said.

'Different in what way?' said Donal.

'It will be bigger, for one thing. The biggest yet.'

Donal was thrilled to hear that, but he didn't allow it to show. He nodded approvingly and waited.

'Have you got much more of that junk left?'

Again Donal's heart leaped. 'Plenty of it,' he said.

'Pick out the best you have,' said Aidan. 'They can exchange it for supplies the same as the others. But they're going to have another mission as well. One that will work far better.' He smiled smugly. 'Your idea was all right, but it was limited. I was way ahead of you, you know. I've been planning this for some time. It takes a great mind to come up with a truly brilliant idea.'

Donal held his breath. His brother's 'brilliant ideas' had already caused death and misery to hundreds of innocent people.

'And I'll send plenty of your men along with them, too,' Aidan continued. 'As many as you can give me. I want at least forty civilians, more if we can spare them from the terraces, so we'll need at least six soldiers, maybe ten.'

It was too good to be true. Fifty people sent into Tír na n'Óg meant fifty souls rescued from the living hell that life had become on this side. And even better than that, it meant another fifty loads of Donal's hoarded treasures sent across with them, to where they would be safe for ever. But Donal knew better than to show too much enthusiasm. So he took some time to think and gave the appearance of carefully weighing up the possibilities. Finally he said, 'I can't see any objections to that plan.'

'Ah,' said Aidan, 'but you haven't asked me what

I'm sending them in for this time, have you?'

Donal's heart sank. He knew there had to be a catch.

'No,' he said. 'I haven't.'

His brother could hardly contain his excitement, and Donal saw that smug smile again, and was deeply suspicious of it.

'Guess,' Aidan said.

Donal swallowed his irritation and reminded himself, as he did every day, how important it was to stay on the right side of Aidan.

'I don't know,' he said. 'Firewood again?'

'Nope,' said Aidan. 'Not firewood.'

Donal looked around for clues. There was that pile of books and papers on the coffee table. What had he been researching there? The poitín bottle standing among them looked almost empty.

'Booze?' he said.

'Not booze,' said Aidan.

'Cattle then?' said Donal. 'Sheep? Devaney's poor old goat?'

Aidan shook his head and pulled a piece of folded paper from his pocket. He waved it in the air between them. 'Aengus Óg,' he announced.

Donal couldn't believe his ears. 'Did you say Aengus Óg?'

'I did,' said Aidan grandly. 'I'm sending as many people as we can spare to track down Aengus and send him over to me.'

Donal had the sense to hold his tongue. He was quite certain now that Curly Crowley was right and his brother had completely lost his marbles. He needed to stay calm. He needed time to think the thing through properly. The safety of fifty people was at stake, and fifty more loads from his precious collection.

'It's an amazing idea,' he managed to say. 'But I thought you just said you didn't believe in the stories.'

'I said I wasn't sure,' said Aidan. 'But I'm a gambler. Everything you see around you got here as a result of my gambling.'

Donal had heard his brother gloating about his gambling successes a thousand times, but he swallowed his irritation and said nothing.

'It's a gut instinct, see,' Aidan went on, 'and my gut instincts are hardly ever wrong.'

He handed Donal the piece of paper. Donal opened it. The writing was awkward and childish, but carefully done.

Aengus Óg. I have some important matters to discuss with you. Please come and meet me at my residence, at a time which suits you.
Aidan Liddy,
The Castle,
The Stony Steps,
The Burren,
Ireland

Donal tried to smile, but discovered his jaws had locked. 'Erm,' he said.

'Brilliant, isn't it?' said Aidan. 'What's the point in sending people over there to import all that stuff when we can just send for Aengus and get it made here?'

Donal gaped at him. 'Get it made?'

Aidan tapped the side of his nose with a forefinger. The smugness had gone and he was now grinning like an idiot. He gestured again towards the pile of books on the coffee table. 'Halls of gold and all that jazz,' he said. 'Banquets fit for kings. But where does it all come from, eh?'

Donal had a feeling he wasn't expected to reply, and he was right.

'They make it!' Aidan said triumphantly. 'Everyone knows that. Did you ever hear of fairies ploughing the land and slaving over grinders or chopping carrots or sweating over cooking fires? No! If they want a feast fit for a king, then, *bing!* they magic one out of thin air, see? And if they can do that, what can't they do? *Bing!* Storm-proof glasshouses. *Bing!* Terraces that don't get washed away. *Bing!* Spuds that don't get blight. Everything we need, see? Just at the wave of Aengus's hand.'

Donal concentrated on breathing. He was still speechless. Aidan reached over and took the note back from him.

'Brilliant, eh?' he said. 'Every person in our new raiding party is going to have a copy of this. And as well as looking for stuff to bring back, they're all going to go looking for Aengus. The first one to find him gives him this.'

Donal didn't much like the sound of that. When he was nine years old he had seen Aengus turn old Mikey into a pig, and on that occasion he had been trying to be helpful. If he saw a copy of Aidan's message, there was no telling what he might do to the unsuspecting soul who handed it to him. But he supposed that one out of fifty was pretty good odds, and worth the benefit to the other forty-nine. He would not try and dissuade his brother from the plan.

And what if, by any chance, it worked? Donal didn't even dare to contemplate that possibility. They would just have to cross that bridge when they came to it.

25

'Why did you hide from them?' Jenny asked Pup as they continued on their way.

'The soldiers?' said Pup. 'I don't want them to see me going back empty-handed. I might get court-martialled for that. Tough business, you know, being in the army.'

'So what made you want to join up?'

'Want?' said Pup. 'Since when did anyone get to do what they want?'

'I thought everybody did,' said Jenny. 'They did when I was there anyway.'

She told him about the sixteen years she had spent in his world, using ploddy time in order to grow up. She remembered that there were occasions when she couldn't do exactly what she wanted, but she was fairly sure that most people got to choose what kind of career they wanted to follow.

But as she spoke she realized that things had obviously changed a whole lot over there now. Her brother Donal had wanted to be a farmer and a musician, but now, apparently, he was the general of an army. Jenny hoped that he would still be alive when she got there. She had no way of knowing how much time was passing on the other side as she and Pup strolled along beneath the sun.

'It was join the army or starve,' Pup said. 'My family was struggling. Every year that passed, our bit of land produced less food. The rain washed away the soil and the crops along with it, and the slugs ate half of what was left. Then, every few years, there would be a drought that would go on for months and there would be no way of growing anything at all when that happened. We were up against the wall, living hand to mouth. So when I was ten I crept out one night and went to the barracks, and General Liddy let me join up.'

'Ten?' said Jenny.

'Some of us are even younger,' said Pup. 'Some families send their young boys because there's no way they can feed them.'

A blackthorn tree sat on a tight bend in the road, and in its branches a dozen or more odd socks were hanging. Pup stopped and stared at them. 'What are they doing there?' he asked.

'It's a long story,' said Jenny. 'Some things leak through from your world into this one.'

'Socks?' said Pup.

'Among other things,' said Jenny.

'So who do they belong to?' said Pup.

Jenny shrugged. 'Do you ever see your family now?' she said.

Pup began selecting socks from the blackthorn tree. 'No,' he said. 'We're not allowed to leave the barracks except on sorties. But I saw my mother twice since I left home. The first time was a week after I joined up. She came to the barracks to try and get me to go home again, but I wouldn't go. And the second time was a few days ago. She came looking for my brother after he was kidnapped. She thought he'd been taken to join the army, but he hadn't. The general wouldn't do a thing like that.'

'But Aidan would.'

'Obviously. It must have been his men that took Billy, because it wasn't anyone from the army. And there's no way his men would have kidnapped them without him knowing all about it.'

'Them?' said Jenny. 'Was there more than one?'

Pup sat down on a wall and began taking off his boot. 'Three that we know of,' he said. 'Two boys and a girl.'

'And no one knows why? Or where they were taken?'

'No,' said Pup. He peeled off his wet sock and Jenny saw the blisters underneath, burst open and red raw. 'But there is one strange coincidence. The girl who was kidnapped has a brother who is in my troop, and he told me a story about her one day. Apparently her mother went a bit mad when the girl was a baby. One morning she went out to feed the hens and left the baby asleep inside. When she came back in, she started saying the baby wasn't hers, that someone had changed it for a different one.'

Jenny listened in silence. The story was an old one and very familiar. Perhaps the woman really had gone mad and imagined it all, but Jenny doubted it. After all, she herself had been exchanged for a ploddy baby. In her case both sets of parents had agreed to it, but that was very unusual. In the past the people of Tír na n'Óg had just swapped their babies whenever an opportunity arose, and now it sounded as if it had started happening again. She wondered whose baby it might have been. It wasn't always easy to keep track of the comings and goings of the fairy folk.

Pup was pulling on socks, one on top of the other. 'Anyway,' he said, 'the strange thing is that I overheard my mother telling a friend that the very same thing happened to her. I was a lot younger then, and I was up in the loft in bed and she didn't know I was listening. She said the baby was swapped while she was out weeding the cabbages, only a few yards from the house. She said she thought she was losing her mind, but my father agreed with her that it wasn't the same baby.'

'It probably wasn't,' said Jenny.

The top sock was blue with red stripes. Pup seemed excessively pleased with it and admired it from various angles before putting his wet boot back on.

'So you see,' he said, 'there's obviously a connection between my brother and the little girl, if they were both swapped over at birth. And I bet the other child, the third one, is the same.'

'I bet you're right, too,' said Jenny. 'I wonder what Aidan wants with them.'

Pup stood up. 'That's better,' he said, walking a few steps out and back across the road. 'It's almost comfortable. Do you think there's enough time for me to put socks on the other foot as well?'

'Go ahead,' said Jenny. 'You needn't have any worries about time in this place.'

With the thick padding of socks inside his enormous boots, Pup walked almost normally.

'You've no idea how good that feels,' he said to Jenny.

'I'm glad to hear that,' she said. 'It means you can be comfortable even if you can't go back to let your blisters heal.'

'Why would I not be able to go back?' he said.

'You don't listen, do you?' said Jenny. 'Didn't I just tell you about Oisín and the white horse?'

'What has that got to do with anything?' said Pup. 'It's just a stupid old story. You don't think it actually happened, do you? I don't believe any of it.'

'You will,' said Jenny. 'Just you wait.'

They turned right when they came to the New Line and then left, up the narrow path that, in JJ's world, had been the gravel road that led to the Liddy house. On this side it wasn't much more than a large hollowed-out boulder, but it was surrounded by some of the loveliest trees in the land. One of them was gone, stolen by the púca, but there were a dozen or more of them still standing, tall and deep red. And beneath their shade Jenny and Pup came upon the third party of Aidan Liddy's raiders.

This one looked altogether more serious. There were three soldiers. Two of them were healthy young men in the prime of life, and the third was a weedy child, even smaller than Pup. They were guarding fifteen or so hungry-looking people who ranged in age from about five years old to about eighty. Every adult had a brand-new rucksack and there were two dismantled wheelbarrows, and a pile of saws, axes and ropes. There was even a bright orange chain-saw, brand new, and a red plastic petrol container. Jenny wondered if it was the first power tool that had ever come into Tír na n'Óg.

When Pup saw the soldiers he stepped sideways into the shade of the hedgerow trees, and Jenny went on alone.

'Welcome to Tír na n'Óg,' she said as she reached them.

'Thank you,' said an old woman. 'Thank you so much.'

'It's wonderful here,' said an old man. 'Have you heard these trees?'

He sang a long low note, and above their heads the red trees resonated with harmonious tones.

One of the soldiers stood up and approached. 'We're the firewood party,' he said. 'We're going to need everyone out of this area when we start work.'

He was trying to sound authoritative, but he wasn't succeeding.

'Firewood, is it?' said Jenny. 'Well, I wouldn't cut these trees down if I were you. My father wouldn't like it and you'd be in all kinds of trouble. In fact, I don't think you should cut any trees down at all until you've spoken to my father.'

'We don't need to speak to anyone,' said the soldier. 'This is a raid, and we only take orders from the commander-in-chief.'

'I see,' said Jenny.

'And we intend to start work soon on preparing and cutting.' She could hear the determination slipping out of his voice, word by word, and being replaced by a kind of idle contentment. 'But we're just taking a short R and R. Just to get our strength up. We'll start work soon.'

He wandered off and settled himself down in a patch of sunlight on the side of the hill. Jenny didn't think there was much danger of his cutting anything down, and from what she could see of the other two soldiers, they were in the same frame of mind.

'What kind of a place is this, anyway?' said the old man who had been singing to the trees.

Jenny was on the point of answering when rapid movement on the hillside above caught her eye. The approaching figure was unmistakable. He was tall and broad with a huge bushy beard and a heavy cloak. The Dagda, king of the fairies, never came down from his lookout point on top of the mountain. And it seemed to Jenny unlikely that he was on his way to dance a set with the others down on the quayside.

So it probably meant trouble. Jenny gathered her courage and set off up the hill to meet him.

26

'Who are these miserable people?'

The Dagda bellowed the words so loudly that Jenny flinched and backed away from him.

'Calm down, Granddad,' she said. 'They're not doing anybody any harm.'

'No harm?' said the Dagda. 'No harm? Millions of ploddies pouring into my kingdom and you tell me they're doing no harm?'

'There aren't millions,' said Jenny. 'I'd say there are no more than fifty of them.'

'Fifty ploddies is fifty ploddies too many,' said the Dagda. 'And what makes you think it will stop at fifty? No, you'll see. They'll keep coming. There's something going on over there in Ireland. I can smell it.'

'You're right, there, Grandfather,' said Jenny. 'They're in the middle of a catastrophe. People can't grow enough food to survive and the army is stealing everything they have. And for some reason—'

The Dagda interrupted her. 'That's not my problem! They needn't think they can just come in here and take over and treat the place like a rubbish tip.'

'A rubbish tip?' said Jenny. 'They're not treating the place like a rubbish tip.'

'Oh, aren't they?' said the Dagda. 'You haven't seen what I've seen, then. Come here. Come on. Wait till you see.'

Jenny followed him up the hill towards the old rath. Like its counterpart on the other side, all that could be seen was the weathered, grassy remains of a circular earthen bank. But inside it was a series of underground chambers; one of the last remaining places where ploddies could still cross in and out of Tír na n'Óg. And as they approached it, Jenny could see that the Dagda appeared to be right. On the bank of the rath was an untidy sprawl of old cardboard boxes, plastic bin-bags and canvas cases in a variety of odd shapes.

'See?' he said. 'Look at that. The nerve of them, bringing in all that junk and dumping it there!'

Jenny looked back. She could see Pup standing beside an ash tree, following at a distance. She shook her head at him firmly. It was not the right moment to be introducing any kind of ploddy to her grandfather. The Dagda stood with his legs planted firmly apart, his cloak thrown over his shoulder, his hands on his hips.

'I'm not having it,' he said. 'Go and fetch them and tell them to take it all back!'

'Wait a minute,' Jenny said. There was something in amongst the scattered jumble that looked familiar. A small square black bag with shoulder straps. She ran up to it and looked more closely.

'What are you looking at?' said the Dagda, coming up behind her.

'I think I know what it is,' she said, tugging at the buckles and zips. 'I think it's Donal's.'

'Who's Donal?' said the Dagda.

'My brother,' said Jenny. 'My ploddy brother when I was growing up.' She pulled out the old 'black dot' accordion and displayed it triumphantly to her grand-father. 'It is. Look!'

He looked at it blankly.

'It's his accordion,' said Jenny. 'You know what an accordion is?'

'Of course I do!' said the Dagda, who refused to admit that he didn't know everything. Jenny had never learned to play the box, but she was able to get a few notes out of it, and the Dagda stared at her in amazement.

'It makes music,' he said.

'In the right hands it does,' said Jenny, and she missed Donal and wished he was there to play the old box.

'Let me have a go,' said the Dagda.

Jenny handed it to him, and he pushed and pulled at the bellows a few times and fingered the buttons. But he soon lost interest and practically dropped it in his excitement to explore the rest of the things assembled on the bank. He went straight for the biggest case, unzipped it and pulled out a cello. It was a cheap modern one but it was all set up and ready to play.

The Dagda laughed at it. 'Who'd play a fiddle that size?' he said. 'Was it made for a giant?'

'It's a cello, Granddad,' said Jenny. She hadn't thought about it before, but now she realized that centuries, perhaps even millennia must have passed on the other side of the time skin since her grandfather had been across.

'I know that,' he was saying. 'I know it's a cello.'

'They use them in orchestras,' said Jenny. 'They have a big, deep sound.'

'I know that,' said the Dagda again. 'It's a cello and it makes a big deep sound in a norcrystal.' But he had already lost interest in it and now he was upending a black plastic rubbish bag. Books spilled out. He had seen books before.

'Stories!' he snorted. 'Do they think we haven't enough stories of our own?'

Jenny began gathering the books into piles, looking at their spines as she went along.

'This is all poetry,' she said. 'Yeats. Plath. Eliot. You might like this one, Granddad. It's Gerard Manley Hopkins.'

But the Dagda had already moved on. He was like a small child on Christmas morning, emptying boxes and opening cases, continually throwing things aside in anticipation of something more exciting.

'More stories,' he said, tipping out the contents of a box.

'No. That's music.'

The Dagda stopped, a shiny brass French horn in his hand. 'Music?' he said. 'Have you gone mad? How could that be music?'

'It's music written down,' said Jenny, retrieving the scattered books and stacking them.

'You can't write down music,' said the Dagda. 'That's like saying you can read dancing!'

'This isn't your kind of music, Granddad,' said Jenny. 'This is Bach, look? And this is Scriabin, and Mozart and Britten.'

He was still staring at her as if she had two heads.

'I can't read it,' she said, 'but my mum can. Aisling, I mean. She used to play this kind of stuff on the piano.'

But the Dagda had lost interest and had gone back to trawling through boxes and bags. The place really was beginning to look like a tip now. 'Like I said, it's all rubbish. Monster fiddles and norcrystals and corjuns. We don't need any of this stuff. We have our own music and stories. I don't want any more ploddies or their ploddy rubbish.'

'But I keep trying to tell you,' said Jenny. 'It's not rubbish.'

'I don't care,' said the Dagda. 'Enough is enough. Tír na n'Óg is not going to become a refugee camp! I'm going to seal the time skin and that'll be an end to it.'

Jenny knew he could do it. He had done it before, on at least one occasion, and she didn't want him to do it now. There was too much she needed to know about the changeling children and who had kidnapped them, and about her brother Donal and why he had become the general of an army.

'Oh no, Granddad,' she said. 'You can't do that.'

'Why not?' said the Dagda. 'Why shouldn't I?'

'Because . . .' said Jenny, searching desperately for a reason good enough to dissuade him. And finding one. 'Because Aengus Óg is still over there. He went to get tobacco. You can't shut out your own son.'

'Aengus Óg?' said the Dagda, and the colour rose in his cheeks. 'Why is it that my omadaun son is always, always in the wrong place at the wrong time?'

27

The very same omadaun son was riding through the pouring rain, and had arrived at a place where floods came up over what was left of the road. Maureen Ryan made a tolerably good chestnut mare. She wasn't very tall and she was a bit on the lean side, but she seemed to have no problem carrying Aengus's weight, which was all that mattered to him.

They had come about three miles so far. As he rode across the landscape, Aengus had come to understand how it was that the woman in Gort was able to make it worth her while to sell those pathetic bundles of sticks. It was as though a gigantic swarm of locusts had swept across the county and stripped it bare. There wasn't a tree or a bush or a thicket of scrub to be seen. Even the hedgerows had been cut to the ground. The poor miserable ploddies had taken the lot and burned it.

He was pleased to discover that the mare didn't seem to mind at all about going into the water. She went in up to her fetlocks, then to her knees, then to her belly. Aengus drew up his feet to keep them clear of the surface, then gave up and dropped them in. The rain was still coming down in buckets and he couldn't get any wetter than he already was. For a while he quite enjoyed it, sloshing along through the turlough, trailing his feet. But then, without warning, the mare lost her footing and plunged into deep water. Aengus clung to her mane with one hand and the apple basket with the other. She lunged and floundered, searching for firm footing under the water. Eventually she found it and hauled herself up, with Aengus still somehow on board and clinging on for all he was worth.

She stood trembling, blowing hard. She was still up to her belly in water, and Aengus couldn't see what she was standing on now, or what lay ahead or behind.

'Not your fault,' he said to her. 'It's the council that's to blame, I suppose. They never did look after the roads properly.'

The mare snorted.

'Oh, that'd be right,' Aengus said. 'No councils any more with all that's going on. Still and all, you'd think somebody ought to do it.'

He kicked her on and she moved cautiously forward, but she seemed very uncertain of her footing now, and Aengus began to wonder whether they were actually following the road at all. There was no evidence of it. Any walls there might have been were submerged beneath the turlough, and the hedgerows that would have been markers in times gone by were history now. Gone up in smoke. There was no kind of landmark anywhere, other than the occasional rocky or grassy hump that broke the surface here and there. And the rain was falling so heavily that Aengus couldn't even make out the distant hills he was heading for. He and the mare were lost and alone on the endless flooded plain, and neither of them had the faintest idea what to do.

28

Aisling and JJ were sitting on the quay, chewing the rag with the wet people and getting up to date on the happenings in Ireland. They didn't pause for breath when a sparrowhawk landed on a beer barrel and turned into Jenny, but the wet people did, and the conversation came to an abrupt halt.

'There's all this stuff up by the fort,' Jenny said to Aisling. 'Books and instruments. Piles of music.'

'Music?' said Aisling eagerly.

'Boxes of it. But the thing is, Granddad doesn't believe in it and he's threatening to throw it all back and seal the time skin.'

'Why would he do that?' said JJ.

'He's got a bee in his bonnet about refugees,' said Jenny. 'Go up and talk to him, will you? Convince him the music is worth hanging on to. And stop him from sealing the time skin while I go over and find Dad.'

'But Dad's here,' said Aisling, pointing at JJ.

'Not that dad, stupid,' said Jenny. 'The other one.'

★ ★ ★

The other one, stranded on the horse in the flood, had decided it was probably safe to turn into a raven again and go the rest of the way on wings. But the problem of what to do with the apples was perplexing him. He had bought them, after all, fair and square. Well, not exactly fair and square, perhaps, but they were his, nonetheless. He never got hungry in Tír na n'Óg but he did over here, and from what he could ascertain, apples were a rare and valuable commodity. He was reluctant to abandon them.

While he struggled with this difficulty, the weather changed again. A sharp little squall slapped a bucketful of heavy rain against his face. The mare lifted her head and twitched her ears. Another squall, even sharper, lifted a tiny wave that sloshed over the mare's chest and up around Aengus's knees. There was a strange, leaden pause in the rain, and then the wind hit Aengus like an invisible fist; so hard that it almost knocked him out of the saddle. He clutched his precious apple basket in one hand and the reins in the other. He cursed the wind but praised his greed for apples, because without it he would have already been up aloft in that gale. And surely there had never been one like this before? He was certain it would have dislocated his wings and pitched him back into the floods to drown.

Drown? No, he couldn't drown, could he?

The mare shifted beneath him, trying to turn her back to the storm. Had Aengus not been a god he might have pitied poor Maureen Ryan and felt regret at having turned her into a horse and driven her into such a predicament. But he was a god, and so he didn't.

'Here,' he said. 'Keep your rotten apples.' And he flung them, basket and all, into the water beneath the horse's nose, then slithered down from her back. In an instant he was gone, nothing more than a glimmer of shining scales vanishing into the murky depths of the flood.

Aisling, being ploddy bred as well as ploddy born, did not have the ability to fly. So Jenny left her to make her own way across the plain and went on sparrowhawk wings back to the rath. There, to her relief, she found that the Dagda had calmed down a bit. He had discovered a box of tin whistles in an old suitcase and he was working his way through them, playing a tune on each one.

'These are rubbish, too,' he said. 'Look!' He blew a note on one and then another note with the same fingering on another. The second one was several tones higher. 'They're not even in tune with each other,' he said.

'They're not supposed to be, Granddad,' said Jenny. 'They're in different keys. They were made like that.'

'Just what I said. Didn't you hear me? Different keys, I said. They're made like that.'

He appraised the whistles splayed out around his feet like shiny bristles. Then he picked up the biggest of them, the low D whistle, and in no time he was lost in its mellow tones.

Jenny was mesmerized by the brilliance of the Dagda's

playing. She had seen him dance and knew that there was no one in either world to compare with him, but she had never heard him play before. She hadn't even known he could, until now.

She stretched out on the bank in the sunshine to listen. First there was a set of hornpipes, then a barn dance, then a pair of jigs. Jenny knew there was something she ought to be doing, but surely it couldn't be all that important? Not more important than lying here in the sunshine, listening to this beautiful music, surely? Nothing could be, could it?

29

The salmon that swam beneath the dark waters of the vast turlough was not the salmon of wisdom that was told of in the old tale of Fionn Mac Cumhail. He was a lost and bewildered fish who felt very small and had no more idea where he was going underneath the water than he had when he was a man on horseback up above it. So the fish that was Aengus Óg decided his best bet was to swim in a straight line and keep going in the same direction. That way, sooner or later, he was certain to reach land.

But it wasn't as simple as it sounded. There were lumps and bumps of hillocks and rocks there on the lake bed, and they had to be swum round. Some of the larger ones that broke the surface had to be investigated in case they turned out to be a shoreline. And when they turned out not to be a shoreline but a bit of a rocky island instead, then the fish was left with the difficulty of trying to remember which way he had been heading when he found it.

Once, discovering he had been deceived three times by the same protruding outcrop of limestone, the fish reared up into the shape of a man, who climbed out on to the rock and bellowed his rage at the world. But the world roared back even louder, and the storm thumped him so hard that he pitched forward from the rock and slid, silver-scaled again, back into the safe, watery darkness.

30

Since there was no sign of Devaney returning with the goat, JJ decided to go along with his wife for the stroll. Out of habit, he put the Stradivarius fiddle away in its case and shouldered it. He knew it was safe in Tír na n'Óg, but he still felt uneasy being separated from it by any significant distance.

On their way out of the village they met the second party of raiders coming in, closely followed by a pair of black-and-white sheepdogs.

'We're looking for JJ,' a woman said. She was the thinnest person either of them had ever seen, and her skin was dry and flaking.

'That'd be me,' said JJ. 'Just carry on down to the bottom of the village there and you'll find some more of your lot.'

'Are they picking up supplies?' said the woman.

'They're getting everything they need,' said JJ. 'Don't worry yourselves, anyway. I'll be back before you know it and I'll help you get sorted out.'

'Thank you,' the woman said.

'Ah, look at your dogs,' said Aisling. 'They look as if they're trying to hurry you along. Aren't they sweet?'

'Dogs?' said the thin woman. 'We haven't got any dogs.'

'Whatever you say,' said Aisling. But as she walked on her laughter exploded. JJ laughed, too, and put a fond arm around the woman he had loved all his life.

About halfway along the Moy road they spotted Devaney in a roadside field. The goat was literally running rings around him.

'Let's give him a hand,' said JJ, and they crossed the tumbledown wall into the field. They spread out, planning to surround the goat and trap her, but the minute she caught sight of JJ she came straight up to him and pushed a horn into his hand. Devaney ran over. The bits of his face that were visible between his thick beard, moustache and sideburns were flushed and damp with sweat.

'See?' said JJ, handing him the goat's horn. 'That's how it's done.'

Devaney hurled a string of abuse at the goat, who responded by belching up a wad of cud and chewing it contentedly.

'She does it to torment me,' he said. 'I swear I'll give her a hammering this time.'

'Ah, don't,' said JJ. 'It ruins the music. And I'd say she's dying for a tune. We all are.'

To make sure he didn't lose her again, Devaney turned the goat into a bodhrán there and then. He took a stick from his pocket and played a few fluid rolls on the taut drum, then said, 'Right, so. Will we go?'

JJ fell cheerfully into step beside him, his fingertips itching for his fiddle strings. But Aisling caught him by the elbow.

'We're going for a walk, remember?'

'Oh, yes,' said JJ glumly. 'So we are.'

31

Donal had begun by copying out the notes as quickly as he could, but as time went on he slowed down, enjoying the unaccustomed warmth of his brother's luxurious quarters; glad to be safe from the storm raging outside.

It was one of the big ones. Some of the fiercest gusts tilted the top layer of containers, so there was a background percussion of whumps and crashes. But if Aidan noticed, he didn't show it. He paced restlessly, muttering under his breath continually, as though he were rehearsing for the meeting with Aengus Óg. Every so often he would stop at the sideboard and refill his glass, and Donal was reminded of the early days of his army, when every man had a ration of grog every evening. It was a long time since any of them had seen a drop of it. He doubted that even the goons saw much of it these days. Aidan's capacity for the stuff was a source of constant amazement to him. Donal had been expecting his liver to pack up for ten years or more, but there was still no sign of it happening. He wasn't sure, but he suspected his brother got through a bottle of that rotgut a day, if not more.

Donal wrote neatly and carefully. He was tempted to be creative with the messages – *People trafficker, contact Aidan Liddy* or *Please do not turn the messenger into a pig!* – but Aidan was too close and, far too often for Donal's liking, he leaned over his shoulder and said, 'How many's that?'

The goons dozed over their hand guns in the corners and Donal wasn't surprised. He was sleepy himself. The room, like most of the container-built quarters in the castle and the barracks, had no windows and stank of too many men. The ventilation grille, which Aidan had thoughtfully installed, had three pairs of socks stuffed into it to keep out draughts.

'You're sure they put a value on all that stuff you're sending over?' said Aidan, dropping into a chair to take his considerable weight off his feet.

'Certain,' said Donal. 'Like I told you, music and stories are the only things the fairies are interested in. Good job I rescued it all, isn't it?'

'Maybe we should keep it back,' said Aidan. 'Use it to bribe Aengus Óg when he gets here.'

Donal was seized with anxiety at the prospect, but he kept his cool. 'We can do that as well,' he said. 'There's a whole container load, after all. No harm in giving him a taste of what's on offer.'

'Hmm,' said Aidan. 'It doesn't matter anyway. I have something of far more value to bargain with.'

'What's that?' said Donal.

That infuriating smug smile returned to Aidan's face. 'Never you mind,' he said. 'All will be revealed in good time.'

Donal returned to his writing. Aidan got up and began noisily searching through his DVD collection. He picked one out and put it in the player, but he didn't turn it on.

'How long do you think it will take?' he said.

'For someone to find Aengus Óg?' Donal, unlike Aidan, had been to Tír na n'Óg, just once, when he was nine. On that occasion Aengus had been sitting on the quayside playing his fiddle, and that was where Donal always imagined him to be.

But he wasn't about to tell Aidan that, in case he decided he didn't need to send so many people after all. 'It depends,' he went on. 'There's a very good chance that he'll be in the village, but then again he could be any-where. He often goes wandering around the place.'

'Do you think it's a wild-goose chase, then?' said Aidan.

'Oh no,' said Donal. 'Not at all. I'm sure someone will find him.'

'But Tír na n'Óg is a big place, isn't it?'

'It's as big on that side as it is on this side,' Donal said. 'A whole world, just like our own. I wouldn't let that worry you, though. I doubt that Aengus goes all that far from Kinvara.'

'Hmm,' said Aidan, and Donal returned to his writing

to conceal his anxiety. He was sure his brother was getting cold feet. But when Aidan spoke again he said, 'Maybe fifty isn't enough. Maybe we should send more.'

Donal breathed deeply and tried not to show his excitement. 'Well, I'll just keep on writing until you tell me to stop, shall I?'

By the time B-Troop returned Donal had written out more than a hundred notes, and he was warm and dry. He had even been treated to a cup of tea with tinned milk, divinely hot and sweet and sticky. He was in good spirits, but the report from Colonel Crowley was disappointing. They had raided the settlement in Carron, as ordered, but there were only eleven people left there to be rounded up.

'Never mind, never mind,' said Aidan. 'We'll send out again tomorrow. Belharbour.'

'Belharbour is already cleaned out,' said Donal. 'Most of it is under water.'

'Glencolmkille then,' said Aidan. 'High time we raided Glencolmkille again.'

'Does that mean we're going to have to wait?' said Donal.

'No, no,' said Aidan. 'Strike while the iron is hot and all that. How many gardeners have we got?'

Gardeners. Only a man as deranged as Aidan could refer to the half-starved people who were working on the terraces as 'gardeners'. But Donal didn't care. Some of them were going to be in for a nice surprise.

'Eighty-three altogether,' he said, 'unless any of them have died since they were sent out this morning.'

It wasn't a joke. The mortality rate among Aidan's 'gardeners' was sky-high.

'Eighty-three,' said Aidan. 'We'll send them all. They won't be needed any more when Aengus Óg arrives. Plus eleven from Carron makes ninety-four. How many notes did you write?'

Donal struggled to remain calm. 'A hundred and three,' he said. 'But I can always write more.'

'I have one,' said Aidan, adding his original to the pile. 'We'll send ten soldiers. The oldest ones this time, not the youngest. We don't want any more cock-ups.'

'Right,' said Donal. 'I'll get it all organized.'

He went out into the open courtyard in the centre of the castle and headed for the exit, but his way was blocked. One of the ground-level containers was empty and had a portcullis at one end and a drawbridge at the other, but both of them were nearly always kept closed. The regular traffic came through a narrow laneway between two container walls, and the soldiers of B-Troop were coming through it now, carrying in the booty from Carron.

It was a poor haul. Half a dozen chickens, drenched and skeletal, tied in pairs by their feet, too weak and shocked even to flap. A sack of oats, all hairy and green with sprouts. Three baskets of potatoes, all of them stinking of blight, and a few buckets of slimy carrots and turnips. It was as well for these people that they had been captured and dragged from their homes. They wouldn't have held out for much longer on those pathetic stores.

Donal smiled to himself. He knew they would be terrified now, huddled together in one of the lock-up containers, convinced that they were facing a fate worse than death in Aidan's labour camps. But they would soon be in a much, much better place, if everything went according to plan.

Donal had to concentrate to prevent himself from running. He couldn't believe that he was being given this opportunity to send the entire dispirited workforce through to safety in one fell swoop. And ten of the most deserving from his army as well.

His spirits sank slightly at the thought, remembering the rumblings of mutiny that morning. It would have to be dealt with somehow. Nothing could get in the way of his plan.

32

The fish finally found the shore and Aengus walked up through the shallows and sat down on a rock. The storm was still raging, throwing punches from every direction. Whichever way Aengus turned, it still managed to hit him in the face. He was not a happy camper. The most obvious thing for him to do was go home – just slip through the time skin into the sunshine and leave the storm to take swings at thin air. But there was, he now saw, a fatal flaw in that course of action.

He had been lucky when he did it before, but he might not be so lucky again. From what he was hearing, tobacco was hard, perhaps even impossible, to come by. As it was, he might, just might, find there was still some left in Aidan Liddy's monstrous metal castle, but if he left and went home, there was a very high likelihood that this ridiculous world would do its stupid time thing and go running off without him. So even if he came straight back again, thirty years might go speeding past while he was gone. Or more. A hundred. A thousand. And then what would his chances be of finding his favourite brand? Zero, that was what.

Aengus raged against the day he had taken up the filthy habit. It had seemed quite harmless when he first tried it. A new fad, brought across from America or England or somewhere. Great craic, it was, puffing away like a dragon. But it wasn't so much fun when the stuff got its nasty claws into you. When you found it wasn't you that was running the habit but the habit that was running you.

Not that there was any danger of him dying from it. First sign of a smoker's cough and he could go back home and stay there. He wouldn't get better but he wouldn't get worse, like some of the poor ploddies did who had nowhere else to go. What bothered him, though, was the extent of his desperation. He was horrified by how dependent he had become on the damned stuff. On this trip he had already been knocked out of the sky, faced guns and got soaked to the skin. Now he was sitting in the storm to end all storms, and if he wanted time to stay put, he had no choice but to wait it out. Was he really prepared to endure all that for the sake of his flaming pipe?

The answer, unfortunately, was yes.

33

When Jenny next looked up, she saw that Pup was lying on the bank nearby. His eyes were closed but she didn't think he was asleep. He seemed to be as enchanted by the Dagda's music as she had been, and she was pleased to see it. Even at rest like that, the hardships of his young life were apparent in the gaunt lines and unhealthy colour of his face. The world he had come from was clearly very different from the one she had left.

She picked out a high D whistle and joined in with her grandfather. They played a set of reels, and afterwards the Dagda said, 'Isn't it great? That one is all high and whistly and this one is deep.'

'Yeah,' said Jenny. 'But they're in the same key so they go together. High D and low D.'

'I know that,' said the Dagda, though he didn't. 'And did a ploddy make these?'

'Yes,' said Jenny, deciding against going into the details of factories and manufacturing. 'A ploddy made them.'

'Hard to believe,' said the Dagda. He began another tune and Jenny played along. She noticed that the Dagda's eye kept straying towards Pup, who was still flat on his back on the grass. When the set of tunes ended, he leaned over and prodded him with the long whistle. Pup sat up.

'You,' said the Dagda. 'There are loads of whistles here. Start up a tune, why don't you?'

'I can't,' said Pup. 'I don't know how.'

'Pick something else then,' said the Dagda, waving the whistle at the instruments spread out among the bags and boxes on the bank. 'What's that thing over there, Jenny?'

'It's another kind of accordion,' said Jenny. 'A piano accordion.'

'Play that, then,' said the Dagda. 'Play the piano corjun.'

'I can't,' said Pup. 'I can't play anything. I never learned.'

The Dagda looked at him in total disbelief. The boy might as well have said he'd never learned to breathe. Jenny looked on, thinking it best to stay out of it.

'Well, dance then,' said the Dagda, fitting his fingers to the holes in the whistle. 'Will you have a reel or a hornpipe?'

'I can't dance either,' said Pup.

'How can you not dance?' said the Dagda. 'You have legs, haven't you?'

'I never learned,' said Pup.

The Dagda looked affronted, and Jenny was afraid

he might do something terrible to Pup.

'It's true, Granddad,' she said. 'He's not making it up.'

The Dagda looked amazed, then decisive.

'Well,' he said. 'We'll have to do something about this, won't we?'

34

Donal hunched up his collar and ran for the barracks as fast as his aching legs would carry him. He was drenched again by the time he got there but he didn't even notice. He was preoccupied with bin-bags, hoping against hope that Aidan would release another few rolls of them from his supplies. If the weather didn't change, they'd be needed to protect the loads of treasure on their way into Tír na n'Óg.

He thought he knew how to persuade Aidan. The notes he had spent all afternoon writing would need protecting as well, or they would disintegrate before they got as far as the souterrain beneath the ring fort. So he would need some of those little resealable bags as well, and if he was opening the container anyway . . .

'Sergeant Mooney!' Donal roared, with an exuberance that he hadn't experienced since he was a child. A sleepy young man appeared at one of the bunkroom doors in his shirtsleeves and socks.

'Where's your uniform, man?' Donal bellowed.

Mooney disappeared and returned a moment later, his

jacket on, his boots unlaced. He had never heard his general give orders with such authority.

'Go to the terraces and bring all the gardeners back here,' Donal went on.

'What, now, sir?'

'Yes, now!'

'But there are still four hours of daylight,' Mooney said.

'This is not a discussion!' Donal roared at him. 'Tell the guards there that the commander-in-chief has given the order. And get them all back here pronto, understood?'

The sergeant saluted and raced off, his laces whipping around his ankles.

Donal shouted again. 'Colonel Crowley!'

Crowley was already in his doorway, his uniform buttoned and his boots laced. He regarded Donal with a shrewd curiosity.

'Assemble the men,' Donal said. 'I want to see every single one of them in the mess hall in fifteen minutes.'

Curly saluted, and Donal set off back to the castle, his mind still fixed on the matter of plastic bags.

35

Aengus sat on his rock and glowered. He knew that there were better ways for him to sit out this storm. The salmon would be far more comfortable, lolling in the shallows, and even a hare might be able to crawl into a hole or a crevice and get away from the wind. But he had worked himself into far too bad a temper to do anything as sensible as that, and with every minute that passed, every gust of wind that doubled him over, every stinging shower that drove into his eyes, his mood darkened even more.

Pup sat on the grass, the whistle in his hand, trying his best to understand what the Dagda was showing him.

'It's just a simple polka,' the Dagda said. 'Simplest polka there is. "Breeches Full of Stitches", it's called. Everyone starts out with this one. Come on, try again.'

Pup put the whistle to his mouth.

'That's it,' said the Dagda. 'Don't bite it. Now. All six fingers over the holes. And blow. And now four fingers. No no, not those four!'

Jenny sighed and looked out across the plain. There

were two figures making their way along the Moy road, strolling arm in arm. Aisling. And JJ had come with her.

'Two!' the Dagda was saying. 'Can't you even count? This one and this one. Now blow.'

Jenny tried to remember why it was that Aisling was coming up here. And that reminded her that she had been on her way somewhere as well. With Pup. Where was it they had been going?

'No no no no no!' said the Dagda. 'Look, let's try something different, shall we? Let's sing it first so you know what it's supposed to sound like.'

'Sing?' said Pup.

'Yes, sing,' said the Dagda. 'La-la-la la-la. You know. Sing?'

Pup was shaking his head.

'You can't be serious,' said the Dagda. 'You're not telling me you don't know how to sing.'

'I never learned,' said Pup.

Jenny feared the Dagda might be goaded into inflicting some dreadful retribution on Pup for his musical ignorance, but his reaction could not have been more different. His bearded face melted into a picture of compassion and Jenny thought she could see the filmy beginnings of a tear in his eye.

'You poor, poor child,' he said. 'But how did it happen? How could you have possibly been so deprived?'

36

It was more like half an hour before all the men, including the stragglers from B-Troop and the guards from the terraces, were assembled. Donal left Sergeant Mooney and a handful of younger men standing watch over the frightened 'gardeners' and the captives from Carron. As an afterthought, he ordered Colonel Crowley to join them. Curly gave Donal a hard look.

'Something going on you don't want me to know?' he said quietly as Donal passed him.

'You have your orders, Colonel,' said Donal. 'I presume you are not questioning them.'

The mess hall was the largest covered space in the whole complex. It was made from four containers, their adjoining walls removed and the open edges welded together. Here the men crowded in for their meals, eating from rickety chairs and tables cobbled together from old pallets. Some of them were lounging in these now, creating an irritating creaking chorus that was louder than the storm outside. Normally Donal's pep talks were accompanied by this noise, but he decided that this one would not be.

'Attention!' he roared.

The men got to their feet and stood straight.

'Right,' said Donal. 'I told you this morning that I wanted four men for a mission. Well, that has changed. I now want nine.'

There was silence, and the men expected a renewed round of pleading and badgering for volunteers. But this time was different. Donal walked along the stiff rows, peering into the faces of the older men or the ones who looked exceptionally ill. One man, barely more than a boy, had dreadful skin cancer caused by the vicious sun that came out between the storms. He wasn't long for this world. Donal put him at the top of his mental list. Three times he strolled along the lines, adding names, removing them, adding them back again. Eventually his mind was made up.

'If your name is called, step forward.' He barked out the nine names that had made it on to his final list. The lucky ones, even if they didn't know it.

'What's it for, sir?' one of them said.

'Silence in the ranks!' Donal snapped. 'This operation has been run along sloppy lines for far too long and there'll be no more of it. This is an army, and orders are to be obeyed and not questioned. Anyone who doesn't like it has the option of a free transfer to the terrace construction works.' He paused for effect, noticing as he did so that there was an almost total silence. The storm had abated.

'Any takers?'

There were none. The men had all served their turn standing guard over those deadly, futile works. That was closer than any of them wanted to be.

'Right,' said Donal. 'Let's go.'

By the time they left the barracks, the puddles were already warming up and the rising steam was affecting visibility. In conditions like that it would be easy for a prisoner to slip away unnoticed, and Donal ordered Crowley and Mooney and their group of young soldiers to come along on guard duty as far as the ring fort.

There was no need now for any of the bags. Donal went ahead and opened up his own container in the castle. In closely guarded pairs, the messengers were brought in and loaded up, according to their capacity, with books or pictures, music or instruments. Even the smallest children took something – a block of manuscript paper, a box of oil paints, a clarinet or a roll of prints.

Aidan was there as well, personally handing out the messages one by one and leaving no one, whether soldier or prisoner, in any doubt about what they were expected to do. When the last person had been given their load, Donal surveyed the empty space in his container. It was disappointingly small. His boxes and crates were packed tightly from floor to ceiling, and every chink and gap between them was plugged with an unframed picture or a small, bubble-wrapped sculpture. There were things stowed away in the back that he could never hope to get into Tír na n'Óg, and he sometimes wondered what he had been thinking of when he brought them here. But even without those particular things, there was still four or five times more in the container than had been taken out. It was proving to be a much bigger operation than he had expected. And how many more people, being realistic, was Aidan likely to allow through? None, unless he got some results pretty soon.

He set one last box aside, then locked up the container. At the back of the queue, Curly Crowley was standing guard, his rifle shouldered, his eyes hard and bright and sceptical. When the last in the long line had collected their load and their message and begun the march down the hill, Donal joined him. He was carrying the heavy box which, if he remembered rightly, contained coffee-table books full of photographs – reminders of landscapes and civilizations going or already gone. They walked down towards the ring fort together.

'You going through yourself then, Donal?' said Curly, gesturing towards the box.

'Not me,' said Donal.

'You know this is madness, don't you?' said Curly.

'Trust me,' said Donal. 'Madness or not, you'll thank me for it soon.'

'Thank you?' said Curly. 'Why should I thank you?'

'Because you're going through with them.' Donal offered him the box but Curly didn't take it.

'No way, Donal,' he said. 'I'm not going into that hole.'

'Take the box, Crowley,' said Donal. 'That's an order.'

For a long, long moment the two men stared at each other, and the rising mist shifted around them like a silent observer. Then Curly turned and saw that there were living observers there as well; some of the younger men who had been helping to guard the line. It was a critical moment. If he refused to obey the general's order, then the entire command structure would be undermined. Either that or he would have to make a challenge and take over the army himself. He locked eyes with Donal again, considering it. Then he looked away, and something inside him seemed to give. It was as though, in that moment, he acknowledged his illness and his exhaustion, and resigned himself to whatever fate was in store for him. He reached for the box and took it.

'Very well, sir,' he said.

37

Aengus Óg stood up and stretched. The storm clouds were trundling away inland, wagging their squally tails behind them. Above his head the sky was blue and clear, and the sun was already pricking the skin of his face with its sharp rays. It felt good, after the battering he had taken.

He looked in all directions across the turlough, but a steamy mist was beginning to rise and he could see no sign of the chestnut mare. He was sure she'd had the sense to find her own way home – not that he really cared much either way. He regretted the loss of the apples, though. He could have murdered a good crisp one now.

But at least he would soon have his tobacco. In a burst of enthusiasm he launched himself into a glossy black beating of wings and climbed into the promise of the sky.

Donal stood and watched Curly Crowley, the last of the straggling line, disappear into the hole in the ground. It hurt him to part from his closest friend in such a way and, not for the first time, he hoped he was doing the right thing. The older he got, the more dreamlike his memories became. The raven that appeared from nowhere and turned into a man. The same man, Aengus Óg, turning Mikey into a pig. The púca, growing to an immense size, punching his fist into the ground, pulling it out with a tree in it. A red tree so that his father could make fiddles as good as the old Italian masters.

Could any of it really have happened, or was he suffering from some kind of terrible delusion? It all seemed absurd, but then, so did all his other memories of those days. Shops piled high with every kind of thing imaginable. Warm, dry motor cars speeding from place to place. Aeroplanes that could take people from one side of the planet to the other in twenty-four hours. And food. All that food. Amazing, delicious things from other worlds. Bananas, oranges, pineapples. Meals you could get ready made, just for the effort of going out and buying them. Anything you wanted, all year round. And had there really been mobile phones? Surely it had never been possible to stand in the middle of an Irish field and talk to someone in America or China without even a wire connecting you? From Donal's perspective now, the possibility of a land without time didn't seem any more unlikely than these other kinds of magic.

The púca was definitely real, and so was Mikey's ghost. Unless he really had gone mad, he was talking to them just that morning. And if they were real, then the rest probably was as well. He had to keep believing in what he was doing, otherwise he might not find the strength to go on. He had to believe that the hundred people he had just sent down that muddy hole were going to find themselves in a better place.

That sound came again, that slow beating of wings. He looked up, but the mist was too thick for him to see the sky. The sound receded, then came again, lower this time, closer. The raven burst out of the mist, barely above the level of his head. It banked hard and circled him, and again he had that unsettling sense of recognition. He shook his head and turned away. Anything was possible, in the end, but for the time being Donal preferred to believe that he was imagining things. It was a bird, that was all.

38

The Dagda's compassionate expression was rapidly changing to one of bewildered concern as the ploddy boy proved as incapable of singing as he was of playing the whistle.

'Is he having a game with me?' he asked Jenny plaintively.

'I don't think so,' said Jenny.

'I'm not,' said Pup. 'We never had any instruments or anything. They weren't allowed. The commander-in-chief hates music. He banned it, and if his soldiers ever heard anyone playing or singing, they were arrested.'

'Never mind, never mind,' said the Dagda. 'It's never too late to learn. Try again now, come on.'

He hummed a line of 'Breeches Full of Stitches' and the boy sang something after him that bore no resemblance to it at all. Or to any kind of music, for that matter. The Dagda looked over his head at Jenny. She shrugged. She wasn't exactly worried but something was bothering her, and it was more than the fact that Pup was tone deaf. There was some reason that she had come up here. Pup might remember, if the Dagda ever left him alone for a minute, but she certainly couldn't.

She sighed and, since she couldn't play her nice new whistle with Pup making all that racket, she went back to sorting through the stuff the Dagda had strewn across the grassy bank. Jenny didn't have a tidy disposition and she had never had any interest in accumulating stuff, but there was something disrespectful in the Dagda's treatment of the things and it made her slightly uncomfortable. So she put books and sheet music back into boxes, glancing through them as she did so. She put instruments back into cases. There were one or two she hadn't seen before, but most of them were ploddy basics and nothing to write home about. It wasn't until she came back round to Donal's accordion that the obvious question came to her.

Why? She could see why Donal might want to send his box through. She hoped it meant that he would soon be coming through after it and would play it. But what about all the other stuff? If Pup was anything to go by, and if what he said about music being banned was true, then the ploddies who had brought it through didn't know how to use it.

A movement inside the banks of the rath caught her eye and she turned to look. There were more of them coming, pouring out of the rath with boxes and bags and stacks and cases and pictures. What on earth was it all about?

Jenny stood up to get a better view of them. Like the

last ones, they were extremely muddy, and most of them looked severely undernourished. One by one they emerged with their loads, squinting in the sunshine, bearing the dazed expressions of the newly-arrived in Tír na n'Óg. Ten came through, then ten more. A soldier, two soldiers, then more civilians. And more.

'Granddad?' said Jenny. The Dagda was still engaged with Pup, reduced now to trying to get him to replicate one steady tone at a time. He didn't look up.

The first of the new immigrants had arrived at the bank and were adding their loads to the piles there. Behind them there were still more coming up out of the hole in the ground, like a nest of maggots waking up from a long hibernation. Most of the soldiers with this lot, Jenny noticed, looked pretty infirm, and one of them in particular caught her eye, because his face was covered with awful sores, red raw and bleeding. He stood at the edge of the hole, gazed out at the countryside around him, and broke into a broad grin.

The Dagda had seen them now, and he and Pup were on their feet. Pup was waving in delight at people he recognized, but the Dagda's face was moving through expressions so rapidly that Jenny couldn't keep up with what he was feeling. There was panic first, then fury, then curiosity, then fury again, and it still wasn't clear which of them he would settle upon.

'Excuse me.' A small child was tugging at her sleeve. 'Are you Angit?'

'What?' said Jenny.

The child handed her a crumpled piece of paper, and she was halfway through reading it when she heard a furious roar from her grandfather. Evidently someone had asked him the same question.

'Me?' he was yelling. 'Me? How could you mistake me for that egregious fool? Do I look like an idiot?'

Jenny glanced back at the piece of paper. Aengus. That was what she was supposed to be doing. Finding Aengus and the kidnapped changelings, and getting them all back home. She looked back at Pup. He was shaking hands with one of the soldiers and had the look of a new boy in school showing off to an even newer one.

The Dagda was still roaring. 'Who are you people anyway? What makes you think you can come here and insult people? And why did you bring all that rubbish with you?'

They were still coming: more and more and more. Jenny had lost count.

'What's in those boxes anyway?' the Dagda was roaring, in the same tone of voice. 'Show me that!'

She had to get Aengus back soon. The Dagda wasn't going to put up with much more of this. But as long as people were still coming through, there was no way she could get Pup out with her. It would be like trying to drive the wrong way down a busy one-way street. There was nothing for it but to go ahead without him. He had surely forgotten, in any case. He was happy here. He probably wouldn't even notice she had gone.

39

For safety's sake Jenny went through in the shape of a hare, and it was as well that she did because she popped up two paces from a soldier's boot. He yelled and ran at her, readying his rifle to shoot, but she was never in any real danger. In the blink of an eye she was out of his sight, hidden by the strange, warm, white mist.

She heard him swearing and telling someone else what he'd seen. She could hear other things, too: the shuffle of many feet, the fearful pleading of a young child, a man's voice saying, 'Go on, down you go. Keep moving. Close up the line, there.'

Surely there couldn't be even more people going in? How many was that going to make? Jenny edged closer to the entrance to the souterrain, moving slowly and taking cover among the grey rocks. It was true. There were as many still on this side as had emerged in Tír na n'Óg. One by one they were slithering into the muddy mouth of the souterrain, passing their boxes and bags through to unseen pairs of hands ahead of them and then following them in. Children screamed in fear. Women pleaded with the soldiers. One man dropped the boxes he was carrying and made a run for it, but the soldiers had him within two strides and he was manhandled up to the head of the line and pushed down into the hole. Jenny had to admit that it looked terrifying from this angle. She could well imagine the horror of being shoved into that darkness, and the difficulty in believing that there was really another world on the other side.

When the last of them had gone down, the small group of soldiers that remained stood around the hole, looking in. None of them said anything. One of them was very old, and Jenny thought there was something familiar about his face. He looked a bit like JJ. With a dreadful shock she realized who it was. Her brother, the closest in age to her when she was growing up, had turned into an old, old man.

She crouched behind the rock, her mind reeling. She knew that it happened – she'd seen the effects of it on JJ and Aisling. But that was different somehow. They had been her parents. They were supposed to get old and grey. But Donal was – had been – two years younger than she was. She sat up on her haunches and looked at him again. He was not only old, he was thin and wasted. As she watched, he shifted his weight from foot to foot and made a grimace of pain, which he tried to hide from the soldiers standing around.

Three more of them appeared, rifles first, up out of the hole. They were covered in mud from head to foot.

'All gone through?' said Donal.

'All through, sir,' one said. 'Both chambers empty.'

'Good,' said Donal. 'Mooney? You're promoted to Colonel, as of now.'

'Yes, sir,' said Mooney. 'Thank you, sir.'

'Dismissed, then, all of you. Make your way back to the barracks and await further orders.'

There was a loud swishing sound and a huge raven flew low through the mist and passed above their heads. The soldiers ducked and one raised the muzzle of his rifle. Donal put a hand on it and pushed it down.

'Don't waste ammo,' he said.

In any case, the raven was already gone, vanished into the steamy whiteness. Jenny had recognized Aengus, because gods and their godlings always know each other, whatever form they might take. She was tempted to turn raven herself and follow him but, for the moment at least, there was enough going on here to keep her interest.

The soldiers strode off up the hill and were soon lost in the mist, but Donal stayed for a while at the old fort. The excitement and his displays of authority had exhausted him, and he was beginning to fear that he might not have the energy, mental or physical, to stay the distance and do all that he had to do. If he could only get his brother out of the way, things would be so much easier. Not for the first time, he considered murdering Aidan. He was in a position to do it. He was the only person in the world who had unrestricted access to the commander-in-chief and could be alone with him. The trouble was, he would never get out again. The goons would have him before he was through Aidan's door, and it would be curtains for him. And if that happened, the likelihood was that one of them would take over from Aidan, and they might turn out to be even worse than he was.

In any case, Donal knew he couldn't do it. Murder was not in his nature, any more than being in control of an army was. Some of the things he'd had to do still gave him nightmares. He had gone against his own deepest principles and he could never forgive himself for that. But there was one place where he might at least be able to forget. His longing for Tír na n'Óg intensified. The mouth of the souterrain began to exert an attraction that was almost physical. Why not just go through and be done with it? Regret was one of those feelings that were said not to exist in Tír na n'Óg, wasn't it?

He couldn't, though. Not yet. As long as he had breath, he had to keep going. Every poor wretch that he managed to send through was a life saved. And the other thing, the matter of what each one was taking with them, he sometimes thought was even more important. It was essential that someone, somewhere, even if it was only the fairy folk, should know that the human race had produced more than wars, catastrophes, and ultimately its own slow and painful self-destruction. It had produced things of exquisite and lasting beauty as well. The contents of Donal's container represented the ploddy equivalent of immortality.

40

Aisling and JJ arrived just in time to see the last soldier in the new party arrive through from the souterrain. He was a middle-aged man with red hair, shot through with silver. His face was lined by stress but his eyes were green and bright.

He dropped a heavy box on the ground and took a long deep breath. Pup ran up to greet him.

'Colonel Crowley,' he said. 'Welcome to Tír na n'Óg.'

'Hello, Pup,' said the soldier. 'Well, I'll be damned. The old madman was right all along.'

'Hey, you,' said the Dagda, gesticulating to JJ. 'Come over here.'

JJ went over and joined him on the cluttered bank of the rath.

'What's this?' said the Dagda. 'What's Shakespeare?'

'They're plays,' said JJ, watching him decant the complete works from a plastic box.

'Plays?' said the Dagda. 'Is there tunes in them?'

'Not exactly,' said JJ, searching among the volumes for

A Midsummer Night's Dream. 'But there's one about fairies, if I can find it.'

The Dagda threw *Othello* over his shoulder. 'But why?' he said. 'What are they doing bringing all this stuff over here?'

'I don't know,' said JJ. 'I suppose all immigrants like to bring their culture with them when they have to leave their own countries.'

'Culture,' the Dagda grumbled. 'Is that what they call it?'

He paused to swear at another young ploddy who had the temerity to ask him – again! – if he was Aengus Óg, then made his way over to Aisling, who was trawling through a pile of old scores a few yards away.

'Oh, this is wonderful,' she said. 'These must have belonged to a serious musician. See all these pencil marks? They're really good notes.'

'Notes?' said the Dagda.

'I mean, not musical notes. The black dots are the musical notes but the pencil marks are another kind of note. Reminders to the musician of how to interpret the piece.'

The Dagda gaped at her and she could see he was out of his depth.

'I wish I could show you,' she said. 'I wish I had a piano.'

'A piano?' said the Dagda. 'There's one over there, look.'

'That's not a piano,' said Aisling. She was working hard to prevent herself from laughing, because laughing at the king of the fairies was likely to have dire consequences.

'It's a piano corjun,' said the Dagda. 'Jenny said so. What's the difference?'

'Quite a lot, I'm afraid,' said Aisling. 'A piano is a huge thing.'

'Bigger than that?' said the Dagda, pointing at a double bass in an extremely muddy case.

'Much bigger,' said Aisling, and she was going to go on and explain what a piano looked like, but the Dagda had turned on a ploddy woman who was coming towards them. She hadn't opened her mouth, but she had one of those pieces of paper in her hand.

'No!' the Dagda yelled. 'I am not Aengus Óg. I am nothing like Aengus Óg. Go away! Go away!'

The woman wandered off, too disorientated to be much bothered by the verbal attack. She joined the other newcomers, who were spreading out in all directions, uphill and downhill, scouring Tír na n'Óg for the elusive Aengus Óg.

41

Donal walked back up the hill, on his way to report to his brother. He was pleased with the way the operation had gone, but disappointed to find that he didn't feel like celebrating. There were always more problems ahead, no matter how many were solved in the short term. He found he was already missing Curly Crowley, partly for his companionship but also for the quiet authority he had over the men. Donal thought Mooney would provide that, but whether he would share the other, unspoken understandings remained to be seen. There were those in the army who considered that rounding up old and infirm people and bringing them back was a waste of time and resources. He knew that if they got into power, there would be a lot more quiet shootings and a lot fewer civilian mouths to feed.

By the time he reached Aidan's castle the sun had burned off the white mist and was splitting the stones. The sound of running footsteps behind him made him stop and wheel round. A slight figure was coming up the hill behind him, and Donal's heart soared out of darkness and into the light.

42

'Are you Aengus Óg?' said the Dagda, pushing his hairy face between JJ and his book. 'Are you Aengus Óg?' he said to Pup, and to Aisling, and to one last bewildered ploddy who was approaching him with the same question. 'So where is he then? And why should I bother whether he comes home or not?'

'And where's Jenny?' said Pup, who had just noticed that she was gone.

The Dagda ignored him. 'He's been nothing but trouble since he was born, that son of mine. Meddling in ploddy affairs. Mixing with the riff-raff. Why can't he stay at home and mind his own business?'

'I don't know,' said Aisling to Pup. 'Where is Jenny?'

'And look at all this!' the Dagda went on, regardless. 'How much more of this nonsense do I have to put up with before he bothers himself to come home? We won't be able to move for ploddies, pushing their pieces of paper into our faces.'

'I shouldn't worry,' JJ began.

'Shouldn't worry?' roared the Dagda. 'Shouldn't

worry? It's fine for you to say I shouldn't worry. You're not the one with all the responsibility, are you? I mean, all you have to do is—'

He stopped, silenced by the sound of a plucked string, deep and resonant. He turned, and JJ did too. Aisling had taken one of the better cellos out of its case and was twisting its huge ebony pegs, tuning it up. The Dagda hurried over to investigate.

'Nice one, Aisling,' JJ whispered, and winked slyly at Pup.

43

Jenny threw her arms around Donal. He was wet and cold and his clothes smelled of wood smoke and mildew, but she couldn't let him go. He hugged her back, feeling tension melt from his muscles and tendons, taking the first unconstricted breaths he had taken in decades. She smelled of grass and sunshine. She smelled of Tír na n'Óg.

'What are you doing here?' he said at last, stepping out of the hug to get a proper look at her.

'I'm looking for Aengus,' she said. 'But I'm glad I found you instead.'

The skin of his face was grey and deeply lined but his eyes were unchanged. They were bright and clear and kind.

'Oh, Jenny,' he said. 'You shouldn't have come here. It's a dreadful place now, nothing like it was when you were last here.'

'I know,' she said. 'Pup has been telling me all about it.'

'Pup?' said Donal, his heart leaping again. 'You met up with Pup over there?'

'I did,' she said. 'And loads of others, too.'

'Are they OK?'

'They're fine. A bit confused but fine.'

'Then go back, Jenny. Go and help them settle in. Aengus is sure to go on home in his own good time.'

'It's not as simple as that, though,' said Jenny. 'The Dagda is cutting up rough about all those people that have been going through. And Pup says some children have been kidnapped.'

'I heard that, too,' said Donal. 'But things like that happen all the time over here. People disappear. It's the way things are these days. You can't concern yourself with this world, Jenny. It's too far gone.'

'But I think they're changelings,' said Jenny. 'It sounds like it, from what Pup said. They might be my brothers or sisters or cousins. I have to find out what's happened to them.'

The mystery surrounding the children began to clear in Donal's mind. 'I don't know where they are, Jen, but if it's true that they're changelings, I'm pretty sure that they'll be safe.'

'There's only one place they'll be safe, and that's Tír na n'Óg,' said Jenny. 'I'm not going back without them.'

Donal looked at her again. She had the subtle beauty of her fairy blood, and something else as well. The robust health of a young woman raised in Ireland fifty years before, when food was plentiful and shelter was warm and dry. There was no one who looked like that now.

'OK,' he said. 'I always told the folks that you could look after yourself. I suppose it's as true now as it was then.'

'Of course it is,' said Jenny.

'Then you may as well come along with me,' said Donal. 'I'd like to know what you make of our little brother now.'

44

JJ was trying to persuade Pup that it was too dangerous for him to go back to his own land. Pup heard about Oisín all over again, and about JJ's own adventures in Tír na n'Óg, and soon he was being drawn back into forgetfulness, lolling on the grass, entirely absorbed in the stories. Behind them, further up the bank, Aisling had succeeded in tuning the cello and was plucking a few notes and trying to work out finger positions.

'Give me a go, give me a go,' said the Dagda, wrenching the cello away from her.

'You really need to be sitting down,' she said, and she lugged over a couple of the sturdier boxes and made a seat for him. He barely paused as he sat on it, nestling the cello's neck against his shoulder, the fingers of his left hand stretching for notes. Already he was getting the hang of it, plucking the strings in turn, altering his fingering to get true notes.

Aisling went looking for a bow. The one that had been with the cello was useless. All the hair had been eaten away, whether by insects or by time there was no way of knowing. She found the same thing in each of the three cello cases, so she went over to JJ and asked him if she could borrow one of his fiddle bows. He opened the case and picked one out for her.

'But you went back,' Pup was saying to him, 'and only a month had passed by.'

'I was lucky,' said JJ. 'I might not have been.'

'Well, it can't be much later over there,' said Pup. 'Colonel Crowley and the others who just came through don't look any older than they did when I left.'

'That doesn't mean anything,' said JJ. He was just about to start explaining all over again that in the blink of an eye or the dancing of a set a whole century could pass on the other side, but it all seemed like too much effort.

'In any case,' he finished up, 'you don't need to worry about Jenny. She can look after herself.'

'That's beside the point,' Pup began, but their conversation was interrupted by a cry from Aisling.

'Look, everyone!'

JJ turned to see the Dagda, his great-grandfather, draw the bow across the cello strings. Laboriously but tunefully he began to pick out the notes of 'Breeches Full of Stitches'.

45

The goon on the gate looked suspiciously at Jenny as Donal brought her into the castle, but he allowed her through. Above their heads the raven flew in big, lazy circles, so high that they weren't aware of his presence. But he was aware of theirs, and he was very curious to know what they were doing.

'This place is amazing,' she said. 'How did he get all these lorries piled on top of each other?'

'He hired a big crane on caterpillar tracks,' said Donal. 'It was about forty years ago he built it. Got it all finished inside a fortnight.'

'And what's in them all?' she said.

'Just about anything you can think of,' he said.

There were more goons in the inner courtyard and Donal noticed a bottle of sunscreen doing the rounds. Nothing but the best for Aidan's men. It was a long time since any had been issued to the regular troops, and a lot of them were suffering badly because of it.

Jenny took in her surroundings. There were other people inside the castle as well, taking advantage of the change in the weather. Women were hanging out washing and chopping vegetables outside the kitchen. A boy was pulling a protesting chicken from a wire coop. The raven, still unnoticed, had begun to descend silently.

'Who's the girl?' said a beefy guard who stood outside the door of Aidan's private complex, looking at Jenny with entirely the wrong kind of interest.

'She's the commander-in-chief's sister,' said Donal. 'If you know what's good for you, you'll keep your filthy eyes off her.'

The guard looked doubtful, but he complied. He slid the hatch off a small grille on the door and called through it. 'General Liddy and . . . and guest.'

'Two minutes,' a voice came back.

Jenny and Donal leaned against the wall beside Aidan's door.

'How have you been?' she asked him.

It was too big a question, and Donal was at a loss. He shrugged.

'Married? Children?' Jenny asked.

Donal shook his head. He had never married, because he had been in no hurry when he was a young man, and now no one got married unless Aidan decided they would. A lot of women lived within the castle compound. They were responsible for running the castle kitchen and laundry, and nearly all of them were the wives and daughters of Aidan's private guards. There were a few children there as well, and the thought of them made

Donal feel a momentary self-pity. He would love to have had children. He would have been a far better father than he was a soldier.

'No family,' he said. 'Unless you count the army.'

There was the sound of heavy bolts being drawn and the door was opened by another of Aidan's men. Donal and Jenny slipped inside, and just as they did so, the huge raven dropped from the skies and swooped in through the gap above their heads.

46

Inside Aidan Liddy's custom-built container home, all hell broke loose. The goon who had opened the door reacted too slowly to the sudden appearance of the enormous black bird and slammed the door shut after it had come in. In any case, by the time he realized his mistake, the bird was no longer a bird, but a tall, fair-haired man.

What came next happened too fast for Donal to see, and he had to piece it all together afterwards. Because suddenly the room was full of guns, all pointing at Aengus, and just as suddenly the guns were falling to the floor because the four goons had been transformed into two kittens and two Doberman Pinscher dogs. The fifth gun – Aidan Liddy's own pistol – was dropped voluntarily as he first put his hands up over his head, then changed his mind and lunged for a massive bunch of keys that was lying on the table.

'Not me, not me!' he blustered, waving the keys in front of his face. 'You can't do that to me!'

The two dogs were advancing on Aengus, their lips drawn back over ferocious teeth, their hackles raised.

'Honestly, Dad,' said Jenny, in that scathing tone that teenagers reserve for their parents. 'Dobermans?' And she turned them into two fat Labradors, which made a brief, friendly investigation of everyone and then collapsed to the floor, panting happily.

'Who . . . who are you?' Aidan stammered. He was trembling so violently that the keys, still held in front of his face, jingled like wind chimes.

'Sorry,' said Aengus, stretching out a hand. 'Aengus Óg. And this person here is my daughter, er . . . erm . . .'

'Jenny,' said Jenny.

'Jenny,' said Aengus. 'Exactly. But I wouldn't be able to tell you what she's doing here.'

'Yes,' said Aidan. 'I know Jenny.' He acknowledged her with a nod, which she declined to return.

'But tell me this,' she said, gesturing towards the dogs. 'Why shouldn't we do that to you? I think a pig would suit you very well, from what I hear about your activities around here.'

'Ah,' said Aidan, fumbling at his key ring with hands that still trembled, and selecting a single key, which he held up to show them. It meant nothing. He might as well have been showing them one bristle on a hedgehog. 'Because I have something of yours. And if you turn me into a pig you'll never know where to find them.'

'Don't be ridiculous,' said Jenny. 'If you were a pig, we'd still have the key.'

'Yes, you would,' said Aidan. 'But what use is a key if you don't know what it opens?'

'Oh, to hell with this,' said Aengus, whose one and only interest was how to get his hands on some tobacco. 'I didn't come here to play treasure-hunting games.'

'No, no, indeed you didn't,' said Aidan. 'And I would have arranged a far better reception for you, Aengus Óg, but I didn't expect you to arrive so soon.'

'Expect me?' said Aengus. 'Who told you I was coming?'

'Well . . .' Aidan spluttered. 'I just . . . I assumed . . .'

'You assumed what?'

A voice came through the grille in the door. 'Everything OK in there, boss?'

'Yes, yes,' Aidan snapped. 'Stop fussing!' He turned back to Aengus. 'I just assumed you had come in response to my note.'

'Your note?'

'I sent some people across into Tír na n'Óg looking for you.'

Aengus was beginning to look dangerous. 'You think I came because of that? You think you can summon a god with a note?'

'Oh,' said Aidan. 'No, no, of course not. I wouldn't begin to presume . . . er . . . to assume—' He stopped, tongue-tied, and then went on, 'So why did you come, then?'

Aengus roared so loud that the kittens fled underneath the sofa and the dogs stopped panting and looked guilty.

'I just want a smoke! What does a man have to do around here to get a bit of tobacco?'

47

Aisling had gone back to investigating the music and was searching through a new box. This one was less interesting than the last one, with lots of exam pieces and books for beginners. She did her best to block out the din beside her. The Dagda's fingering was nearly perfect and he was singing along tunefully, but he had dragged Pup in again and his efforts were painful to listen to.

JJ was investigating the fiddles that had been brought across. The first case he opened contained a mass-produced Chinese instrument plastered in livid red varnish. He shuddered and slammed the lid. The next one held an old German instrument that would probably make a half-decent fiddle with a proper set-up. But the third held a delightful surprise. It was one of his own instruments, made when he was in his fifties. It was unmistakable, not only because of the particular Strad model he'd copied, but also because this one had been made on special order for a musician in Galway, and instead of the regular scroll which completed the pegbox it had a lion's head.

The bow that was with it was a good one, too, and would have cost a small fortune when it was bought. Like the cello bow it was completely hairless, but unlike the cello bow it was well worth the effort of rehairing. JJ thought about the white horse down beside the Moy road and wondered how it would react to having a few hairs pulled out of its tail.

Pup was bored to tears. He had quite enjoyed listening to the Dagda playing the whistle, but this singing malarkey was driving him up the wall. He didn't believe any of JJ's guff about life passing by on the other side and people turning to dust. He knew he could go back and look for his brother and he had every intention of doing so. But he had been around enough dangerous men in his life to recognize that this bearded character had a lot of power, and it wouldn't do to get on the wrong side of him. So he could see no alternative but to keep on humouring the Dagda and trying to copy the sounds emerging from the beard.

He wasn't the only one who was coming to the end of his tether. JJ had gone some distance away and was restringing the lion-head fiddle with new strings from his fiddle case, but Aisling, who had perfect pitch, was suffering badly. Pup's desperate efforts were straining her nerves to breaking point. So when she came across a simple piece of music in the beginner's box, it gave her an idea.

'Dagda?' she called. 'How would you like to try your hand at a trio?'

48

'Any particular brand?' said Aidan to Aengus.

'Yes,' said Aengus, and named it. 'And I need a lighter as well. Mine got wet.'

'I think I may be able to oblige you,' said Aidan.

Donal suspected that he could. Tobacco, along with sun block, sugar, tea and toilet paper, had long ago been removed from the lists of army rations and saved for the sole use of Aidan and his guards.

'You wouldn't mind fetching it?' Aidan asked him, selecting a key from his enormous bristling bunch and carefully working it free. 'Container number thirty-seven. Just below yours, I think you'll find.'

Donal took the key and Jenny went with him to the door. He squeezed out under the curious noses of the goons and she pushed it closed behind him and slid the bolts home.

'Nice to see you, Jenny,' Aidan said. 'You haven't changed a bit.'

'Nor have you,' said Jenny. 'You always were a nasty, selfish little brat.'

'Sometimes that's what it takes to survive in this world,' said Aidan glibly. 'Where do you think our Donal would be now if I hadn't built this place and taken care of everybody?'

'Probably playing his squeeze box with Mum and Dad,' she said. 'I don't know why he stayed here for so long.'

'Don't you believe it,' said Aidan. 'Donal loves power as much as I do. Why do you think I put him in charge of the army?'

Jenny couldn't answer that. It didn't fit with her memory of Donal, or even what she had seen of him since she got back. He didn't look or act like a hardened army general. But that, apparently, was what he had become.

It was pouring with rain again outside, and Donal was soaked to the skin before he got to the other side of the central compound. The goons, snug in their waterproof jackets and hoods, watched him suspiciously as he passed between them towards the 'dry' wall of the castle compound. That wall was where the most precious things were stored – the things that could not withstand dampness. An ingenious heating system, powered by a bio-mass boiler, circulated through the containers and kept the contents in a dry and warm environment.

Aidan's ones held, among other things, dried and tinned food, tea, coffee and cigarettes, duvets, pillows, and large quantities of new clothes and shoes. Everything he stored there was either edible, tradeable or comfortable. But the contents of Donal's container were none of those things. In Gort's pathetic market they would have had no value whatsoever. He had picked them all up for next to nothing at the time of the End of Imports. When the cities and towns were looted, Donal's treasures were left behind, untouched and unwanted. He'd had the field entirely to himself. All he had needed was a van.

He climbed the ladder and opened container number thirty-seven. The atmosphere in there was still perfect, conditioned by the pipes that ran along the walls and across the floor. But Donal knew it couldn't be maintained for much longer. The boiler required a lot of fuel to keep it running, and that fuel – logs and sticks and sods of turf – just wasn't there any more. It wouldn't be long before Aidan would be forced to shut it down, and within weeks of that happening these stacked goods would begin to decay.

He walked down the twin aisles, reminded of the supermarket shelves of his childhood. In here were boxes of paper, envelopes, sellotape, medicines. There were packets of pasta and rice and beans, seeds and dried fruit and nuts, all double- and triple-protected by layers of plastic boxes. There were crates and crates of tinned stuff, all decades past its sell-by date. A lot of it would be inedible by now, but some of it was still good, and the castle diet was supplemented by twenty-year-old baked beans and rice pudding and peaches. Donal slid a plastic-wrapped block of A4 paper into the poacher's pocket of his jacket and emptied a box of ballpoint pens in beside it. He took a few boxes of aspirins, opened one, and popped a couple of tablets into his mouth. He felt like a child in a sweetshop and looked around for other things to pilfer from his brother, but there was nothing else he could see that he needed.

It wouldn't do to be away for too long. He found a plastic bag and filled it with tobacco and cigarette lighters, then left the container and locked it up behind him.

Jenny watched Aengus Óg, who was on his knees on the floor, trying to coax the kittens into coming out from under the sofa.

'So what have you been up to?' Aidan asked her.

That was difficult to answer. More than fifty years had passed here since she left to go to Tír na n'Óg, and she certainly didn't have fifty years worth of news.

'Oh, you know,' she said. 'This and that. And you?'

'Just what you see,' said Aidan, gesturing to his surroundings. 'I don't go out much these days.'

'Why have you started kidnapping children, Aidan?' she asked.

'I'm going to get around to that,' he said. 'Let's wait for Donal to come back first, shall we?'

Aengus had captured a kitten, which was hissing and spitting like water thrown on the fire. 'It doesn't like me,' he said. 'Why doesn't it like me?'

'You've got it upside down,' said Jenny, and she was on her way over to rescue the kitten when a knock came at the door.

'I'll get it,' she said, with a warning look at Aidan. She unbolted it and opened it a crack, then closed it again and called through the grille. 'Everybody stand back except Donal.'

She looked again. The goons had withdrawn a few paces, so she let Donal in. He turned and slid home the bolts behind him. Aengus saw the tobacco under his arm and dropped the kitten, which twisted in mid air, landed on its feet and fled back under the sofa.

He reached for the tobacco but Aidan got there ahead of him and took it from Donal.

'Wait a minute,' he said. 'We haven't talked terms yet.'

'Terms?' said Aengus. 'What terms? Do I have to sign for it or something?'

'Nothing like that,' said Aidan. 'Sit down, sit down. Make yourself comfortable. Let me explain why it is I wanted to see you.'

49

The Dagda couldn't read music, but the cello part only had four notes repeated in a simple pattern and Aisling was able to teach him how it went. Since she'd been deprived of her piano she had taken up the flute instead, but for this little piece she decided to try the piano accordion. JJ got another bow from his case and tuned up the lion-head fiddle.

The piece had been designed, Aisling thought, rather than composed. It was incredibly simple and held no musical surprises at all. But its harmonies were sweet, and when they came to the end, the Dagda was inspired.

'Again,' he said. 'Play it again.'

So they did, and then again, and then again. When the Dagda eventually allowed them to stop, he turned to Aisling, a look of amazement on his face.

'You're not going to tell me a ploddy wrote that?'

Aisling laughed. 'Oh, I wish I had a piano. I wish I could play some of the pieces that ploddies have written. You'd love Bach, I know you would.'

'Well, it can't be much better than this,' said the

Dagda. 'Come on, let's play it again.' He lifted his bow and then stopped. 'Is there a part in it that little fella could play?' he said.

But the little fella, when they looked round for him, was nowhere to be seen.

50

'I suppose you've noticed,' said Aidan, 'that things have changed a bit over here.'

'Well,' said Aengus, 'the shops aren't what they used to be, that's for sure.'

'They're not, are they?' said Aidan. 'In fact, it's worse than that. There isn't even anything left for the shops to sell. There are no trees for firewood, no cattle or sheep to eat, hardly any wild animals left to shoot.'

'Shocking,' said Aengus, looking pointedly at the tobacco, which Aidan was holding firmly in his lap.

'And the weather makes it practically impossible to grow food. I saw it coming, of course. I built up a fantastic stronghold here and laid in tons and tons of supplies.'

The braver of the two kittens emerged from beneath the sofa and Aengus made a grab for it. He missed, and it vanished again.

'But even those are running out now,' Aidan went on. 'I'm sure you see my problem, Aengus. I have my household to run and my army to feed. We're all facing disaster here.'

'Come over then,' said Aengus cheerfully. 'Eat up what you have left and come over to my place. Bring everyone. If your bellies are full when you get there, you'll never be hungry again. No time to get hungry in, you see?'

Jenny was surprised to hear Aengus say something as sensible as that. It seemed to her like an excellent solution to everyone's problems. If the tyrant and his army were out of the way, then families like Pup's might be able to hang on and make a go of it. But Aidan was not so impressed by the idea.

'Never,' he said, with absolute conviction. 'There is no way I could go somewhere else and submit to someone else's rules.'

'Do we have rules?' Aengus said to Jenny.

'You don't understand,' said Aidan. 'This is my kingdom. Nothing happens unless I order it. No one eats or sleeps or moves without my permission. You expect me to give up all that?'

'It's not a bad idea though, Aidan,' said Jenny. 'You wouldn't miss any of it once you got to Tír na n'Óg. You probably wouldn't even remember most of it.'

'But I want to remember it!' said Aidan. 'I don't want to wander around in a daze and be subjected to that diddly-aye music and have Aengus Óg telling me what to do.'

'Do I tell people what to do?' said Aengus.

'Well, what alternative do you have?' said Jenny.

'I'm glad you asked that,' said Aidan. 'Because that's why I've asked Aengus to come here. I've been studying the literature, you see. And I reckon Aengus here can sort out all our problems for us.'

'I can?' said Aengus, without taking his eyes off the kitten, which was beginning to creep out again.

'I know what you can do,' said Aidan. 'I know that you can produce feasts and banquets with a click of your fingers. With magic like that, nobody would ever need to go hungry again.'

'What's he talking about?' Aengus asked Jenny.

'Glamour, I'd say,' she said.

The kitten had reached the leg of Donal's chair. The rainwater that had drenched his clothes when he went out to get the tobacco was now dripping into a puddle around his feet, and the kitten had walked into it by accident. It was shaking its paws in irritation, one after the other. Donal reached down quietly and picked it up.

Aengus watched, annoyed. 'Why should we do tricks for you, just because you tell us to?' he said. 'We're not performing monkeys.'

Aidan waved his keys again. 'Because I have something you want.'

'I know that,' said Aengus, and there was a flash of danger in his eyes now. 'You have my tobacco.'

'Is that all?' said Aidan. 'Really? You don't want your children back?'

'My children?' said Aengus. 'I'm not missing any children.' He pointed at Jenny. 'This one here is my youngest.'

'Is that so?' said Aidan. 'Well, I have three of your changelings in my possession. They must belong to somebody.'

'Oh, wait a minute,' said Aengus. 'Now you come to mention it, I might have another one growing up somewhere. But we never worry about them. They make their own way home when they're ready.'

'Well, these ones won't,' said Aidan, waving the keys again.

'Oh, that won't bother them,' said Aengus. 'They're—'

Jenny elbowed him in the ribs. 'Dad! You have to take this more seriously!'

'Do I?' said Aengus. 'All right, then. If you say so, Jen. What is it he wants?'

'Food,' said Aidan. 'Feasts.'

'Glamour,' said Jenny.

'Oh, all right,' said Aengus. 'We can probably rustle up a bit of glamour if that's what you want. But it won't do you any good, you know.' He reached out and pulled Donal's woollen hat off his head and dropped it on to the table, where it turned into a chocolate pudding. 'Let's see,' he went on. 'What else?'

As Aidan watched, his gun turned into a loaf of hot, crusty bread, the plastic fruit into muffins, the stack of fairy books into a leg of roast lamb surrounded by crisp, golden potatoes. Steam rose from the food and the room filled with mouth-watering smells.

'Happy now?' said Aengus. He turned to Donal. 'Give me a go of that furry thing, will you?'

The kitten was purring contentedly in Donal's lap, but the moment he handed it to Aengus it stopped and started wriggling and mewling.

'That's exactly what I meant,' said Aidan. 'I knew it! I knew that it would work.'

'There's only one snag as far as I can see,' said Jenny.

'And what's that?' said Aidan.

'Well, see for yourself. Go on. Have a taste of the chocolate pudding.'

Aidan hesitated for a moment, then plunged two plump fingers into the pudding and licked them. 'Mmm. Delicious,' he said, putting the fingers back in and scooping out another mouthful. 'Scrumptious.'

'Why is it squawking?' said Aengus, trying to restrain the struggling kitten.

'Other way up, Dad,' said Jenny. 'I wouldn't eat too much of that now, Aidan. You might regret it.'

Donal, who had been watching quietly throughout, suddenly came to a realization. 'It's not real, is it?' he said. 'It's just made to look irresistible. That's what glamour does.'

'Didn't you know that?' said Jenny.

But Donal didn't answer. The realization had brought with it a sudden stark insight into another kind of glamour. It was a long time ago now, but he saw it all quite clearly: how the media and the advertisers had created their own kind of glamour to seduce whole populations into a kind of insanity. Food that was bad for people, drink that turned them into mindless thugs, countless tons of useless rubbish, all dressed up by advertising glamour to appear like things people couldn't live without. And the human race had fallen for it hook, line and sinker, becoming what the business moguls and advertising chiefs had wanted them to become. Consumers of limitless glamour, all of it ultimately worthless.

And where had it got them? To this. A world used up and overheating, and the human race on its way down the drain.

Aidan had stopped eating and was looking distinctly uncomfortable.

'Look,' said Aengus, who had finally got the kitten the right way up and was cradling it against his chest. 'In all fairness I don't think this is the answer to your problems. All this impending disaster stuff isn't my department. You'd be much better off having a chat with my father.'

'Your father?' said Aidan. The chocolate pudding was giving him a stomach ache and it had left a distinct aftertaste of sodden wool and wood smoke.

'The Dagda,' said Aengus. 'He might be able to help you. All kinds of powers, my father has. He can fix anything. He might even be able to sort out your climate for you. And he'd definitely be impressed by your thing with the bunch of keys. He's mad about his family, the Dagda is. Except for me, maybe.'

'That sounds good,' said Aidan. 'So how can I get to meet him?'

'Come over,' said Aengus. 'I'll tell you where to find him.'

'Oh, no,' said Aidan. 'You're not going to fool me with a trick like that.'

'Right,' said Aengus. 'Tell you what. Give me that tobacco and I'll go and fetch him for you. Is that a deal?'

Before Aidan could answer, Aengus snatched the bag from his grasp and vanished. The tobacco, being inanimate, vanished with him. The kitten, being in essence a ploddy goon, did not.

Even Jenny was surprised by the suddenness of Aengus's departure. In the moment it took her to wonder whether it might be a good idea to go with him, she lost the opportunity. Because Aidan acted like lightning. Before anyone could react, he leaped to his feet and, with astonishing speed, was behind Donal and had a gun to his head.

Another gun. Jenny winced. She should have suspected he would have one, but she hadn't.

'Don't try anything,' Aidan said. 'If you disappear, I'll shoot him.'

She ran through her options in her mind, but he was ahead of her at every step. 'Do you think you can, Jenny, eh?' he said. 'Can you turn me into a pig quick enough, do you think? Only takes a fraction of a second for my trigger-finger to act, you know. Would you risk it?'

She wouldn't, and he knew she wouldn't. She said nothing.

'He was your favourite brother, wasn't he, Jen?' Aidan went on. 'Donal and Jenny, always off around the place together.'

It wasn't how Jenny remembered it, but it was true that she had been closer to Donal than to any of the others.

'You wouldn't want anything to happen to him, would you? You'll stay with us for a while, at least until your clever grandfather turns up.' As Aidan spoke, he was backing towards the door. He called through the grille and, with the gun still aimed at Donal's head, drew the bolts with his free hand. Two goons burst in, bristling with weapons. But it seemed that reinforcements weren't the only things Aidan had on his mind.

As soon as the men were inside the door, he snapped out an order.

'Get me a drink,' he said.

51

Aengus sat on the hill in the lee of the stony steps and eagerly filled his pipe. But the tobacco was disappointing. It was little more than dark brown dust, and when he lit the pipe, it flared up and singed his hair. The smoke burned his throat and made him cough.

'A pox on these ploddies anyway,' he said. 'Can they never get anything right?'

He packed the pipe again, tighter this time, and managed to get enough smoke into him to finally calm his cravings. But it was not a nice experience, and he was still coughing and spitting out bitter tobacco dust when he put away the pipe and set off down the hill.

At the bank of the rath he discovered a strange scene. His father was sitting on a box with an outsized fiddle between his legs, and Aisling appeared to be teaching him how to read.

'That's D there,' she was saying. 'And so the next one up is E.'

'Hello, Aengus,' said JJ. 'You know the white horse down there on the road?'

'What about it?' said Aengus.

'Is it quiet?' said JJ. 'Would it mind if I pulled some hairs out of its tail?'

The Dagda looked up from the music score and noticed Aengus Óg. 'There you are,' he said. 'What have you been up to this time?'

'Well,' said Aengus, 'since you ask—'

'Wait a minute,' said the Dagda. He closed his eyes and concentrated for a moment, and the others felt a strange, subtle jolt beneath their feet.

'What was that?' said JJ.

'Barricades are up,' said the Dagda. 'No more coming and going. Let's see the ploddies try and get through now!'

On the other side of the time skin the jolt was felt as well, but it was a gentle sensation and nothing like the storms that rocked the container castle every day. No one took any notice of it except Jenny. She had never experienced it before, but her instincts told her what it was, and a tentative exploration with her free hand confirmed her fears.

She was filled with despair and terror. Like all the fairy folk she was not inclined to worry, and although it wasn't very nice being held captive by her brother and his nasty henchmen, she'd had no doubt that she would, sooner or later, manage to get away. But that subtle tremor in the world's edge represented a death sentence to her. If she couldn't get back to Tír na n'Óg, she was condemned to sharing the ploddies' miserable and doomed existence. She was no different from anyone else trapped on this side and subject to the irreversible effects of time. Like them she would now have to live with the awful fact that, sooner or later, she would die.

'You sealed the time skin?' said JJ to the Dagda.

'But Jenny isn't back yet,' said Aisling. 'And I think that little lad might have gone back through as well.'

'That little lad who was here?' said the Dagda. 'The one who couldn't play?'

'Maybe you could open it and then close it again when they come back,' said JJ.

'Actually,' said Aengus Óg, 'that might not be a bad idea. Thing is, Dad, there are a few of us still over there.'

'What?' said the Dagda.

'And I said you'd go over and sort it out.'

'What?' roared the Dagda.

'And stop it raining and blowing. You should see the storms they get over there. Serious stuff.'

'What?' bellowed the Dagda.

Aengus went on doggedly. 'And the thing is, that son of his has turned into a bit of a warlord and by all accounts he's making everyone's life a misery.'

'Whose son?' said the Dagda.

'JJ's,' said Aengus. 'And he's got some of our kids locked up somewhere and he says he won't let them out unless you go over there and put everything right.'

The ground was trembling beneath their feet again, but this time it had nothing to do with the time skin. The whole of Tír na n'Óg was affected by the Dagda's momentous rage.

'How dare he?' he roared. 'How dare he take my children hostage and make outrageous demands of me?'

'That's exactly what I said—' Aengus began, but the Dagda ignored him.

'I will not go over to that godforsaken place under any circumstances. I will not make deals with a despot. I will not even enter into a discussion!' He looked around wildly in his fury, and his eye fixed on JJ, who was in the act of trying to make a quick getaway.

'You!' he called. 'This is all your fault!'

'Me?' said JJ. 'How could it be my fault?'

'Because it's your corrupt offspring that is causing all this trouble.'

JJ might have pointed out that the Dagda washed his hands entirely of Aengus Óg's indiscretions, but he was aware of what might happen to him if he didn't play his cards very carefully indeed.

'Well, I'm sorry if you think that,' he said, 'but—'

'But nothing!' said the Dagda. 'Get over there and sort this mess out!'

'Get over there?' said JJ.

'He can't,' said Aisling, stepping over to JJ and clutching his arm.

'Of course he can!' said the Dagda.

'Actually, Father,' said Aengus, 'I think she might be right.'

'I don't care what you think, Aengus Óg,' said the Dagda. 'That white horse down there is bored out of its brain. It'll do it the world of good to get a bit of exercise.'

JJ gasped. The white horse. He knew, as everyone did, that it was the one that had taken Oisín across the time skin and come back without him, but it had never occurred to him that it could do it again. 'Now hang on a minute,' he said.

'I will not hang on,' said the Dagda. 'If you value your skin, JJ Liddy, you will do as I say. Get up on the white horse and go over to Ireland. And don't come back until you have set my children free!'

Aengus strode over and threw a hearty arm around JJ's shoulders. 'He's right, you know. You've nothing to worry about. So long as you don't get down from the horse you'll be grand.'

'Oh yeah,' said JJ. 'Just like Oisín was grand.'

'Well, he fell off, the old eejit,' said Aengus. Then he raised his voice and said, very loudly, 'And anyway, you can't go over because my genius of a father has just sealed up the time skin.'

There was a grunt from behind them and they felt a second jolt, just like the first.

'That's the job,' said Aengus. 'Come on, JJ. Let's go and find the old nag.'

Reluctantly JJ went with him. Aisling set out to join them, but the Dagda called her back.

'I have a job for you as well, Mother of Ireland's Woes.'

'Oh, great,' said Aisling sourly.

'I want you to find all those ploddies that are wandering round as if they owned the place and bring them back up here.'

52

Jenny felt the second jolt and breathed a sigh of relief as she was reprieved from the sentence of death. She didn't know what all the opening and closing meant, but she very much hoped that Aengus Óg hadn't just gone to sleep somewhere and that help was on its way. She needed it badly. Two of Aidan's other men were sitting in there with them now, but Aidan himself was keeping the gun to Donal's head, not trusting anyone else to do it.

'You might give me my men back now,' Aidan said, gesturing towards the dogs and kittens.

'I prefer them the way they are,' she said.

Aidan said nothing, considering whether it was worth making an issue of it, and decided it wasn't.

'How long are we going to stay like this?' said Donal.

'Sorry, brother,' said Aidan. 'I hope you're not taking it too personally.'

'It feels pretty personal,' said Donal, 'having a loaded gun pressed into your head.'

'It's not, though,' said Aidan. 'You just happen to be a useful bargaining chip. I have four of them now, you see.

Four fairy children. That ought to make some impression on your grandfather, don't you think, Jenny?'

'Is that what we're waiting for?' said Jenny. 'Do you really think the Dagda is going to come running over and wave his magic wand?'

'I certainly hope so,' said Aidan. 'I'm already getting bored. And if I run out of patience, we're going to have to think of something else, aren't we?'

'Like what?' said Jenny.

'Leave it with me,' said Aidan. 'I'll come up with something.'

53

Crossing over into Tír na n'Óg had not caused Pup the same problems it had caused the others in his party. He had remembered who he was, what he was supposed to be doing, and that his brother had been kidnapped. But returning was quite different. After he emerged from the souterrain he stopped and sat on the bank, examining his gun and wondering how he'd come by it, and what he was supposed to do with it, and why.

The rain fell and the wind picked up, and eventually Pup had to get up and go in search of some kind of shelter. As soon as he did so, his feet put him on the path that led up the hill, and when the barracks came into view he remembered that they were his home. He couldn't clearly recall where it was he had just come from, but he knew it was a better place than this was.

He was amazed by the reception he got. When the sentries at the gate saw him coming, they raced into the courtyard and raised the cry.

'Pup's home! They're coming back from the other side! Pup has come home!'

By the time he went in, all the doors were open and men were streaming out of their quarters to greet him. He was inundated with questions.

'What's it like?'

'Where are the others?'

'What's the food like?'

'What have you brought back?'

'Where's the loot?'

The questions jogged his memory, and before long it all came back to him. He remembered his mother visiting the barracks to tell him his brother had been kidnapped, and how he tricked his way in and confronted the commander-in-chief. He remembered the execution order, and thinking that his life was over. But he had been rescued from that by the one person who had always made his life in the barracks worth living. So the soldiers got no answers, but only another question.

'Where's the general? I have to report to General Liddy.'

'He's up at the castle,' Mooney told him. 'But tell me this. Did you see Crowley over there? Did he get there safely?'

'He did, sir,' said Pup. 'And he was delighted to find out it was all real after all. You should have seen his face.'

'Well, I'm Colonel here now that Crowley's gone,' said Mooney. 'You can report to me since the general isn't here.' But when he saw the disappointment in the young soldier's face, he went on, 'All right, then. Go up to the castle and find him, then come back here and tell us all about your adventures.'

So Pup set out for Aidan's castle. It wasn't far, not much more than a couple of hundred metres, but the closer Pup got, the slower he went. What if the sentry at the gate didn't send him to the general, but to the commander-in-chief? Would he remember him? Would he decide to have him shot by firing squad after all, particularly as he had returned from the mission empty-handed and without the rest of his party?

He sat down beside the path. The rain had stopped temporarily but the wind was growing stronger by the minute, and Pup had a sudden clear memory of the calm warmth of Tír na n'Óg and wondered why he had bothered to come back. His brother. It was because his brother had been kidnapped. But what could he do about it? Confronting Commander Liddy had led nowhere, and he still had no better ideas.

He was on the point of returning to the barracks when a pair of the commander-in-chief's guards emerged from the castle and came in his direction. It would look bad to get up and run now, so he stood in the path and waited.

'What are you doing there, soldier boy?' one of them asked.

'I'm on my way to report to General Liddy, sir,' said Pup.

'Oh, are you?' said the goon. 'Well, the general is

indisposed just now. He's not feeling too good. And since you're here you can save us a trip to the barracks.'

'Yes, sir,' said Pup.

'The general sent us with a message for Colonel Crowley. He says he's unwell and, until he gets orders to the contrary, Colonel Crowley is to take charge of the army.'

Pup opened his mouth to speak, then closed it again.

'Got that?' said the goon.

'Yes, sir,' said Pup.

'Off you go then,' said the goon. 'Quickly. There's a big storm on the way.' And they both turned and went back towards their warm, comfortable quarters in the castle.

54

JJ leaned on the gate and watched as Aengus tacked up the white horse. He didn't seem to be entirely sure which bit of leather went where, but the horse was clearly delighted to get some attention and stood waiting patiently while Aengus worked it all out. It dropped its head into the bridle, opened its mouth for the bit, made no objection when Aengus tugged at its ears and forelock and put a finger in its eye while he was reaching for the throat-lash. In fact, JJ had the impression that the horse would have tacked itself up if it could have.

But none of that made him feel any more confident about his upcoming mission or his prospects of success. Leaving aside the very real possibility of falling off and being reduced to a clatter of mouldy old bones, there was also the small matter of what he was supposed to do when he got there. He had never had any success in imposing discipline on his youngest son and he held out no hope that anything would have changed in the twenty-five years or so that had passed over there since he had last seen him. The very notion of telling Aidan to get his act together and stop causing trouble was absurd. The whole mission was a wild-goose chase, and an extremely dangerous one at that.

But what alternative did he have? There was no opposing the Dagda on his home turf, and there was no hiding from him either. And although he hadn't been threatened with any specific sanctions, he could imagine a whole variety of unpleasant destinies if he refused to follow orders.

'That should do it,' said Aengus, patting the horse on the shoulder and leading it forward. 'Up you get.'

JJ was not a rider. A weekend at a trekking centre in Donegal with his oldest daughter, Hazel, was the extent of his experience. He remembered the bit about putting your foot in the stirrup and hauling yourself aboard, but he didn't remember the bit where the saddle slid sideways and you landed on your rear end in the grass.

'Oops,' said Aengus. 'Girth isn't tight enough.'

JJ stood up and brushed himself down. There were no bones broken, but all the same, it was not the kind of start he might have hoped for.

55

The goons were right. There was another storm on the way, and by the time Pup had covered the short distance back to the barracks it was already blowing at full strength. Rain was hitting the containers sideways on, and forcing its way through cracks and rusted seals.

The other men were eagerly awaiting his return.

'You were quick,' said Colonel Mooney. 'Did you see the general?'

'No, sir,' said Pup. 'But I have a message. Can I give it to you in private?'

'All right, Pup.'

Now that Mooney was promoted to Colonel, he had moved into Crowley's cramped quarters beside Donal's. As soon as the door was closed behind them, Pup said, 'There's something wrong, sir.'

'Go on,' said Mooney.

'I met two of the commander-in-chief's men. They said the general was ill and they were bringing a message from him.'

'A message for me?'

'That's the thing, sir,' said Pup. 'It wasn't. It was a message for Colonel Crowley and it was about taking command of the army until the general came back. But it couldn't have been from him, could it, sir? Because he knows that Colonel Crowley has gone to Tír na n'Óg. He knows you're the colonel now.'

'How ill is he?' said Mooney.

'I don't know, sir. But he'd need to be very bad indeed to forget something like that, wouldn't he?'

'You're right,' said Mooney. 'I wonder what's going on.'

'I wonder, too, sir,' said Pup.

56

The horse set out along the road at a jaunty but not particularly rapid pace. This suited JJ just fine. He was in no rush to get to the next bit – the dangerous bit – and a mile or two on this side would give him a chance to get used to being in the saddle.

But the horse had other ideas. Without warning, it turned off the road into a field, accelerated into a canter and burst through the time skin. JJ wasn't even given the chance to gasp. Luckily for him, his subconscious mind had grasped what had happened immediately and had firmly closed his mouth. Because it took a full two seconds for him to understand that he was underwater. The horse had gone from beneath him and he was floating, but he was still holding on to something – the reins, of course – and between his fists he could feel the long mane stream-ing. He grabbed a handful of it and clung on for all he was worth.

His head broke the surface and he sucked in air, but it was full of water, too, and he coughed and hacked as, beneath the waves, the powerful swimming of the horse towed him along. He could just make out the white shape of its ears and nose breaking the surface, but its body was far beneath him and he had no contact with it at all.

What frightened him more than anything was that the air above him had almost as much water in it as the sea below. There was a mighty wind blowing, full of rain, and it was churning the surface of the sea into a boiling froth of white-caps and flying spume. He was being towed help-lessly through a breathless nightmare and it had to be hell. He was certain that the stupid horse had got it all wrong. This had definitely not happened to Oisín. The horse in Oisín's story might have come up out of the sea, but there was nothing in it that he could remember about conditions like these.

It felt to JJ as though he would never be released from this torment. Time, the tyrant of all tyrants, had him in its grip again and would never let him go. But eventually he felt the horse's feet touch solid ground and its back rose up beneath him, collecting him neatly into the saddle. It waded up through the shallows and JJ felt his nerves begin to unfrazzle. But there were more dangerous times to come, and the first one was when the horse suddenly stopped and turned into a road drill. That was what it felt like to JJ anyway, as it planted its four feet and shook itself violently. He lost his stirrups instantly, and was seized by a sudden panic, convinced that the horse was trying to get him off. But it didn't go on for long, and when it finished, he realized that it had just been shaking the water off itself.

At least, that's what he thought it had been trying to do.

The next crisis came when he and the horse had a disagreement about which way to go. Once he felt secure enough to look around properly, JJ got a glimpse of the shapes of the hills and realized where he was. The sea level had already begun to rise before he retired to Tír na n'Óg, but it had got a lot higher now. It had eaten away at the foot of Sliabh Carran and created brand-new cliffs that stretched away to his right and left. But here, just where they had emerged, there was a slipway. A few boats had been dragged out, high above the reach of the waves, but they were all rotten and full of holes, and it was clear they hadn't been used for a long time. If there were regular storms like the one that was churning up the surface of the sea now, JJ guessed that people had given up trying to catch fish, from this point at any rate.

The slipway met the sea at the end of what had once been the old Carron-to-Kinvara road. JJ would have liked to veer off to the right across country and see what had become of his old house, but the horse had other ideas. It set off along the remains of the old road – clearly the going there was more to its liking. JJ found the courage to pull on the rein to turn the horse's head and even to give it a couple of kicks, but when it tossed its head and started going backwards, he chickened out and let it have its own way. He was in enough trouble as it was, and there was no sense in trying to make more of it.

57

Colonel Mooney went up to the castle and brought Pup along with him. At the small door to the laneway they knocked, and a sentry pulled back a sliding panel and peered out at them through a barred window.

'What do you want?' he said.

'To see General Liddy,' said Mooney. 'I'm his second-in-command. I've come to clarify orders for tomorrow's manoeuvres.'

'General Liddy is indisposed,' said the sentry. 'I thought you had been informed.'

'I have,' said Mooney, 'but there are some issues I need to discuss with him. Perhaps I might be allowed to visit his bedside, just briefly.'

'Wait there,' said the sentry, and closed the panel.

Mooney and Pup waited. The rain blinded them and the gusts of wind made them stagger. But the sentry returned very soon, and opened the panel again.

'Your orders are to round up replacements for the terrace work crews. Everything else as per usual.'

He closed the panel again. Mooney looked at Pup and

shook his head slowly. Then he knocked on the door again.

The panel was yanked open. 'What now?' said the sentry.

'Can't take orders from you, I'm afraid,' said Mooney. 'They have no validity unless they come from the general or the commander-in-chief himself.'

The goon slammed the panel so hard the whole door shook.

In Aidan's quarters the tension was becoming unbearable. Donal was stiff from holding himself still, afraid that any attempt to relax might set off Aidan's trigger-finger. Jenny was not faring much better. She kept trying to work up the courage to do some quick magic, and she watched Aidan for any sign that he was losing concentration. But there was none, and she was afraid to take a chance. If anything happened to Donal, she wouldn't be able to live with herself.

Aidan was not one bit happy about the intrusion by Mooney, and when his sentry returned a second time, his mood became explosive.

'What the hell does he want?' he said.

'Why don't you go yourself?' said Donal. 'He'll accept orders from you.'

'You must think I'm an idiot,' said Aidan. 'I'm not moving an inch until the Dagda gets here.'

'And what if he doesn't?' said Jenny. 'He might not,

you know. And then there's the time difference. Even if Aengus has told him and he's on his way, there's no way of knowing when he'll actually get here.'

Aidan took a swig of his drink. 'Sit down,' he said to Donal. 'Just here, on the floor.'

Donal sat down, carefully and painfully, at Aidan's feet. The muzzle of the gun never left the back of his head. With his free hand Aidan reached for paper and a pen. He plonked it in front of Donal.

'Write something,' he said. 'Get the idiot off our backs.'

'Like what?' said Donal.

'You're the flaming general! You work it out!'

58

The gale was furious and the horse walked with its head low and its ears flattened. Its feet slid in the rubble that had once been the metalled surface of the Carron road. The rain made visibility poor, and JJ couldn't see for more than a few metres in any direction, but it was enough to give him an idea of how much the place had changed. The hazel and whitethorn that had once made this lane so pleasant were all gone. Here and there a few brambles were moving into the space left by the trees, clinging low to the ground to survive the winds, but other than that the land-scape was bare and bleak.

There was no evidence that anyone lived in the place at all, and JJ wondered whether the time thing had fooled them all again. Maybe he had come through much later than Aengus had come back, and everyone was already gone. There was just no way of knowing, and there was no possibility of turning back until he had at least found out. In any case, the horse had a mind of its own, and JJ had no intention of entering into another battle with it if it could be avoided. So, for the time being at least, he decided to sit back and let the horse go where it wanted.

In some places the road disappeared completely, or turned into a rapid stream, and JJ found himself disorientated on more than one occasion. But he was not, he realized, dazed and bewildered in the way he had been the two previous times when he returned to his own world from Tír na n'Óg. He remembered exactly where he was and why he had come, and he remembered, anxiously, what it was he had been sent over to do. He supposed it was the horse that made the difference. As if it were a little piece of Tír na n'Óg, detached from it but still possessing its magical and timeless qualities.

How else, in fact, could JJ possibly be there, riding through a time in which he should have been long dead. The thought sent a shockwave through him and he looked at the ruined road in a completely different light. To touch it meant instant death, and his reaction to the thought was to grab the horse's mane and grip its body with his legs. The horse responded with a patient sigh, as though it was well used to insecure riders, and JJ wondered how many times it had done this. Maybe it hadn't just been Oisín. Maybe this was the horse's regular job and it had carried dozens of ploddies over from Tír na n'Óg to revisit the land of their birth. And that possibility raised another uncomfortable question.

How many of those time tourists had the horse taken safely back?

59

Mooney and Pup waited, hunching their shoulders against the gale and trying to guess where the next windblown waterfall from the top of the containers was going to land. It was taking a lot longer this time for the sentry to come back, and Pup hoped that nothing was going wrong inside.

Eventually they heard his footsteps. The panel opened and a piece of paper was shoved through it. Mooney took it and squatted on his heels, creating a shelter with his body to enable him to keep the wind and rain from the note. He opened it.

> *You are in command, Colonel. Do what needs to be done.*
> *Signed:*
> *General Donal Liddy*

'Is it from the general?' said Pup.

'I think so,' said Mooney.

'What does it say?'

Mooney read it out loud.

'Does it make sense to you?' said Pup. 'Do you know what needs to be done?'

'I'm not sure, Pup,' said Mooney. 'I have an idea, but we'd better go back to the barracks and have a careful think about all this.'

The silence and tension settled back into the room when the sentry was gone. After another few minutes had passed, Jenny began to wonder whether, in fact, she was making the right decision. What if the time skin closed again and she couldn't get back? Would Aidan really shoot Donal if she disappeared? She probably wouldn't know either way in any case, and what she didn't know couldn't hurt her.

Donal didn't look very happy anyway. He was very old, and maybe a quick death wouldn't be such a bad thing for him. She couldn't understand why everything always had to be so complicated in the land of the ploddies. It was all so much simpler at home.

So should she go or shouldn't she? She came to her senses just in time. Of course she couldn't. But she wished the Dagda would hurry up and get there. Or someone. Anyone. And soon.

In the strained silence, everyone could clearly hear when another knock came to the outside door of the castle. Everyone, even the goons, stiffened. It couldn't be those soldiers again, could it? They wouldn't have the neck, surely.

★ ★ ★

Outside the castle JJ waited for a reply to his knock. Rain was running off his saturated clothes and collecting in a puddle around the horse's feet. It shifted restlessly.

A panel in the door flew open and a furious voice yelled, 'What is it now?'

JJ cleared his throat. 'It's Aidan's father,' he called into the gloom beyond the barred window.

'Whose father?' said the sentry.

'Aidan's,' said JJ. 'Aidan Liddy.'

There was a stunned silence, and then the voice said, 'Are you referring to our commander-in-chief?'

'I suppose so,' said JJ. 'If that's what he's calling himself these days.'

There was another silence, and then the voice said, 'Wait there.'

JJ waited. The horse turned its tail to the wind. The wind changed direction. The horse shifted away from it again. By the time the sentry came back JJ was several metres away from the door and couldn't hear a thing he said. With a combination of bullying and pleading he succeeded in getting the horse up beside the castle again.

'What?' he shouted through the bars.

'The commander-in-chief says he has no father,' the sentry called back.

'Oh, damn and blast him,' said JJ. 'Of course he has a father. Tell him I'm back from Tír na n'Óg to visit him and he better let me in before I drown!'

60

'There's definitely something fishy going on,' said Colonel Mooney to Pup. 'I don't think I believe the general is ill.'

'Nor do I,' said Pup.

'He didn't send the first message anyway, the one to Colonel Crowley. He sent him through to Tír na n'Óg and promoted me himself, so there's no way he would have sent that message. Unless it was a deliberate code in itself.'

'Then what is he saying in the note? What does he want you to do?'

'I think I know, Pup, but I'm not sure.' Mooney led the way across the inundated parade ground to the container where he and the general had their private quarters. 'If I'm in acting command then I'm entitled to use the general's office,' he said. 'And we just might find some clue there to what's going on.'

The stove was out in the little sitting room, and condensation was dripping on to the furniture. Mooney took a quick look around but there was nothing there apart from wet clothes hanging on their rail above the fire and a shelf of books, their pages all swollen from the damp and stuck together. The door to Donal's private room was secured with a padlock, but it was so ancient and rusty that it yielded to one good tug from Mooney. He slid the bolt across, and he and Pup went in.

It was a tiny space. The general's narrow bed took up most of the far wall, and a short rail at the foot of it held his few clothes on hangers. A heated pipe ran along the near wall, fed by a boiler in the stove, and above it was a plank, narrow and warped. It was covered with candle-stumps and melted wax, and Donal had obviously been using it as a desk. At one end stood five unopened boxes of resealable plastic bags and a cup of ballpoint pens. In the middle, protected from the damp by a larger plastic bag, was all that existed of the general's paperwork. Mooney opened the bag. There was an A4 pad, nearly used up, and beneath its top leaf was a stack of handwritten pages.

It didn't take Mooney long to ascertain that there was nothing there in the way of military secrets. Each of the pages was a neatly torn half of A4, and all of them were exactly the same. He handed the top one to Pup. Pup could read, but not very well.

'What does it say?'

Mooney picked up another one and read it aloud.

'*If you cannot stand it any more, there is a way out of this world. Go to the old fairy fort below Aidan Liddy's castle and down into the hole you will find in it. Go through two underground chambers, and when you come to the far wall, keep going. It is not a real wall. You will find yourself in a world far better than this one and you will be safe there for ever, provided you mind your manners.*

'*Trust me. All I have written is true. And if you are reading this note for a second time, then it probably means you have nothing left to lose.*'

Pup turned his page over. On the other side, and on every one of the two hundred or so other notes, was a beautifully drawn map of the area, with the beacon marked in red, the Liddy castle in blue, and the circular outline of the fairy fort in green.

Colonel Mooney gathered up the notes again and put everything back in the bag, exactly as he had found it. 'You know,' he said to Pup, 'if I had come across these a few hours earlier, I would have been convinced that the general was completely insane. But you tell me it's all true?'

'Oh, it is, sir. I swear on my mother's life.'

'And I believe you,' said Mooney. He flattened the bag to push any remaining air out of it before he sealed it. Then he turned his back to the narrow desk and leaned against it thoughtfully. Eventually he said, 'You know what I think, Pup?'

'No, sir,' said Pup. 'What do you think?'

'I think it's time we went and found out what has really happened to our general.'

61

The sentry was gone a long time and the horse turned and kept turning, shook its head and stamped its big feet restlessly. JJ could get no wetter but he was getting colder, and some of the gusts of wind were so strong they threatened to knock him off the horse. He was in a foul temper by the time the sentry returned, and his mood wasn't improved when the man came out with a mouthful of gobbledygook.

'The commander-in-chief says if you're his father, what did the cat eat and what did the cow eat?'

'What?' said JJ. 'What did you say?'

'He wants to know what did the cat eat and what did the cow eat?'

'Oh, for God's sake,' said JJ. 'I'm getting blown away out here. Can't you just open the flaming door?'

'Not till you give me the answer,' said the goon smugly.

The horse turned round again and a blast of wind hit it so hard that it was driven against the side of the castle, trapping JJ's leg.

'Mice,' he yelled desperately. 'Mice and silage!'

But into the silence that met his words, a tune arrived and began to play itself inside his head.

'No, wait, wait,' he called out. 'That's not right.' The tune in his head played on, and now he remembered its name. And it made sense. Aidan had always hated the music that the rest of his family loved, but he couldn't avoid hearing the tunes, and their names as well. And what better way of getting JJ to identify himself than by asking him the names of some old family favourites?

'It's a candle,' he said. '"The Cat That Ate the Candle". And the other one's a tune as well. "The Cow . . ." What was it? "The Cow That Ate the Blanket", that's it! So that's his answer. A candle and a blanket.'

The sentry didn't answer, but there was an odd creaking sound from somewhere near the door. The white horse started walking backwards again and JJ swore at it and tugged furiously on the reins, with absolutely no results. Then he saw why, and he felt guilty and slightly stupid, because the horse had far sharper senses than he had and was getting out of the way of the end of a container that was being opened just beside them. He had given the right answer and the goon was letting down the drawbridge.

When it reached the ground, the horse stepped on to it. JJ looked down the length of the container and saw a heavy mesh gate at the other end being raised like a portcullis. He urged the horse forward, but it refused to move until the gate was fully raised, then it dashed forward and out the other end before either exit could close and trap it inside. JJ appreciated the logic of it, but he wished the horse would let him make at least some of the decisions. At the other end it stopped again, and this time JJ pulled firmly on the reins and pretended it was his idea.

62

Just a stone's throw away, the barracks was buzzing with activity. Colonel Mooney was barking orders and men were jumping to carry them out, putting on their combat gear, packing emergency rations, and queuing, for the first time in years, to receive live ammunition.

Pup, along with one of the sergeants, was handing it out, and the men in the line took the opportunity to ask him, finally, what it was like in Tír na n'Óg.

'Fantastic,' he said. 'I'm going back there as soon as I've sorted out a few things over here.'

'What's it like?'

'The sun always shines. There are socks hanging off the trees. And people playing music. And no one worries about anything.'

'I'm volunteering next time,' said a young lad of about Pup's age.

'And me,' said the squaddie behind him.

'And me,' said the next.

A lot of the guns in the army hadn't worked for years and were just carried around for show. Some of the others did work but the stores had no ammunition to fit them. But there were still eighty or so working weapons left in the barracks, and Colonel Mooney was busy identifying them and making sure they were put into the most reliable hands.

'It may be necessary to use them,' he told the chosen marksmen. 'But no one is to fire without specific orders from a commanding officer.'

The men understood, and even the hardest of them would obey. Ammunition was in short supply and not to be wasted. But they were excited, too, and ready for action. No one other than the colonel and Pup yet knew what kind of action they were preparing for, but every soldier in the barracks had a keen sense of anticipation. Though no one dared say it, most of them had the feeling that this was the moment they had all been waiting for.

Aidan got one of his men to open the door into the court-yard. Outside it there was a grey-haired man on a large white horse.

Jenny had the best view through the door. 'It's JJ,' she said.

'Are you sure?' said Aidan.

'Positive,' said Jenny.

Aidan removed the gun from Donal's head. 'Don't anyone try anything,' he said. 'The gun's in my pocket and it's still aimed straight at you. Understand?'

Donal and Jenny nodded. Aidan stepped towards the

door and stood sideways on, keeping all angles covered.

'Hello, Dad,' he said. 'You're just about the last person I expected to see.'

JJ blinked. The fat man standing in the doorway was nearly bald and had hardly any teeth. He had no idea who he was, so he took a guess.

'Aidan?'

'Who else?' said Aidan. 'Welcome to my castle.'

JJ was speechless, stunned by what the passage of time had done to his son.

'Why don't you come in?' Aidan went on. 'My men will look after your horse for you.'

'Ah, well, no,' said JJ. 'I can't get off the horse, you see?'

'You can't get off?' said Aidan.

'Well, I can,' said JJ, 'but it wouldn't be my preferred option.'

'Ah,' said Aidan. He had just been studying the literature, so the story of Oisín was fresh in his mind. 'The white horse trick, eh?'

'That's the one,' said JJ.

Aidan considered the situation. The rain was still sheeting down and there was no way he was going outside in it. There was only one other option. He stood back from the doorway.

'Then you'd better bring it in with you, hadn't you?' he said.

★ ★ ★

Mooney divided the army into three sections and put a sergeant at the head of two of them. The first of them left the barracks by the rear entrance and went downhill towards the ring fort, then turned to their right and made for the old Carron road. The second squad went up the hill, bypassing the stony steps as though heading directly for the beacon. The third, which he was to lead himself, waited in the barracks. When the others were in position, they would play their part.

63

On top of the mountain the púca had returned from his foraging and was talking to Mikey's ghost while he chewed the cud. The army sharpshooters had long since eliminated the herds of wild goats that once roamed the area, so the púca's vigil up there had been as lonely as Mikey's. Now that they had finally become friends, they found that they had a surprising amount in common.

As the first troops were leaving the barracks and JJ was trying to persuade the horse to go through Aidan's narrow doorway, the ghost and the púca were discussing the demise of mankind. The púca maintained it was the fairy folk who had started the rot by charming the ploddies with their music and dancing and their sly, seductive ways. They had persuaded the people of Ireland to switch their allegiance from the púcas, who were nature gods, and worship the Dagda and Aengus instead. And as the people of Ireland had changed their religion once, there was nothing to stop them doing it again, and they were easy prey for the Christian missionaries when they came along. But when the worst god of all began to woo them, they didn't even realize that they were changing their religion again.

'Mammon,' said Mikey, sending the púca a single grim image.

'Exactly,' said the púca. 'The great god of money. Sly one, that. The poor old ploddies lined up in their millions to sell their souls to him and had no idea what they were doing.'

'True, true,' Mikey thought. He found that the púca, who could read all kinds of winds and trends, understood his method of communication even better than Donal did. In fact, if he spoke a sentence in his mind, the púca seemed able to hear it. 'We were a hopeless lot, but you have to give us credit for some things.'

'Really?' said the púca, who had no time at all for the human race. 'Like what?'

'Well, we fought some terrible wars and did some unspeakable things to each other, but we created some pretty good peacetimes as well. We can be good neighbours as well as good enemies.'

'I suppose so,' said the púca, 'for what it's worth.'

'And then there are the sciences and the arts.'

'Not too impressed by the sciences,' said the púca. 'Your technologies were responsible for most of this.' He made a vague gesture across the plain, which Mikey took to imply the state of the world. 'But tell me what you mean by the arts.'

'You know,' said Mikey. 'Music. Poetry. Literature. Fine

art. Things that bypass all the day-to-day strivings and squabblings and speak directly from soul to soul.'

The púca yawned and belched up a fresh mouthful of cud.

'As a matter of fact,' Mikey went on, 'my good friend Donal has a bit of a problem in that regard.' He explained about the cultural treasures Donal had gathered, and the problems of getting them through to Tír na n'Óg.

The púca folded his goat feet beneath him, closed his eyes and chewed on implacably. He appeared to have gone to sleep, but when Mikey finished talking he opened his eyes again, took a moment or two to stare into the middle distance and read the winds, then left.

64

By the time JJ and the white horse were inside, there was no room to swing a cat, not even one of the ginger kittens. Aidan ordered the two goons who were still human to move some of the furniture back against the walls, and then wait outside. He was confident about keeping control now. JJ's arrival had added a second weapon to his armoury.

Donal went up to JJ, who leaned down as far as he could to hug him. They were both wet, but Donal was at least warm and wet. JJ was so cold his fingertips were blue.

'Well, isn't this nice?' Aidan said. 'A regular family reunion. All we need now is Mum.'

'And Hazel,' said Jenny.

'And Sally,' said Donal.

'Any word from either of them?' said JJ. 'Sally and Hazel, I mean, not Mum.'

Donal shook his head. His oldest sister, Hazel, had still been in Cork when he had last heard from her, and his younger one, Sally, had joined up with like-minded people to build an eco-village in County Mayo. They had all kept in contact until the world changed so radically, but there were no phones or letters or emails now and, short of making journeys that would be extremely arduous and even more dangerous, there was no way for Donal to know whether they were alive or dead.

The living room had turned into a menagerie. The kittens had overcome their anxieties and were chasing each other over the furniture. The dogs were hogging the rug in front of the fire, and now there was this horse, which looked much bigger in the confined space than it had out in the open.

'So what's on your mind, Dad?' said Aidan. 'Or more to the point, what's on the Dagda's mind? Did he send you over with a message?'

'Erm . . .' JJ was having difficulty settling in. It was partly the terror of being on the horse in someone's living room, and partly the shock of seeing his two sons transformed, overnight as far as he was concerned, into old men. He had to concentrate very hard before he could remember what he was doing there. 'Not exactly a message as such,' he said.

'No?' said Aidan.

'No,' said JJ. 'More like a kind of a job.'

He sighed. He had hoped to come up with some ideas on the way but he'd had no luck. Aidan was what? Around sixty, he supposed. He was as fat and soft as the two dogs snoring on the hearthrug, but he was still Aidan, and JJ knew he would have no more influence over him now than he'd had when he was a child. Aisling ought to have come instead. Aisling had ways of dealing with him – at least she had when he was small. He wished she was there with him now. The horse could probably have carried the two of them. He hoped and prayed that he would get to see her again, and fondly imagined that she was sitting staring into space on one of the grassy slopes of Tír na n'Óg, thinking the same thoughts about him.

She wasn't though. She was busy trying to follow her own orders from the Dagda, even though her heart wasn't in it. She had no desire to see those wretched people sent back through the souterrain to whatever dreadful fate lay in store for them on the other side. But there was no future in disobeying the Dagda. He would have his way in Tír na n'Óg no matter what anyone said or did, and Aisling passing her existence as a toad would be of no benefit to anyone.

So she was trying her best to round up the ploddies, but she was not having much success. The ones she found, even the soldiers, were all very pleasant and cheerful, and they all listened politely to her instructions. Most of them even set out in roughly the right direction. But again and again she encountered the same people, wandering around with the same dazed and delighted expressions. All of them remembered meeting her before but none of them remembered where it was they were supposed to be going.

★ ★ ★

'The thing is,' JJ said to Aidan, 'you have to stop it.' It sounded as pathetic to JJ as it did to the others, but once it was out of his mouth he couldn't put it back.

'Stop what, Daddy?' said Aidan. He sounded as if butter wouldn't melt in his mouth, but everyone there knew him well enough to hear the bitter sarcasm behind his words.

'All this nasty business of bullying people and stealing their food and making them into slaves and stuff.'

'Oh, Dad!' said Aidan. 'Who have you been listening to? It's not true at all. You never did understand the way the world works, did you? Too much of that fairy blood in your veins.'

At that moment JJ was wishing he could disappear through the time skin and regretting that he didn't have more fairy blood, but he said nothing, and Aidan went on, 'Someone has to take charge, you know. You can't have a society without some kind of government. What you don't realize is that I'm protecting all those poor unfortunate people. I have their best interests at heart, even if they don't always realize it.'

'How do you work that out?' said Jenny.

'Protection, Jenny, that's what. It's your brother's department mainly. The presence of our army stops other gangs from moving in and taking over the area. And they would be worse, you can be sure. In some parts of the country, those raiders have been through and left no one alive behind them.'

'Hang on, though,' said JJ. 'That doesn't account for the way you've been treating your own people.'

'But you've got it all wrong,' said Aidan, and again he had that saccharine tone in his voice. 'It's amazing how people manage to distort the truth. It's all very simple, you see. All governments impose some kind of taxation. Even you must understand that.'

'Well, yes,' said JJ, 'but—'

'And we collect our taxes in kind instead of in cash. Food instead of money. That's all.'

'Yes, but—'

'And if some of our poorer citizens find themselves in difficulties, then it's our duty to help them out, wouldn't you say?'

'Yes, but—'

'Unfortunately we can't afford unemployment benefit like they did in your day. As you can see, our world has changed a lot. But we can't just abandon them, can we?'

'No, but—'

'No. So we find useful work for them on government projects instead. Full employment, see? Every single citizen housed and fed. I know it isn't perfect, but things are very different now. Look at what we're having to deal with.'

He paused for dramatic effect, but the storm failed to respond to his cue. The wind had dropped again.

And it made conditions just perfect for Colonel Mooney's advance parties.

On two sides of the castle, soldiers were scaling the walls. They worked efficiently and in absolute silence, standing on each other's shoulders to make a human ladder and hoisting the smallest boys to the top. Once up there, they tied ropes to the crane lugs and dropped them back down for the others to climb up. Everyone stayed on their bellies, well out of sight of the courtyard. Still shrouded in their waterproof hoods, the goons on guard below hadn't the first idea that there was anything going on.

'Anyway,' Aidan was saying, 'all this just goes to show you why we need the Dagda's help so badly. I was hoping that he'd pay us a personal visit, but apparently he doesn't think we're worth the effort.'

All three of the others became aware of the warning signs entering Aidan's face and voice. They had lived with him for long enough to know when one of his tantrums was coming on and they all, with the possible exception of Jenny, feared the mayhem he could wreak.

'All I was asking for was a little bit of magic,' he went on. 'Simple stuff for the king of the fairies. Turn these awful storms off. Put everything back the way it was.'

'I'm not sure about that,' said JJ, but Aidan wasn't listening.

'I'm not asking for much. I'm not looking for a

Mediterranean climate or anything. I don't want to grow olives and lemons, just cabbages and spuds like we used to have. I want to get some cattle up and running again. I want fresh milk and meat. I don't mind a bit of wind and rain. I just want it back the way it was!'

'Yes, but—' said JJ.

'I wouldn't need to tax people then.' Aidan was red in the face and close to tears. 'I wouldn't need to build terraces that keep sliding down the flaming hillside if the soil stopped running away and the shops were open again.' He spun round to face JJ. 'He wouldn't come, though, would he? No. He sent my old dad to slap my hand and tell me to behave myself. Well, you better go back, JJ. Take your stupid white horse out of my living room and tell the king of the fairies to get his fat backside over here!'

'I can't,' said JJ.

'What do you mean you can't?' said Aidan.

'I mean I can't. For once in your life, will you shut up and listen?'

Aidan stared at him, then turned in fury and kicked first one dog, then the other. They yelped and bolted through the heavy velvet curtains into Aidan's bedroom. The kittens vanished and the horse threw up its head.

'I'm listening,' said the commander-in-chief.

JJ took a deep breath. 'The Dagda wants his children back,' he said. 'The ones you're holding hostage.'

'I'm delighted to hear that,' said Aidan. 'That's precisely why I took them.'

'I can't go back without them,' said JJ. 'I'm prepared to put your concerns to the Dagda and ask him to come and see you, but I can't go back without them.'

'Oh, really,' said Aidan. 'Well, you'd better not go back then, had you? Because I'm not going to give up the only bargaining chips I have. Not for a vague promise that he "might" come over. Do you think I'm mad?'

'Yes,' said Jenny and Donal in unison.

'I wasn't asking you!' Aidan roared. He turned his back on his father. 'So, if you've nothing better to offer, you might as well clear off.'

'But what do you expect me to do?' said JJ. 'Wander around on this horse for ever?'

'Why not?' said Aidan.

'Because . . .' JJ hadn't really thought about it, but now some awful eventualities besieged his imagination. 'What if the horse gets tired and lies down or something? What if I go to sleep and fall off?'

Aidan grinned broadly, showing his yellow gums. 'Poor Dad. What a predicament.'

'Don't listen to him, Dad,' said Jenny. 'We'll think of something.'

'Shut up, Jenny,' said Aidan, and a look of pure malevolence came over his face. 'I've just had an idea. Would you like a fighting chance, JJ?'

'Of course I would,' said JJ.

'Then I'll give you one,' said Aidan. 'What would you say to the idea of a little bet?'

65

The ghost's talk about Donal's cultural mission had reminded the púca of another kind of culture, one of which he was particularly fond. It was a weakness, he knew, a silly little foible, but the opportunity, now that it had presented itself, was too good to ignore.

He had to admit that it was a cunning plan, and he rather wished he had thought of it himself. There were other ways of doing it, of course, but if Aengus Óg got a whiff of the púca's personal involvement, he would be sure to do his utmost to stymie his little project. Doing it this way was much, much safer.

The things he needed were small and light and easy to transport, but he had to travel quite a distance to get them. Although he could not, like the fairies, transform himself into a raven or a hawk, he did have ways of covering distances on foot at great speed. He used one of them now: became a white colossus striding across the mountainside, unseen by anyone in the thick, warm mist that followed the passing of the storm.

★ ★ ★

The third time Aisling went through the village, she was joined by a pair of sheepdogs, who seemed tremendously eager to help. She had devised a plan for collecting the immigrants together instead of directing them and had gathered a crowd of about thirty, who were dawdling along in roughly the right direction. The dogs paced backwards and forwards at the back of the group, hustling the stragglers and nipping at their heels. Aisling had never worked with dogs but she had seen them on TV, so she gave them commands and sent them speeding away in different directions to gather any nearby ploddies she might have missed.

'Come on now, keep going,' she said to a couple of children who were sitting on the kerb, playing marbles with beach pebbles. They got up happily and skipped along the street, but an elderly man and a soldier had started wandering off in the wrong direction and she had to go back for them.

Why couldn't the Dagda just leave them? They weren't doing anybody any harm. Her body as well as her mind was rebelling against the job she had been given, and she found that she was walking more and more slowly. She was, she realized, beginning to despise herself for following the Dagda's orders.

66

'What kind of a little bet did you have in mind?' asked JJ nervously.

'Here's the deal,' said Aidan. 'If you win, I give you this clever little key here which belongs to the place where the fairy children are hidden.'

'And tell him what it opens,' said Donal.

'And where it is,' said Jenny.

Aidan shot them both a look. 'All those things,' he said to JJ. 'And you can take them home with you to the fairy patriarch and ask him very nicely if he'd care to pay me a visit.'

'OK,' said JJ. 'And if I lose?'

'Very simple,' said Aidan. 'Piece of cake, really. All you have to do is get down off the horse.'

In the silence that followed his words they could all clearly hear a loud rumbling, creaking sound, coming from nearby. Aidan crossed to the door and called through the grille.

'What's the noise?'

'Drawbridge, sir,' came the reply. The voice was

muffled, as if it came through a very thick scarf, but there was nothing unusual about that in the weather they were having.

'Why are you opening the drawbridge?' Aidan barked back.

'Maintenance, sir,' the voice said. 'Just discovered a kink in the chain.'

Aidan closed the cover. 'Well?' he said to JJ. 'What do you think?'

'Don't do it, Dad,' said Jenny.

JJ had no intention of doing it, but he was intrigued all the same, and he wanted to know what Aidan was prepared to risk.

'So what's the game?' he asked.

'Cards, I thought,' said Aidan. 'A few hands of poker, perhaps?'

'Poker?' said JJ.

'Pontoon if you prefer.'

'Aidan,' said JJ, 'I'm your father, remember? You've been using marked cards since you were eight years old. I had to go to your school and pay back all the money you swindled out of your classmates.'

Aidan laughed with delight. 'It's a fair cop,' he said. 'We can toss for it instead. Best of five.'

'Not that, either, Aidan. Not if you're still using that weighted coin.'

'I've an idea,' said Donal.

'Have you now?' said Aidan. 'Let's hear it, then.'

'Drink him for it.'

'You what?'

'Have a drinking contest. Whoever is left standing, or conscious at any rate, is the winner.'

Both men stared at him blankly. Jenny stared at him as well. His wet clothes were steaming in the warm room, and it made him look like a cartoon character whose brain was overheating. The idea sounded insane, but he seemed to be quite serious about it. And if Jenny had to choose one person in either of the worlds to trust with her life, it would be Donal. So she backed him up.

'Yeah. Sounds like a brilliant idea to me.'

Aidan edged backwards so he could inspect the poitín on the sideboard without taking his eyes, and the gun in his pocket, off his brother.

'You might have an idea there,' he said. There were two full bottles and a bit left in a third. They wouldn't need anything like that amount. Aidan knew his father had enjoyed a few pints when he was a young man, but in later years he had given it up entirely because it sent him to sleep. In a straight drinking contest, glass for glass, Aidan knew he could drink JJ under the table.

'I'm up for it,' he said. 'Are you, Dad?'

JJ hoped Donal knew what he was doing. But in the event that he didn't, at least JJ would know nothing about it. If he fell off the horse in an alcoholic stupor, then he'd never feel himself turning into a heap of old bones.

'I suppose I am,' he said.

67

The two dogs, for all their apparent enthusiasm, never came back to Aisling. As she traipsed along behind her little herd of willing ploddies, she caught a glimpse of them in a distant field, chasing each other and rolling in the grass like a pair of puppies. The sight of them made her stop and think, and she sat on a grassy bank beside the road and pulled a summer stalk to chew on.

She wasn't going to do it. Somehow she had decided that without even realizing it. She wasn't going to deliver these refugees back to the Dagda so he could throw them out. It was obvious that there was no future for them in Ireland. Sending them back there amounted to an act of murder, or at least manslaughter, and she was simply not going to do it.

As for the consequences, she would put up with them, whatever they were. The sheepdogs had reminded her that there were worse fates than being an animal. And for all she knew, toads might have more fun than any of them. Whatever it was like, it had to be better than living with the knowledge that she had been complicit in sending these innocent people to their deaths. She wished JJ was there so she could tell him what she was doing and why. She hoped that he would make it and that she would see him back here in Tír na n'Óg again, even if he didn't notice her peering out from beneath a rock or flying over his head.

A child sat down beside her and leaned against her shoulder. One by one the other people sat down beside the road, or on it, or wandered away into the adjoining fields. They were happy, and Aisling was, too. Whatever happened happened, and at least she would be facing it with a clear conscience.

68

Aidan reversed to the sideboard and collected two shot glasses. He put them on the table and returned for the bottle, never once taking his left hand out of his pocket or his eyes off Donal.

Donal reached for the glasses, but Aidan snatched them up from the table.

'Whoa, whoa,' he said, hugging them to his chest like a small child with a bag of sweets. 'What do you think you're doing?'

'You can't take part in a contest and be the referee as well,' said Donal. 'I'll pour the drinks and hand them out.'

Aidan stared at him suspiciously.

'He's right, Aidan,' said Jenny. 'You can't have it all your own way.'

Aidan set down the bottle and the glasses. 'No funny business, then,' he said. 'Equal measures. And you pour them right in front of me, there on the table.'

'OK by me,' said Donal. 'Is that OK by you, Dad?'

'Fine by me,' said JJ, although the whole thing was anything but fine by him.

Donal picked up the bottle and, under Aidan's eagle eye, poured two perfectly equal measures. Aidan reached for one of them but Donal put a hand over it.

'Hold on a minute now,' he said. 'There's something we need to sort out before we start.'

'What's that?' said Aidan.

'The key. And directions to the place where the children are being held. If you pass out, we won't know where to find them.'

'But I won't pass out,' said Aidan. 'Never happened before. Won't happen now.'

'Then the deal's off,' said Donal. 'No point in having a contest only one side can win.'

'All right, all right,' said Aidan. 'But you don't expect me to tell you now, do you?'

'No,' said Donal. 'Write it down.'

'Write it down?'

'Yes. And sit on the piece of paper. If you fall, we take it. If you win, we never see it.'

Aidan looked carefully at Donal and then at Jenny. 'No funny business, then. You haven't forgotten the other thing, have you? The thing in my pocket? Because it's still there.'

'What thing in your pocket?' said JJ.

'Don't worry about it, Dad,' said Donal. 'We haven't forgotten, Aidan.'

'Right.' Aidan took the writing pad and, without taking his left hand out of his pocket or his eyes off Donal, wrote something on the top sheet, then tore it off and folded it.

'And the key,' said Jenny.

Aidan searched through the bunch of keys until he found the one he was looking for, then levered it off the ring. He wrapped it in the handwritten note, then put the little package into his back pocket. 'Happy now?' he said. 'Are we finally ready?'

Donal handed one of the glasses to Aidan, then picked up the other one and turned towards JJ on the horse. The instant his back was to Aidan, he casually slopped at least half of the poitín on to the front of his jumper, where it made no impression at all on the soaking wet wool. JJ reached out his hand and Donal pushed the glass well into it, so JJ's fingers closed right around it and hid the level of the drink.

'Sláinte,' said Aidan, throwing back his drink in one go. JJ followed suit, and his reaction left no doubt in anyone's mind that there was poitín in that glass. It was throat-scorching stuff, and JJ coughed and gagged and waved his hand in front of his mouth as if he'd just bitten into a chilli pepper.

'Nice stuff, eh, Dad?' said Aidan. 'We make it ourselves out the back, just like in the old days. It's getting scarce now though, what with the shortage of spuds and all. You're honoured to be getting a drink of it. I hope you appreciate it.'

JJ nodded weakly. His eyes were streaming and were

fixed with dread upon Donal, who was pouring the next round. But once again, as soon as he turned his back on Aidan, Donal spilled half the drink down his jumper. He did it with no sudden or obvious movements, just a careful tilt of his wrist at exactly the right moment. JJ wrapped his hand around the glass and raised it to his other son.

'Down the hatch,' he said.

They both drank, and again JJ gasped and coughed, but not quite so badly this time. His throat was getting used to the stuff, and besides, the small measures that he was swallowing down were already beginning to enter his bloodstream and numb his senses. By the time the third and fourth glasses had been knocked back, he was beginning to enjoy himself and think that old Aidan might not be such a bad fella after all.

Jenny looked on anxiously. From the chair where she was sitting she could see what Donal was doing, but she wasn't convinced it would work. Although he was drinking at more than twice the rate that JJ was, Aidan still looked the more sober of the two.

'Another bottle,' he said, standing up to go and fetch it. But on the way back he betrayed himself by the hint of a misplaced step, and by dropping too quickly into his chair. There was just a chance, then, that JJ might hold out.

Donal opened the new bottle. 'Round five,' he said.

69

'What are you doing?' said the Dagda. 'Why are you all sitting in the road?'

Aisling hadn't heard him approach. 'Oh,' she said. 'We were just having a bit of a rest.'

'Rest?' said the Dagda. 'Why would you want to rest? Don't you realize how anxious I am to get them all going?'

Aisling summoned her resolve. 'I'm sorry, Dagda,' she said. 'I don't want to help with what you're doing.'

'What?' he said, astonished. 'How can you say that? I need your help. I order you to help.'

'I don't want any part of it,' said Aisling. 'I think you're wrong to do it.'

'Wrong?' said the Dagda.

'If you're determined to go ahead with it, then you'll just have to manage without me.'

'But I can't,' said the Dagda. 'I can't possibly.'

Aisling said nothing more and, seeing that his attempts at persuasion were having no effect, the Dagda decided to adopt cruder tactics.

'Right,' he said. 'Up you get, you lot. Come on. That's it. Straight on up the road to where you came in.'

The ploddies responded peaceably. Soldiers picked up their guns, children picked up their pebbles, the whole sorry, ragged lot started out along the road.

'You'll follow along, I dare say,' the Dagda said to Aisling. 'Because it seems to me you can't possibly mean what you say. I suppose you're having a bad mood or something – would that be it?'

Aisling stayed where she was, amazed to find that she had defied the Dagda and he had left her not only in one piece, but still human as well. Maybe he wasn't as dangerous and unreasonable as she had been led to believe. And if that was the case, maybe there was just the slightest chance that she could make him see reason and get him to change his mind. So, as he had suggested she would, she got up and followed quietly along behind.

70

'Round nine,' said Donal, filling the glasses again.

'Bring it on, bring it on,' said Aidan, but the hand that reached for the glass missed it by a mile.

Jenny looked from her father to her brother and back. It was not easy to tell who was winning. Both men were swaying and grinning, and both were slurring their words. Jenny considered the possibility of doing some magic, but as if he read her mind, Aidan pulled out his gun and began waving it around in a way that filled her with terror. He was definitely losing his grip, and it meant that Donal was taking even more dangerous risks with JJ's drinks. His jumper was completely saturated and was beginning to drip. The floor was becoming damp and slippery and the stink of poitín made the room smell like a distillery. But Aidan was much too drunk to notice any of it.

This time Donal emptied the glass down his jumper before handing it to his father.

JJ raised the glass to his lips and upturned it. ''S empty,' he said. 'Gimme a full one.'

Aidan swallowed his in one gulp. 'Mine too. 'S empty 's well. Gimme another.'

Donal poured. The level in the second bottle was going down rapidly and he hoped, for his father's sake, that he wouldn't have to open a third. Because JJ was becoming voluble, making grandiose declarations of incontrovertible truths and tossing his arms around, and his balance on the horse was looking increasingly precarious.

'I love you all, all of you,' he said. 'D'you know that? 'N' I sushpecially love Aidan. I don't care what anyone says. He's my black sheep and he's done very well for himself. I don't care what he's sushposed to have done. He's my shon.' And, as if this were an insight of particular genius, he said it again. 'He's my shon!'

'Lesh drink to that,' said Aidan, emptying round ten.

'Where's mine?' said JJ, wobbling dangerously.

The horse, which had been quiet and patient throughout, was now taking an intense dislike to the proceedings and was beginning to get restless. There wasn't much room in there for it to move, and it bumped into the walls and the furniture as it shifted around.

'Whoa there,' said JJ, making several wild and ineffectual attempts to grab the reins.

'Round nine,' said Aidan. 'Where's round nine?'

'It's round eleven,' said Donal, handing him another glass.

Aidan emptied it down his throat and handed it back.

'Shame again,' he said. 'And whatever you're having your-shelf.'

Donal refilled it, but this time he didn't even bother giving one to JJ. Aidan was beyond noticing. He swigged the next drink down, handed back the glass, and collapsed sideways on to the rug with the dogs.

'Bull's-eye!' said Donal. 'You've won, Dad. Well done!'

'Exshellent,' said JJ. 'What have I won? Shall we drink to it?' The horse shifted again, trying to turn round in the small space. 'Where'sh everybody gone? Why is everything whizzing round?'

Jenny bent down and took the note from Aidan's pocket. She unfolded it and read what he had written.

'Oh no,' she said. 'Oh no!'

Donal was trying to calm the horse, which was rapidly approaching a state of panic. 'What is it?' he said.

She handed it to him. All that was written on it was:

You people really are idiots, aren't you?

And for a moment Donal was inclined to agree. The horse was barging around, desperate to get out, and JJ was swaying in the saddle and singing 'Whiskey in the Jar'.

'How are we going to get out past the goons?' said Donal.

'I don't know,' said Jenny. 'There are too many for me to deal with at the same time, and Dad's a bit of an easy target on that horse.'

'*Ring da ma do da ma . . . dilly . . . diddy . . . daddy . . .* How does it go again?' said JJ.

'Wait a minute,' said Donal to Jenny. 'If you turn me into a bird, can I turn myself back?'

'No,' said Jenny.

'Then you'll have to go,' he said, quickly scribbling a note. 'Take this to the barracks and get it to Colonel Mooney.'

He opened the door cautiously, just wide enough for the swallow, with the note in her beak, to burst through. But what he saw on the other side made him catch hold of the bird before it flew off. There were plenty of guns aimed at the door, but they weren't in the hands of Aidan's goons. And the first face he saw belonged to Pup.

Jenny changed back into herself, and she and Donal ran out to congratulate the army. Pup and Mooney told them how it had all come about, and Donal promoted Pup to Captain on the spot. Jenny recommended them both for medals. Strictly speaking she wasn't entitled to do that, but no one seemed to mind.

'I have a job for you, Captain Pup,' said Donal. 'Take as many men as you need and drag that drunken brother of mine down to the old fort. Take his guards as well, and the kitchen staff.'

Jenny turned the dogs and kittens back into men for their trip down to the souterrain, and it was only then, as Donal continued to add detail to Pup's orders, that she remembered JJ and looked around the courtyard. She couldn't see him.

'Dad?' She looked inside Aidan's quarters. 'JJ?'

But there was no sign anywhere of him or the white horse. And the drawbridge and portcullis were both wide open.

This time the horse ignored the ruined road and made a bee-line for the sea. It was going straight down the precipitous drop towards the fairy fort, slipping and sliding on the rocks. On its back, JJ jerked and swayed like a puppet with three of its strings broken. His head was still spinning but he was sobering up very fast indeed. He couldn't believe he'd been stupid enough to agree to a drinking contest, and the entire episode seemed like a lunatic dream. He couldn't remember what the contest had been for, or what he was doing here in the first place. What he did remember was the importance of staying on the horse at all costs, and his entire attention was taken up with clinging on for dear life.

When he saw the banks of the rath ahead of him, he was gripped with a sudden wild hope. Could he go through that way, like he had done on previous occasions? Was that why the horse was taking him there? Maybe it was safe to get off inside the rath. It was fairy territory, after all. Everyone knew that, even the ploddy farmers who protected the old ring forts so carefully. Maybe they

were like embassies, little bits of home territory in foreign
lands where stranded citizens could take refuge. But the
horse, it soon turned out, was not heading for the fort. It
bypassed the outer bank, ignoring JJ's efforts to steer
it, then came to an abrupt halt beside a large boulder.

JJ badly needed the reprieve. His head was throbbing
painfully, and he was dizzy and nauseous. What he wanted
more than anything else was to be off the horse and to feel
his feet on solid ground, but he had just enough sense left
in his head to remember what would happen to him if he
got off here. So he took the opportunity to get his feet
back into the stirrups and readjust his hold on the reins,
thumbs up, the way he had been taught at the trekking
centre. Because the horse had lost its calm entirely. It was
agitated, snatching at the bit, and JJ got the impression it
was waiting for him to do something. Tentatively he
kicked it on, but instead of going forward it began to move
sideways, edging towards the boulder until JJ's knee was
trapped between the saddle and the rock.

'Hey!' he said, pulling hard on the opposite rein.

The horse turned its head in response, but its body
didn't follow. On the contrary, it now leaned right into the
boulder, rocking backwards and forwards as if it were
trying to scrape JJ off. His trapped knee ground painfully
against the weathered stone.

'What are you doing? Stop it!' JJ flapped the reins and
kicked as hard as he could with his free leg. The horse at
last moved away from the rock, but if JJ thought it had

decided to cooperate with him, he was badly mistaken.

In the skies high above, Jenny was searching for him. She had started out along the track that ran between Aidan's castle and the Carron road, and now she was returning in a direct line above the open hillside. She saw something down there that surprised her. Inside the roofless walls of the old Liddy house, brambles and ivy had grown up tall and strong. From most angles there was nothing else to be seen, but when she was directly overhead, her sharp hawk eyes could make out something underneath the foliage. A white panel, stained and flaking, its edges only a stone or two lower than the walls which surrounded it. It was a shed or something, with a flat white roof. She was on her way to get a closer look when she spotted the horse careering down the hillside with JJ still astride, arms flapping.

She swooped low and crossed in front of them in an effort to cut them off. The manoeuvre was almost fatal. The horse swerved violently, and JJ was thrown out of the side of the saddle. If his life hadn't depended on staying on, he would almost certainly have let go, but as it was he managed to hold on, one knee hooked over the saddle, both arms around the horse's neck. With all the strength he possessed, he succeeded in dragging himself upright, but now he had lost his stirrups again, and the reins had somehow got snapped when he dropped them, and the horse was still plunging at lunatic speed down the hillside.

A hundred metres ahead of him, JJ saw the

sparrowhawk drop out of the sky and turn into Jenny. But the horse saw it too and veered to the right, leaving her standing there helplessly as it went thundering past. Now the ruins of the old house were coming up fast and, equally fast, JJ was nearing the point of exhaustion. He was fit, but he was still an old man, and his heart wasn't up to all the excitement. Nor were his bruised seat-bones, or the overstrained muscles in his legs and arms. He knew that he couldn't hold on for much longer, and it occurred to him that if he could only reach the old house, he might not mind letting go. It would, after all, be a fitting place for him to lay his old bones to rest.

The horse, for once, had the same idea as JJ. It galloped headlong down the hill, crossed the stony wastes that had once been JJ's prime meadows and leaped a patch of brambles to arrive, sweating and trembling, in the spot where JJ's kitchen had once stood. It was gone now, its remaining walls barely knee-high, but the walls of the living room were still standing, all covered with ivy, and so high that he couldn't see over them. In the old doorway was a huge rock, and above it was a window made of milky glass or perspex or something. Behind it, peering out like a frightened ghost, was a face.

72

When Aisling reached the banks of the rath, she discovered that nearly all the refugees had been rounded up. Aengus Óg was there, sitting on a box, and she suspected that he had been drafted in to help as well, because he had the sulky look of someone who has done what they were told but bitterly resents it.

'Right,' said the Dagda when he saw her. 'Excellent. Let's get going, shall we?'

Before Aisling could reply she noticed Aengus standing up and looking towards the entrance to the souterrain. There were more people coming through: a few women and girls first, then a whole string of men wearing identical waterproof jackets.

'Oh, yes!' said Aengus, with sudden enthusiasm. 'I forgot about that. I left this gorgeous little creature behind me the last time.'

'What gorgeous little creature?' said the Dagda, eyeing the young women suspiciously.

'You know,' said Aengus. 'Those funny little furry little cat yokes.'

And one by one, he turned all Aidan's uniformed guards into ginger kittens.

On the other side of the souterrain, Captain Pup was obeying his orders to the letter. At least, so far he was. He had sent the castle party through, the domestic staff first, then the goons, and after them he had sent all but two of his handpicked team of squaddies. The ones who were left were his best friends, and as they stood guard over the slumbering figure of their former commander-in-chief, the three boys talked about their past lives in Ireland and their future ones in Tír na n'Óg.

The Dagda, just like his son, was instantly kitten smitten. He ran around the rath until he succeeded in trapping one of them under a rock and catching it. He was delighted with it, laughing and cooing and talking to it in baby talk. But when he came back to Aisling's side he grew serious again.

'Come on,' he said, indicating the refugees, who were lounging happily on the grass. 'What are you waiting for? Why haven't you got started yet?'

'Because I'm not going to,' said Aisling. 'I told you that before, and I haven't changed my mind.'

'But why?' said the Dagda. 'I don't understand. What have I done to offend you?'

'You haven't offended me,' Aisling said haughtily, 'but what you're intending to do offends my principles.'

'Huh?' said the Dagda. He momentarily relaxed his grip on the kitten, which took the opportunity to race up his arm and launch itself into space.

'Look at them, Dagda,' said Aisling. 'There's nothing for them in their own country except misery and starvation. They're happy here. They're doing nobody any harm. It's immoral of you to send them back.'

'Send them back?' said the Dagda, absently accepting the struggling kitten from the small child it had landed on. 'Who said anything about sending them back?'

'But . . .' said Aisling. 'But why have you rounded them up and brought them all here, then?'

'Because here's where all the music and the instruments are,' he said. 'So here's where we'll have to have the norcrystal.'

'Orchestra?' said Aisling.

'That's what I said. Orchrista. We've got enough people, haven't we?'

'Well . . . yes,' said Aisling.

'So what are you waiting for?' said the Dagda.

73

Up at Aidan's castle, Donal's soldiers were ransacking the stores and carting off whatever they fancied. They began with the clothes, and soon every man was kitted out in new boots, shirt, jeans and, best of all, new waterproofs. Then they moved on to the food. There were none of the old staples left – bread and biscuits hadn't been seen for years – but there was still some good stuff. There were crates full of tinned beans and peas and sweetcorn, rice pudding and peaches and sweetened condensed milk. There were jars of jam and chutney and pickles, some of them mouldy and inedible but some miraculously preserved against all the odds. Donal would have turned his nose up at the ancient food when he was a child, but today's survivors had strong stomachs and this was the finest of fare for them. There would be a feast in the barracks tonight.

In the morning they would feast again, then Donal would send them over to Tír na n'Óg, with as much of the treasure from his container as they could carry. This world had reached its end game and there would be no more need for armies now that Aidan had gone. Donal planned to join them before too much longer, but he had one last time-consuming job to do first. He hoped he would have enough strength left to carry it out.

When the last of the rejoicing squaddies had returned to the barracks, the sun was sinking rapidly. But there was still another half an hour of light left in the sky, so Donal decided to have a sort through his container and choose which things would go and which would have to be left behind. He climbed the ladder, opened the container and went in.

There was another of JJ's handmade fiddles, and he put that beside the door to go, and then a box of modern novels that he had picked out when he had still had time to be choosy. He was just going through a stack of children's picture books when he heard a strange sound on the roof of the container. It was like footsteps, but hard little ones; nothing like a man. He turned towards the open doors, just in time to see the púca changing himself into his long form and swinging down into the container.

'Good evening, Donal,' he said. 'You're the very person I was looking for.'

74

When he got over the initial shock of seeing the face, JJ urged the horse forward. It complied, and he might have realized that it did so too willingly if he hadn't been so intrigued by what he had found. The ancient plastic windows made it difficult to see the face, but it was clear that it belonged to a child, and behind it were two more, looking out eagerly. The kidnapped children. Who else could it be? JJ had stumbled across exactly what he had been sent here to fetch.

He remembered it all now that they had stopped for a moment and he was no longer fighting with the horse. The drinking contest. Donal cheating. The written note. The key. He had won, so surely he must have the key. Moving gingerly and still fighting waves of nausea, he checked in all his pockets. He couldn't find it, and nor could he remember anyone giving it to him.

'Don't worry,' he said to the children. 'I'll soon have you out of there.'

The door didn't look very strong. It belonged to an old caravan, which had been cleverly concealed inside the ruins of the house. If he could just move that big rock, it shouldn't be too difficult to get it open, even without a key. He coaxed the horse forward, and again, too willingly, it obeyed him. It almost seemed to sense what he wanted, and positioned itself as close to the big rock as it could get, so it was easy for JJ to reach down and—

'Dad!' came a voice from behind him. 'No! Don't touch it!'

JJ straightened up and turned to see Jenny racing through the rubble towards him.

'Don't worry, sweetheart,' he said. 'I've found the children. I was just—'

He stopped mid-sentence and broke into a cold sweat.

'Just doing exactly what Oisín did when he fell off the horse,' said Jenny.

'Oh my God,' said JJ. 'I was, wasn't I? Lucky you came along.'

The horse turned and glared at Jenny, and she got the distinct impression that it didn't agree. It tossed its head, swivelled on its hind legs and, with JJ still somehow clinging on, set off again for the sea.

75

'Have you been drinking?' said the púca, sniffing the air.

'Not me,' said Donal. 'My father and my brother. It's a long story.' He had changed his clothes along with the rest of the men, but Aidan's poitín had somehow soaked right into his skin and he was sure he could taste it as well as smell it.

The púca looked around the container. 'Such a marvellous idea. So clever of you to think of it.'

'It was Mikey's idea, really,' said Donal. 'I just expanded on it a bit.'

'All the same,' said the púca, 'it's a great achievement. Do you have a copy of *The Grafter's Bible*, by any chance?'

'I've got several Bibles,' said Donal. 'I don't know which versions they are.'

'Not that Bible,' said the púca. '*The Grafter's Bible: A Layman's Guide to the Propagation of Fruit Trees.*'

'I'm not sure,' said Donal. 'It might be in one of the boxes. I did get some farming and gardening books, but I doubt whether they'll get through.'

'Not get through?' said the púca. 'Why would they not get through?'

'There aren't enough people left now,' said Donal. 'Not here anyway. So most of this stuff will have to stay where it is.'

'That would be a shame,' said the púca. 'Of course, there's always the chance that I might be able to give you a bit of help.'

Donal stared at him, struck with a vision from his childhood. The púca's fist reaching between the worlds and returning with a tree in it. He had seen it with his own eyes. He swallowed hard, refusing to allow hope to engulf him. Because if the púca could do that, what was to stop him doing the same thing in the other direction? If he could pull things out of Tír na n'Óg, he could surely push things into it as well.

'I see that you remember,' the púca said. 'It would be no bother to me at all, you know. I could put the whole lot through for you if you like.'

'That would be fantastic,' said Donal. 'You have no idea what it would mean to me.'

'But naturally,' the púca said, 'I'd have to ask for a little favour in return.'

Donal remembered his terror of the púca when he was a child. He ought to have realized there would be a catch. The hopes that had dared to surface sank back into the depths they had come from.

'What kind of favour?' he asked.

The púca held out a bunch of sticks, some of them hairy little roots, others twigs cut from a tree. 'I'd like you to take these over with you and look after them for me. It's completely harmless, just a bit of good rootstock and some cuttings from my favourite trees. I may need them again one day and it would be nice to know they were somewhere safe.'

'I don't see a problem with that,' said Donal.

'There isn't one,' said the púca. 'But I would rather Aengus Óg was kept in the dark about it, if it's all the same to you. We're not exactly the best of friends, and he'd be certain to try and thwart me if he knew what I was doing.'

'OK,' said Donal, hope emerging afresh. 'I don't see why he needs to know anything about it.'

'Excellent,' said the púca. 'So I can rely on you to keep them hidden? Just these few little precious things? Will you keep them with you?'

'I could do,' said Donal. It was, after all, a small price to pay for getting the rest of his stuff across.

'So where would you put them?' the púca asked.

Donal opened his jacket and showed him the poacher's pocket.

'Oh, isn't that wonderful?' said the púca. 'You know, old Mikey is right about some things. You people are not entirely useless. That's an extremely clever idea.'

'There's loads of room in it,' said Donal. 'They'll be quite safe in there.'

'But you'll have to take those other things out, presumably,' the púca said.

'Oh, I will,' said Donal. 'But I'm not going over just yet. I have some work to do first and I'll need the things that are in there.'

'Oh.' The púca sounded disappointed. 'Well, would you mind if we tried it out? I'd just like to be sure that my stuff will fit in there.'

'No bother,' said Donal. He took out the rolls of plastic bags and the A4 pads and the ballpoint pens. The púca stretched out his hairy arm and placed the rootstock and cuttings carefully inside. The tops protruded slightly.

'Do you think they'll be safe?' he said.

'Oh, yes,' said Donal.

'Even if you do up the jacket?'

Donal demonstrated, buttoning the jacket up to the top.

'And they won't get broken if you sit down, or when you go to sleep?'

'No,' said Donal. 'I'll make sure they don't.'

'Good,' said the púca, and with a speed that caught Donal completely off guard, he stepped out on to the ladder and slammed the container doors closed.

The horse careered down the hillside, leaping rocks and scattering stones. The setting sun was directly ahead, fiercer than any searchlight, making it impossible for JJ to see where he was going. He had given up trying to influence the horse's behaviour and was concentrating hard on holding on to anything he could find. The empty stirrups bounced wildly, hitting him in the thighs and once, when he was pitched forward, on his nose. It was the nightmare to end all nightmares, and it felt as if it was never going to end. At the bottom of the hill, where the encroaching sea met the foot of the mountain, its storm-driven waves had eaten away a sheer cliff, about ten metres high. And the horse, which couldn't see much better than JJ could, had no idea it was there.

When Aisling surveyed the ragtag bunch of humanity gathered before her, she began to wonder whether she might not, after all, harbour some fascist tendencies. Because the idea of trying to turn a hundred tone-deaf refugees into a functioning orchestra was absurd. It filled her with such panic that she almost wished she had sent them all back where they came from after all.

She didn't know where to begin, but the Dagda was striding through the crowds as if it was all perfectly simple.

'Here,' he said, handing the piano accordion to a bent old woman. 'You play this. And you, that tall fella over there – you play this dirty great big fiddle thing. The muddy one, that's right.'

It was ridiculous. If Pup was anything to go by, these people wouldn't even be able to sing. They didn't have the first rudimentary concepts of music. She would have to start them all from scratch, get them listening first, and maybe doing some clapping exercises. But there was the Dagda, surrounded by a gang of children, handing out whistles as if they were lollipops. And, predictably, the first thing they did was blow into them as hard as they could.

Aisling glanced up at Aengus, who was watching from the sidelines, his handsome face creased with laughter. 'Right!' she said, with the volume and tone she had often borrowed from her first headmistress. 'Everybody stop blowing and listen. Aengus Óg is going to play us a tune.'

One moment JJ and the horse were hurtling down the stony hillside; the next, completely without warning, they were in mid air and the brilliant surface of the sea was soaring up to meet them. They hit it with a crash and JJ gasped at the sudden cold shock.

It was just as well he did, because that last snatched breath of Irish air had to last him a long, long time. The horse did not stay on the surface, but plunged straight down beneath the waves and stayed there, swimming strongly through the gloom, dragging JJ in its wake. The sea bed wasn't far below but the horse stayed above it, ploughing through the seaweed that grew there. As the oxygen began to run out in JJ's lungs, he was gripped by the awful realization that the horse wasn't going to take him back through the time skin to Tír na n'Óg. It had never intended to do that. He remembered it rubbing his leg against the boulder on the hillside. He remembered how cooperative it had suddenly become when he wanted to move that stone that was up against the door of the caravan. He wondered again how many people the white horse had taken out of Tír na n'Óg and back to Ireland. And he wondered whether any of them had made it back again. Because he saw now that bringing people home wasn't the horse's job. Twice it had tried to get him off with the old rock trick, and now it was trying to drown him.

All his instincts were telling him to let go, but he knew that he couldn't. If he lost the horse and returned to the surface, he was as good as dead. He could never again set foot in Ireland, and he would not be able to stay alive in that storm-tossed sea for more than a few hours. Whichever way he looked at it, his prospects were not good.

* * *

Jenny circled above the place where JJ and the horse had gone in. She flew lower, certain that she would soon see the two white heads appearing above the waves. But they did not. She circled more widely, in case they had been carried away by the tide, or by some strong current, but there was no sign of them anywhere in the bay.

Jenny hoped they had gone through and were safe in Tír na n'Óg. There was nothing she could do for them now, in any case, so she turned and flew back to where the children were anxiously waiting in the mobile home.

Every night, two of Aidan's goons came down to check on the children and take care of their basic needs. It took both of them working together to shift the huge rock that was propped against the door, and Jenny had no hope of moving it on her own. She struggled for a minute or two, then tried a different tack. Inside the mobile home the children squealed and retreated when they saw the grizzly bear appear, but a moment later it was gone, and they weren't at all sure it had ever really been there. The rock was gone as well, and the door swung open freely on bent hinges.

Jenny thought about Aidan and the ruse with the key. It had all been a lie. There was no need for a key to open this door.

77

On the floor of the souterrain, Aidan Liddy woke up and groaned.

'Oh, God. Oh my head! Where am I?'

It was what Pup and his friends had been waiting for. All three of them were small but they were strong, and before Aidan knew what was happening, they had bundled him through the fluid wall and into Tír na n'Óg.

'Go on,' said Pup to the other two. 'Your turn now. Get him out the other side before he tries to come back.'

'And you?' said one of them. 'Aren't you coming through with us?'

This was where Pup, unknown to anyone, was departing from the strict orders Donal had given him. He was, in fact, supposed to go through with the others and stay there, but he had no intention of doing so.

'Don't worry about me,' he said. 'I'll be through soon after you.'

There was a moment of hesitation, then the soldiers saluted and disappeared through the wall. Pup waited for a minute to make sure no one returned, then he picked up the stump of candle and made his way back through the long stone chambers and out into the open.

It was almost dark, and a few hazy stars had appeared inland. But above the sea there were none, and Pup sensed the approach of a new band of rain clouds. He wished he didn't have to face that. He longed to be with the others, out on the bright side where no storms could get him and there was nothing to worry about at all. But there were things he had to do first, before he could go.

On the bank of the rath Aengus Óg paused in the middle of a reel and put down his bow. High up on the mountainside, just below the stony steps, there was an explosion of flying rocks and dust, and when it settled he could see that an enormous rusty box had appeared there.

Aengus was enjoying JJ's lion-head fiddle. He picked up the bow and carried on playing. Most of the ploddies forgot about the explosion and lounged back to listen, but a few of them, led by Aisling and the Dagda, set off up the hill to investigate. So nobody noticed when Aidan Liddy, flanked by two young soldiers with rifles, emerged from the mouth of the souterrain and collapsed on the ground, clutching his head in both hands.

'That god-awful music as well!' he groaned. 'I always knew that this place would be hell!'

78

JJ's lungs and mind were both on the point of collapse. The need for air had become painful and he had to battle against the urge to open his mouth and fill himself with sea water. His life – both his lives – were flashing in pictures across his mind's eye. It was all over for him now, he knew.

But the horse, too, had reached the end of its endurance. Though it came from Tír na n'Óg it had no more ability to breathe underwater than any other horse, fairy or ploddy. With the last of its strength it pushed for the sea bed, broke through the time skin and landed itself and the astonished, gasping JJ on the firm, warm plain of Tír na n'Óg.

Pup was just about to set out for the barracks when he heard voices on the other side of the fort. He went towards them and soon he could make out Jenny's face in the half-light. And not only Jenny. There were three children there as well, and one of them was his brother, Billy. Pup ran up and hugged him, then listened to the story of the midnight kidnap and the long, frightening imprisonment in the old caravan.

'And now we're going with Jenny,' Billy finished up. 'Over to Tír na n'Óg where we won't be hungry or frightened or cold ever again.'

'Where you belong,' said Pup.

'Why?' said Billy.

'Where you came from in the first place,' said Pup. 'Or your parents, anyway. Isn't that right, Jenny?'

'Actually,' said Jenny, 'I'm not so sure. But we're going over there anyway, aren't we, lads?'

'Are you coming, Pup?' Billy asked.

'I am,' said Pup, 'but not just yet. I have to help the general with something. But I'll be there before you know it.'

After the crash, and after the clatter of settling rubble, silence descended. And not just silence, but peace; a sense of absolute calm and contentment that Donal remembered experiencing only once in his life before, long, long ago. He knew this was not supposed to be happening. He hadn't wanted to come here yet. He had things to do; responsibilities; there were people who still needed his help. But no matter how hard he tried to hold on to them, his troubles dropped away from him one by one, until at last he couldn't even remember them, no matter how hard he tried. He knew there had been one last thing, vitally important, that he had set himself to do, but it wouldn't come back to him. It was gone beyond retrieving.

The accumulated exhaustion of decades of sleepless nights pressed down upon him now. Taking care not to bruise the púca's precious apple stock, he sank down on to the floor of the container and fell into a deep, deep sleep.

79

The barracks was a shambles. The fuel stores had been raided, and huge fires had been lit all around the parade ground. Soldiers were sitting and sprawling everywhere Pup looked. They had clearly been making free with the commander-in-chief's liquor as well as his food. There were very few of them still awake, and among those who were, few were capable of stringing a coherent sentence together. But finally Pup found Colonel Mooney, who was just about able to tell him that the general had stayed behind at the castle and still hadn't come back.

So Pup walked back out into the night and over to the dark castle. The place was silent, inside and out. The drawbridge was down and Pup went in, still half expecting to be challenged or shot at, even though he himself had seen the commander-in-chief and his henchmen through to the other side.

'General Liddy?' he called. His voice bounced back metallically from the empty containers.

'General?' he called again.

A rat scurried across the open mouth of a raided storeroom, but there was no other sound. Pup stood in the centre of the circular courtyard and looked around at the massive steel walls, and it was then that he noticed. Despite the dark, the break in the skyline was obvious. One of the containers was missing.

It was like waking up one morning and discovering Sliabh Carran had disappeared. Pup stepped closer and looked up at the empty space. It wasn't impossible to move those containers. A team of men with ropes and pulleys and levers could get it moving, and a pile of rocks could be constructed to lower it gently down to the ground. Pup had seen it done once before. But it was a massive undertaking and it took time to organize and more time to carry out. There were no signs of that kind of activity, and in any case, why would they want to do it and leave a gap in the castle wall?

As he stared, Pup became aware that there were pipes sticking up like broken veins around the gap, as though the container had been wrenched out carelessly by some massive force. He realized, even before he worked it out from the numbers, that it was the general's container that was missing, and for some reason this made the disappearance even more sinister. He stepped backwards, called out once more, then ran out across the drawbridge before the unknown force that had taken the container could decide to lock him in.

He didn't want to go back to the barracks and face

those stupid drunken squaddies again. His heart had been full at the prospect of seeing the general, and telling him why he had disobeyed his orders and come back, instead of going through to Tír na n'Óg with the others. It was to help him, that was why. It was still what he wanted to do, and he realized there was one other place General Liddy might be. Pup knew where he went every day, though he didn't know why. He looked up at the sky. He could see no stars now, but there was enough light filtering through the clouds for him to see his way, and there was no rain yet. So he pulled his jacket tight around him and set his oversized boots on a course for the stony steps and the top of Sliabh Carran.

80

JJ threw himself off the white horse and lay face down on the warm, sweet-scented grass.

'Home,' he said. 'Home, home, home.'

He was wet. His seat-bones were sore and his hands were blistered from clinging to wet reins and wet mane. His arms and legs were hurting and his nose had been bleeding and was still blocked from the blow the stirrup had given it. That is the way he would always be in Tír na n'Óg, where no kind of injury got better. He rolled himself carefully on to his back and gazed into the blue sky that never rained, and squinted at the bright sun that never set. He wouldn't get better but he wouldn't get worse, either, and the aches and pains seemed like a small price to pay for the privilege of being back here again.

The horse was wandering off across the field, its reins dangling. JJ was seized with a sudden, furious urge to get back on it; to show it who was boss and make it carry him down to the village to see what was happening. But a cold shock ran through him when he realized the mistake that would be. Because the next person who got on it would be taken, just as he and Oisín had been taken, out of the land of eternal youth and back to the place where death was just a careless moment away.

He went after the horse anyway, but he didn't get on it. He took off the saddle and bridle and, instead of hanging them neatly on the gate where Aengus had found them, dropped them in a heap at the bottom of the hedge, where they would be very hard for anyone to find. With luck, he would be the last rider that white horse ever took across to Ireland.

One of the children up beside the container spotted JJ appearing on the plain far below, and pointed it out to the others. Aisling's eyes had never been particularly good and she couldn't see that far. But the description of the white horse and a man with white hair getting up and running after it was all she needed to hear. JJ was home and safe and, from the sound of it, as eccentric and unpredictable as ever.

'Are there any children with him?' said the Dagda to the sharp-eyed ploddy.

'No, sir,' said the child. 'Not that I can see.'

'Hmm,' said the Dagda. 'I'd better go down and see what he's been up to.'

'Wait, Dagda,' said Aisling. 'Let's just see what's in here first.'

One of the soldiers opened the doors of the container. When the Dagda saw Donal sleeping inside, he said, 'Another ploddy. Ingenious, aren't they? The ways they find of sneaking across.'

'I think I might know this one,' said Aisling. She looked more closely and her heart passed through shock, then through sadness and into joy as she recognized her Donal, nearly as old as she was now, but still her beloved son.

The Dagda made to prod him with his boot, but Aisling stopped him.

'Let him sleep,' she said. 'He looks as if he needs it.'

So she and the other ploddies began to unload the boxes and crates and bags and cases, working carefully around Donal, who slept right through it all. Outside on the rocky ground, the Dagda eagerly ripped everything open and ordered any scores and instruments to be carried down to the orchestra.

As the workforce dwindled, he sent an order for re-inforcements to come up and help. Meanwhile the unpacking went on. They were nearly at the back of the container when a tall soldier lifted a box from the top of a roof-high stack and Aisling caught a glimpse of the things that were standing behind it. She gasped, and began hurriedly to dismantle what proved to be the final wall of boxes. Because there was something there that she had never expected to see again; something that would make her life in Tír na n'Óg complete.

There were two pianos, but she was only interested in one of them. It was her own one; the old Bechstein that her parents had given her when she first married JJ.

'Dagda!' she called. 'These are pianos!'

'What are?' he said, coming in and helping her move the last of the boxes. 'Those things that look like sheds?'

Aisling pulled up a box to sit on and opened the keyboard lid of the Bechstein. It looked OK. All the keys were still there, anyway. She played a few notes, and then a couple of scales and arpeggios. It was out of tune and some of the keys were a bit sticky, but it was not half as bad as it should have been after . . . what? She glanced across at Donal to get an idea. Twenty-five years? Thirty? It wouldn't be a problem. JJ had tuned the piano for her in the past and he'd surely figure out a way of doing it again. And in the meantime it was an awful lot better than nothing.

She adjusted the height of her seat with a few large books and tried out the pedals with her feet. Then she began to play.

As Pup approached the beacon, he thought for a moment that he saw a man standing on top of it, but when he got there, all he saw was a big white goat. It wasn't, however, an ordinary goat, and when it stretched out and took on a form that was almost human, Pup began to wonder whether he might have got lost when he was under the ground and come up into some entirely different kind of world. Nothing was right here any more. The squaddies were all drunk, a container had vanished, and now this. The weird goat even spoke.

'A soldier boy,' he said. 'Or a boy soldier. Which is it?' Pup was too surprised to answer, and the púca went on, 'What brings you up here at this time of night?'

Pup found his voice. 'I'm looking for General Liddy.'

'General Liddy?' said the púca. 'Now, which of the Liddys would that be?'

'Donal,' said Pup. 'General Donal Liddy.'

'Ah, Donal,' said the púca. 'Well, he's not here, as you can see. But I happen to know where he is.'

'Really?' said Pup. 'Where is he?'

'In Tír na n'Óg,' said the púca. 'It seems to be all the rage this summer. They're all flocking over there for a bit of sunshine.'

'Not the general,' said Pup. 'He can't be.'

'I assure you he is, though,' said the púca. 'I put him there myself. Him and his big trunkful of memories.'

'You did that?' said Pup. 'You moved the container?'

'Piece of cake.' The púca yawned and sighed and said, with a drop of acid in his voice, 'Is there anything else I can help you with?'

'No,' said Pup. 'I'll be going back, I suppose.'

He turned and started down the side of the barrow, but the púca called out after him. 'Soldier boy?'

'Yes?'

'There's someone here who wants you to take a message.'

'Who?' said Pup. 'Who's there?'

'It's just an old ghost,' said the púca, and fear crawled over Pup's scalp. 'He wants you to give a message to General Liddy. Are you intending to follow him over to Tír na n'Óg?'

'Yes.' Pup's eyes searched the surrounding darkness but he could see no sign of any ghost. 'But I have some things to do first. It won't be for a while.'

'Doesn't matter,' said the púca. 'There's no mad rush. But when you do see him, tell him Mikey says goodbye.'

'Mikey?'

'Mikey says goodbye. Can you remember that?'

'I can,' said Pup.

As he walked back towards the stony steps, a wind began to snake around his heels, threatening worse to come. Above him there were no stars at all, but out of the corner of his eye he caught a glimpse of something bright and shining. It seemed to float along the edge of his vision for a while, before rising up and vanishing among the clouds.

'Mikey says goodbye.' He repeated the words to himself to make sure he didn't forget them. 'Mikey says goodbye.'

81

Into Donal's dreams came a sound from his childhood. His mother's favourite piece, played so often that everyone thought of it as her theme tune. In the dream he was on the sofa, and Jenny was under the television, pulling the plug out of the wall. Aidan was a toddler, wandering around with a hammer.

The Dagda stood enraptured, his eyes closed, his hands drifting around him as though he was searching for something in mid air. Indeed, Aisling realized as she watched them that he probably could, and did, pull music out of the air. He *was* music, from the tips of his gently tapping toes to the fly-away hairs on the top of his head. With the right kind of guidance he would make the conductor to beat all conductors. Her fingers moved automatically through the familiar piece but her mind was already racing ahead. Whatever it took, she would knock the starry-eyed rabble of Tír na n'Óg into an orchestra and hand it over to him.

When the piece came to an end, the Dagda opened

his eyes and blinked. 'How did you do that?' he said. 'That yoke is a whole orchrista in a shed.'

'Not quite,' said Aisling. 'It's just a piano.'

The Dagda nodded sagely. 'Without the corjeen bit.'

'Without the corjeen bit,' said Aisling.

'But come here,' said the Dagda. 'You're not going to try and tell me a ploddy wrote that? What you just played?'

Aisling thought about it. The piece was an old one, from the baroque period, by a French composer called Couperin. But if, as JJ had discovered on his first trip to Tír na n'Óg, the people of Ireland got their music from the fairy folk, who was to say that it wasn't the same all over the world? The name of the piece said a lot. It was called, translated into English, *The Mysterious Barricades*.

Aisling smiled to herself. 'I used to think so,' she said. 'Now I'm not so sure. It's quite possible that I was wrong.'

Despite the nerve-racking encounter with the goat and all the talk of ghosts, Pup did not seek out the company of his comrades-in-arms at the barracks. Instead he steeled his nerve and went back to the castle to make preparations for the days and weeks ahead. Because if the general really had gone through to Tír na n'Óg, then it was all up to him now. He would have to manage on his own.

Some of the containers had been unlocked and left with their doors wide open, and the rats had called their friends and relations from all over the county to come and help themselves. In every corner, cats and kittens watched, or slept, or washed themselves, all of them full of rodent and enjoying the break before they began hunting again. Under the sofa in the ransacked living room of the commander's quarters, Pup found a bunch of keys. By the light of his candle-stump, he began to unlock and search the containers that the soldiers hadn't got around to breaking open. He was amazed by what he found. Boxes of toothpaste gone hard with age and toothbrushes still perfect in their plastic packaging. Crates of tools, never used but welded together by rust. Boxes of candles and matches, soaps and shampoos, pots and pans and glasses and cups. One whole container was packed full of electrical machines that had never been used and never would be. He had no idea what any of them had been for.

Tinned food was heavy and there was only so much that Pup could carry with him, but he had the commander's keys now and some of the padlocks they opened, and it gave him an idea. He picked an empty container on the second row and claimed it for his own. Into it he packed everything that he thought he could possibly need over the weeks ahead, and more besides, to be safe. A pile of new waterproofs and six different pairs of boots, all in the right size. A dozen wind-up torches and the same number of Swiss Army knives. Boxes of paper and plastic bags and pens.

The rest was food, and he laboured at that for most of the night, stocking his storeroom high. He didn't intend to be around long enough to eat it all, but a person who has experienced as much hunger as Pup had can never take enough precautions against it. The rats and the cats worked alongside him all night, and from the sounds of it they were all getting fed. So when Pup was finally satisfied with his provision store, he locked it up securely, then lit himself a little fire and cooked himself a feast.

82

At first light, Colonel Mooney distributed painkillers to his men to help them over their hangovers, and those who had the stomach for it ate a massive breakfast. An hour later they abandoned the barracks and set out for the rath.

Pup watched them and waited until he was sure no one was coming back. Then he packed a brand-new rucksack with as many of the provisions as he could carry and made his way down to the barracks. The place was a mess: a rubbish tip of discarded cans and bottles, torn cardboard boxes, dirty pots and pans. There were piles of vomit in all the corners and the stink from the latrines hung over the whole place like a malignant mist. The rats were already busy but Pup ignored them as he made his way to General Liddy's quarters. Nothing had been touched since he was there with the colonel, and he spent an hour transferring Donal's meticulously written notes into separate, sealable bags. When he was done, he packed them into the top of his rucksack and set out on the road.

His first port of call was his home place, where his mother and sister were still just about hanging on. They were delighted to see him, and amazed by the news he brought. They spent a day together, and the next morning Pup gave them one of Donal's notes and went on his way.

When the Dagda came back to the rath and discovered the children there with Jenny, he was delighted, and announced that JJ was off the hook. But when another hundred or so bewildered soldiers appeared, he was not so pleased.

'That's too many. We don't have enough instruments for all these. They'll have to go back where they came from.'

Aisling neatly distracted him by commandeering the entire army to bring the Bechstein down from the stony steps. She supervised the operation herself, dividing the army up into ten lifting parties which took it in turns to carry the piano. And through all the tramping around inside the container, and the shuffling for position, through all the barked orders and warnings, through all the grunts and groans of the lifting parties, Donal slept on.

Down at the rath, Pup's mother and sister came through into Tír na n'Óg. Billy raced over to welcome them and Jenny followed. She was pleased to meet them and delighted to hear about what Pup was doing over there and that he was well. But something had been puzzling her. Jenny had tested the children's godling skills with a few simple lessons, and there was no doubt at all that the other two children who had been kidnapped by

Aidan's men were of fairy origin. But Billy, she was certain, was not. He could neither step through the time skin nor change a kitten into a piglet – or anything else, for that matter. So something was wrong with the story, and she asked Pup's mother to clarify it for her.

'Oh,' she said, 'I had a baby swapped on me all right. But it wasn't Billy. It was his brother that was the changeling. It was Pup.'

And so, ironically, the boy who was doing his best to rescue the surviving people of Ireland turned out not to belong to the race of people that he was working so hard to save. Nor did he know, although sometimes he suspected, that he didn't need a fairy fort to get into Tír na n'Óg but could step through the time skin wherever he chose.

When he left his mother's house, he called to the few neighbours who still survived and told them about Tír na n'Óg. After that he made it up as he went along, delivering his notes at every inhabited house he was able to find in the bleak and barren country. To begin with he returned to the castle regularly, to stock up on provisions and, when he ran out of them, to painstakingly write out more copies of Donal's original note. But as time went on, his mission took him further and further afield, and in those places where his message met with a good reception he found that people were willing to share their meagre meals with him and he had no need to carry so much food. And he found, as well, that he could see no natural end to the job he had set out to do. No matter how far he travelled there were always more people to be reached, and how could he save one family and leave the next to its fate?

So, on his final visit to the castle, he packed a minimum of tins and jars and filled the rest of the space in his rucksack with paper and pens, and a spare pair of boots. Then he took a new waterproof jacket and set out to walk the roads of Ireland.

83

Donal dreamed that he was riding in the car with his father, along the Moy road to Kinvara. There were huge new houses all along the way, signs of the new wealth in the country. He dreamed of fat people driving fat cars, of ride-on lawnmowers, of rubbish bins overflowing by the roadside. He dreamed of being at home with a roast in the oven in the dry, warm kitchen, and his mother coming in from the garden with her arms full of fresh sweetcorn.

Some people called the wandering boy a madman, others a saint or a prophet. Some welcomed him and his message, and believed every word he said. Others shot at him or threw stones. Once a bullet hit him in the elbow and he lost the use of that arm for nearly six months. Another time a gang of raiders came across him on the road, and they beat him up and left him for dead. They took his rucksack and his supplies, but they left his precious notes, which were what mattered most to him.

Donal dreamed of television, of the programmes he used

to watch. They played in his head, like dreams within his dreams. People getting famous, people winning money and prizes and cars. It was all so easy. And the advertisements in between promised more. You could have anything you wanted. You could borrow money for the asking, and you could buy anything you wanted with it.

On Pup went, through dangerous territories governed by other warlords like Aidan, and through peaceful parts, where people pulled together and helped each other out. Here and there along the way he picked up stories about other raths, and when he took people down into them to test them, all but one of them worked. But Pup never went across himself. He was afraid that if he went into Tír na n'Óg again, even for a little look, he would never be able to bring himself to come back.

And still he had work to do. In friendly homes he dried out his wrinkled paper and wrote new notes with new directions, and he got help from some of the older folks, who could write as well as the general himself had done. And when he was rested and refreshed he went on again, to the next house or hamlet or village. Avoiding dangerous warlords wasn't too difficult because people were always willing to tell him where they were, but avoiding the weather was not so easy.

Donal dreamed of shopping malls. He dreamed about the bright lights, the heat, the endless open doors of shops like mouths, sucking people in. He dreamed of money changing hands, of shelf after shelf piled high, of lorries and warehouses and factories, all crammed full of things. He liked the things. He wanted the things, even though he realized he had no idea what any of them were supposed to be for.

In the third year of Pup's wanderings the next drought hit. For fifteen weeks no rain fell. Wells ran dry. Gardens dried up, fruit trees died, and people went over to Tír na n'Óg in droves, through their nearest forts. The drought was barely over when the first hurricane hit. It tore through sturdy houses as if they were cardboard boxes and toppled boulders from hilltops where they had stood for thousands of years. It thrust its snarling snout into every remaining sheltered spot in Ireland, uprooting orchards, demolishing terraces, making a muddy soup of vegetable gardens and washing away topsoil by the ton. Whole hillsides lost their grip on the rocks beneath and slid down into the valleys, taking houses and gardens with them.

Sheltering in a waterlogged cave, Pup sat out the storm. And when, after three hungry days, it passed, he set out again to see how many survivors it had left in its wake. There weren't many, but there were still enough to make his work worthwhile. For another two years he walked on, passing on his message by word of mouth when the last of his paper dissolved into mush. But as people became fewer, so too did the meals he was given in their houses, and a time came when he realized that he could go on no longer, whether or not his work was done. So he guided himself by the sun and by the old signposts which still stood at some of the major crossroads, and eventually he got back to the Burren and Sliabh Carran.

Donal dreamed of supermarket shelves. Mile upon mile upon mile of food. In his dream he smelled hot bread. Then the scene changed and he was in Aidan's grubby containers, walking along the rows, looking for something. It wasn't there. There were goats and ravens in there, and there were storms and deluges raging in the corners, but the thing he was looking for was not there. Where had Aidan put it? Why couldn't he find it? A little red Hohner accordion with twenty white buttons and one single black one.

The effects of the tornadoes were astonishing. The beacon was half its original size, its stones scattered across the mountain top. Further down, the castle and the barracks had been picked up and tossed down the hillside, the containers strewn around as if they were no heavier than cardboard boxes.

Pup sat at the foot of the stony steps and looked down on it all, the end of a civilization written clearly across the landscape. The only thing that hadn't changed since he last saw the place was the huge white goat that stood a short distance away, watching him. Pup waved to it, and it stood on its hind legs and waved back. It reminded him of something, and he knew it was time, at last, to go home. Just as an experiment, he decided to try going through the time skin right there, just where he was.

84

'Pup!' said Jenny, when she saw him walking towards her down the hillside. 'Great to see you!'

He was ragged and hungry and battered and tired, but he had to admit that it was great to see her as well. She had been much older than he was last time they met, but she wasn't now. She was just about right. He smiled, using muscles he'd forgotten he had.

Jenny smiled back. 'I'm glad you waited behind,' she said. 'You needed the time to catch up.'

'I'm glad, too,' he said. There was a silence that threatened to become awkward, and Pup remembered just in time that there was someone else he wanted to see. 'Where's the general? I mean, your brother Donal. There's something I have to tell him.'

Together they walked through a throng of people, in the middle of which JJ was trying to teach a soldier how to string a cello.

'Is that the last of them now?' said the Dagda, looking up from a page full of lines and black dots. If he recognized Pup, he gave no sign of it.

'I think so,' said Pup.

'It had better be,' said the Dagda.

They walked up to the container on the hill, where Donal was still dreaming his way through his past life. Jenny woke him gently and he sat up, one hand going instinctively to his side to protect the púca's sticks.

'Pup?' he said. 'Is that you?'

'It is, General,' said Pup.

'But you've grown up. How long have I been asleep?'

'No time at all,' said Jenny. 'Don't worry so much.'

'What have you been doing, then?' said Donal. 'Why did you stay behind?'

'To finish what you started,' said Pup. 'To hand out all those messages you wrote. And a few more, besides.'

'Ah, Pup,' said Donal. 'I always knew you had a heart of gold.'

'And I have a message for you as well,' said Pup. 'Mikey says goodbye.'

'Mikey?' said Donal. 'Is Mikey gone?'

'I can't answer that, General,' said Pup. 'I never saw Mikey at all. But it seems likely that he has. Everything's gone, General. There's nothing left of that old world at all.'

PART TWO

THE MIDDLE

When the musicians and dancers gathered on the quay in Kinvara learned that the Dagda had come down from the mountain and was mingling with his people at the rath, they decided to go and take a look for themselves.

In Ireland, the second hurricane set in. It was closely followed by a third, but by then there was hardly anyone left alive to see it.

Aisling decided that the ploddies needed to learn the first principles of music. She set Jenny to teach some of the smaller children to sing. She herself was trying to round up the adults for dancing lessons, and she wanted Pup to help her, but Pup wasn't going anywhere. He refused to join in with Jenny's singing group but he wouldn't leave it, either. All he wanted to do was lie on the grass, soak up the sunshine and keep half an eye on his darling girl.

Between the storms the scorching sun beat down. It melted the last of the Greenland ice and the seas rose even higher, inundating coastal areas all around the world. In South America and Indonesia, horrendous droughts finally put an end to the last of the rain forests, and lightning strikes set them ablaze. The smoke from them shrouded half the planet.

Aengus and JJ were in negotiations over the lion-head fiddle. JJ was happy to give it to him, but Aengus insisted on paying him for it. The problem was, JJ couldn't think of anything at all that he wanted.

'Dad,' Jenny called. They both turned their heads. 'Is Pup my brother?'

'How should I know?' said Aengus. He sat down on the grass and took out his pipe. 'Where did you find him?'

'He just appeared like all the others,' said Jenny. 'But you must have a way of knowing.'

Aengus peered hard at Pup, who was listening anxiously. 'You don't look much like each other. I shouldn't think you're related.'

'That's not good enough, Dad,' said Jenny.

Aengus poured tobacco dust into his pipe and regarded it gloomily.

The great deserts that had formed around the equator spread further north and south, creating an arid band of ferocious temperatures around the middle of the globe. At the poles the storms raged on.

'Why does it matter, anyway?' said Aengus.

'You know perfectly well why it matters!' said Jenny, trying to conceal a rising blush.

'Oh, I see,' said Aengus. 'You two are—'

'No we're not!' Jenny snapped.

'But we might be,' said Pup, blushing as well.

Aeons and aeons passed away.

Aengus Óg lit his pipe, which flared up in his face. The children in the singing group held their noses because of the smell of singed hair.

'Give it up, Dad,' said Jenny.

'I think I might have to,' said Aengus, waving his hand to divert the hot smoke away from his eyes.

And slowly, slowly, slowly, the oceans absorbed carbon from the atmosphere.

'But anyway,' Aengus went on, 'I can see the predicament you two are in. You're thinking you might like to make a little visit over to the other side for a while?'

Jenny and Pup both coloured again, and looked everywhere except at each other. Aengus poked an elbow through the time skin, like someone testing the temperature of a baby's bathwater.

And the Earth's atmosphere cooled. The storms brought snow instead of rain, and ice began to form again at the poles. It spread outwards, glaciers formed, blizzards forged ahead of them and paved their way towards the equator.

Aengus whipped his elbow straight back and rubbed it hard.

'I wouldn't go back there just yet, anyway,' he said. 'It's a wee bit cold.'

The glaciers lifted the stones of the beacon, and the dented remains of Aidan's warehouses, and the broken walls of the Liddy house, and the caravan that had been hidden inside them.

'Where were you born?' he asked Pup.

'Not far from Carron,' he said. 'Between there and Liddy's castle.'

'And what kind of house was it?'

'An old one,' said Pup. 'I mean a really old one. Built out of stone, not blocks.'

'Hmm,' said Aengus. 'Not enough information.'

The glaciers powered on, scouring all mankind's ruined hopes and vanities from the face of the land and depositing them deep beneath the oceans.

'What did your mother look like?' said Aengus.

'She's here,' said Pup. 'That's her over there.' He pointed to a crowd of people who had gathered to listen

to Donal. He was playing 'The Cow That Ate the Blanket'
on his old button box.

And then the seas themselves froze over.

'The one beside the girl with the frizzy red hair,' said
Pup. 'The girl is my sister.'

'Oh,' said Aengus. 'I see who she is now. No. That's not
her. I definitely didn't leave my baby with her. I've never
seen her before in my life.'

*And for a time the Earth became a quiet place, muffled in snow
and ice, and nothing but blizzards and gods moved across its
round white face.*

'And anyway,' Aengus went on, 'now that I come to think
about it, my baby was another girl.'

*Beneath the surface the Earth's crust creaked and shifted. Land
masses split apart and new continents were formed, and collided
with each other. Mountain ranges reared up into the clouds. The
last remains of the old human cities were ground into sand and
buried deep inside brand-new land masses.*

Pup and Jenny leaped to their feet and embraced.

'Come to think of it,' said Aengus, 'I wonder where
she is.'

He got up and wandered off to look for her, leaving

his smouldering pipe abandoned on the grass.

Jenny tested the time skin again. 'Not yet,' she said to Pup.

And then, as it had done countless times throughout its long, long history, the Earth began to warm up again. The púca watched patiently for the first sign of life. It began with tiny organisms that had hibernated deep beneath the sea's icy crust. In the warming waters, they started to multiply, mutate and evolve.

While Aengus Óg was looking for his daughter, a fairy woman by the name of Meadbh caught his eye. He caught hers as well. Something in the air, no doubt about it. He made his way through the crowds towards her.

Once the basic building work had been done, the púca came into his element. Seaweed was thrown up on to the beaches and mutated into rudimentary land plants. With a bit of help from the goat god, these became grasses and legumes, then shrubs and trees, and they marched inland as the ice receded and established themselves into forests and tundras, covering every landmass with a thick fur of vegetation.

Whatever the thing was that was in the air, it was contagious. Throughout the assembled orchestra couples were forming, among the ploddies as well as the fairies. The Dagda looked on benignly.

'It's the music, of course,' he said, to no one in

particular. 'It always brings people together.' He caught
Drowsy Maggie's eye and gave her a wink. 'A set!' he
roared to Donal. '"Miss McCleod's Reel"!'

*But the bit the púca loved best was still to come. It began with the
small, cold-blooded things that crept out of the shallows and found
they enjoyed the sensation of warm sand beneath their flippers.
The púca helped them develop lungs to breathe air, then coaxed
them further inland to his grassy plains and forests. They needed
awkward things like noses and eyes and claws, and he helped
them with those as well, and once the basic equipment was safely
up and running, he really went to town. This time round the birds
and beasts were going to be better than ever. Not too big – that
was a mistake he had made before and learned from – but brighter
and more beautiful than anything that lovely Mother Earth had
ever known before.*

JJ and Devaney joined Donal to play for the set, but it
wasn't until Aisling joined in on the piano that the yips
and cheers began to rise up from the watching ploddies.
One by one, timidly to begin with and then with more
confidence, they began to try and imitate the dancing of
the fairies. The Dagda, teamed up with Maggie, spun her
round so fast that she got dizzy.

'They're getting the picture at last!' he said. 'We'll have
the orchrista up and running in no time now.'

But suddenly, mid bar, the music stopped.

'What's going on?' said Aengus, who was partnering

Meadbh in the same set as his father. He looked over at the musicians and saw that the púca had arrived in their midst, and that Donal was handing him something that looked like a bundle of kindling.

'That cloven-hoofed vandal!' said Aengus. 'How dare he gate-crash our party!'

He began to make his way over, but the crowd was thick, and by the time he got there the púca had taken his sticks and gone.

'What was that all about?' he said to Donal.

'Just some bits and pieces he asked me to mind for him,' said Donal.

'What kind of bits and pieces?' said Aengus.

'Gardening stuff,' said Donal, who didn't want to give the púca's secrets away entirely.

'Gardening stuff, is it?' said Aengus. 'Hmm. I wonder . . .'

Taking a chance, he plunged his whole arm through the time skin, and it came out warm and dry. A broad smile spread across his face. To Aisling's horror, he sprang up on top of her precious piano and called out over the assembled dancers, 'Come on in, lads. The weather's lovely!'

PART THREE

THE BEGINNING

1

It was millions of years since any of them had gone through the time skin, and all their clothes had long since passed their degrade-by date. But the fairies were masters of glamour, and a hastily snatched fig leaf or two quickly had them covered, each of them according to their preferred fashion. In any case, despite the amorous nature of their intentions, they found that there were far more interesting things to be looking at than each other.

Because the púca had created a paradise on Earth. Brilliant flowers hung in multicoloured chains from the branches of tall, elegant trees. In the canopy far above their heads, radiant birds fluttered and sang, purple and orange and red. Lovely animals peered down from the trees with large, kind eyes. Spotted bears and striped wallabies fed from bushes that were laden with ripe fruit, and beside them fruit-eating lizards and snakes dangled lazily from the branches. And there were other beasts, too, unknown and unimagined, which jumped and swung and climbed through the forest, each one more beautiful than the last. They all watched the fairies curiously, but none of them were worried by the sudden appearance of this new kind of creature in their midst.

But there was, as Aengus Óg pointed out, one snag.

'No ploddies.'

'There might be,' said Pup.

They pushed further on into the jungle, but soon they had to admit that Aengus was probably right, and that they were the first people to see this place. There was something too clean and fresh about it all – it was impossible to believe that it had ever been seen by anyone else.

'It doesn't matter,' Jenny said after a while. 'It doesn't mean we can't have our children. It just means we'll have to stay and look after them.'

'Stay and look after them?' said Aengus. 'Are you mad? It's all very well for you teenagers, but do you know how old I'll be if I stay here for fifteen or twenty years?'

Jenny took a guess. 'Forty-five? Fifty?'

'No,' said Aengus. 'But anyway, it's impossible. Can you imagine what my father would say if I came home older than he is? My life wouldn't be worth living.'

'Don't be so touchy,' said Jenny. 'It happens all the time.' She turned to Pup. 'Did you know that Aengus Óg is JJ's grandfather? Which means that I'm his aunt as well as his foster daughter. And he's seventy and I'm seventeen. Do you know how complicated that gets sometimes?'

'Well, you stay, then,' said Aengus.

'Hang on a minute,' said Pup, who had been nibbling

on some interesting cherry-like fruit. 'Two parents can bring up more than one child. Once they're on their feet, we can just treat them like a family. Take it in turns to come over and look after the whole lot of them for a year or two.'

Everyone agreed that this was an excellent idea, and so the little party stayed. While they waited for the babies to arrive, they set about building a new rath to replace the one the glaciers had erased, so that they would have a marker to help them remember where they were in this new and strange land, and where it connected to their own rath in Tír na n'Óg. First they built the circular bank in against the side of the hill. Digging earthworks without tools was a tedious business, but the fairies worked languidly, taking long breaks to wander through the forest and eat their fill of the vast array of fantastic foods that grew there. Gradually the rath took shape, and when the bank was finished they began work on the souterrain. But the fairies are not known for their industry, and by then everyone was getting fed up with working, so instead of building a proper underground chamber with stone walls and crawl-holes, they just dug a tunnel to connect with the fluid wall beneath the rath in Tír na n'Óg.

By the end of the first year, each of the seven couples had produced a baby, and by the end of the second year all the babies were crawling and some of them were walking. Since food was easy to come by and required no effort to prepare, everyone agreed that two people would be enough to take care of them.

Jenny and Pup volunteered to take the first shift. Now that the fort was finished and the other parents were gone there was no need to stay in the same place, so the young couple and the seven children roamed the forest, going wherever their fancy took them.

So when the púca came across the fort, it was empty, but that offered him little in the way of consolation. It was leaking some of the strangest and nastiest music he had ever heard, and he reacted in the way any keen gardener does when he discovers that dangerous vermin have invaded his patch. He shuddered and stamped and swore and blocked up the hole with the first thing that came to hand, even though he knew it was useless. He had made some mistakes, he now realized. He had become complacent, too busy creating exotic and beautiful things. He ought to have made some of his snakes venomous again, like last time. He should have covered the forest floor with deadly spiders and poisonous plants, as protection against the fairies.

He resented them coming in and making free with the fruits of his creation, but when he had calmed down a bit, he had to admit that he couldn't see what serious harm they could do. They were all too frightened of time to stay around for long. His best bet, he decided, was to ignore the fort and hope the pests would go away.

2

Tír na n'Óg was in a state of total pandemonium when Aengus got back. Aisling was playing a nocturne on the piano, but apart from a pair of old men who were trying to dance a set to it, no one was listening. The Dagda was striding around with a bassoon in one hand and a hazel rod in the other, trying to herd everyone who had instruments into a quiet corner of the rath. A group of ploddy children were dancing on the steepest part of the hill, a game that required a lot of falling over and laughing. Aidan Liddy, his hands over his ears, was crouching in the middle of a crowd of soldiers, all banging drums and blowing whistles.

Aengus Óg had had enough of orchestras and ploddies. Snatching a kitten up under his arm, he sneaked across to where JJ and the others were sitting around with their instruments.

'Let's go down to the quay,' he said. 'Gather up the old crew and get back to the old ways.'

Keeping a close eye on the Dagda, in case they should be spotted and commandeered for some other occupation, the musicians spread out through the crowds and passed on the message to the dancers. Then, their instruments hugged close to their chests, they set off down the road towards the village.

3

The children were ten years old before Jenny and Pup became exasperated by the job. They longed to go home and they were angry that no one had come over from Tír na n'Óg to take a turn. They loved the children as well as fairy parents could, but they felt time dragging at their spirits and they were ready for a respite.

One of them was going to have to go and get some of the other parents, but there was, they both knew, a great danger in that. Visits to Tír na n'Óg were never simple, and even if one of them went right now, and even if they remembered what they were doing when they got there, there was still no telling how much time would pass on this side before they came back. In the best case it might only be a couple of hours. In the worst it might be decades, or even centuries.

They drew straws and Pup drew the long one, which meant he got to go home, and Jenny was left with the short one, which meant she had to stay. And although the seven children were quite good company now and full of conversation, she still felt lonely when Pup was gone.

★ ★ ★

Pup lay on the bank and listened to Aisling's nocturne. There was a lot of other noise going on and it wasn't always easy to hear the piano, but the bits he did hear were beautiful and lulled him into a pleasant daze. He might have gone right off to sleep if the Dagda hadn't come along.

'It isn't working, it isn't working,' he said. 'Make them read the music. Show them how to do it.'

Aisling sighed and stood up. 'It isn't that easy,' she said.

'Of course it is,' said the Dagda. 'If you can do it, anyone can do it!'

Aisling shook her head. 'Thanks very much,' she said.

'And you,' said the Dagda to Pup. 'What are you doing lounging around there?'

'Erm,' said Pup, trying to remember just what he was doing there. 'I'm looking for a mother.'

'Aren't we all?' said the Dagda.

'Or a father,' said Pup. 'To take a turn in minding the children.'

'The children will be fine,' said the Dagda. 'Come along with me now. I've a job for you.'

He was right. The children were fine. They were teenagers now and growing more independent by the day. They were inclined to go off exploring on their own or in pairs, and Jenny allowed them to, providing they all came back at night to whatever rendezvous was agreed. She had resigned herself now to seeing the project through, and had given up on the prospect of getting any help. But there wasn't all that much longer to go, and she had to admit that the children were much more fun now that they were developing minds of their own.

In the evenings they gathered and made camp, and stayed up late into the night. Jenny sang the tunes and taught them to dance, and she carved crude whistles from reeds and taught them how to play. When they were tired of music, they quizzed her about Tír na n'Óg and asked to be filled in on their heritage and their stories. So she told them about the magical land where no one grew old and no one died and no one ever went hungry. And although the children had no experience of old age or death or hunger, they nevertheless developed a longing to see the land where they belonged, and they were as impatient as Jenny was for all the growing up to be over and done with.

4

One day the púca was up in his favourite part of the forest. It was in the foothills, beside a river, overlooking the canopy of the trees below. The place was his nursery, where he brought on young creations and experimented with new ones. On that particular occasion he was trying to perfect a flying cat. It was quite a challenge because he didn't want to use feathers this time, and the problem was that all his early efforts had turned out looking too much like bats. He wanted to find a new method of flight entirely, one that he could extend, over time, to the spotted bears and the wallabies and the lovely multi-coloured snakes and lizards, but it was proving to be a knotty problem.

He looked up from his work. He could hear voices and he swore beneath his breath. He had located the little family of fairy folk a long time ago, but had decided to leave them alone and stay out of their way. He knew about fairies and their need to borrow time, and he knew roughly how much of it they needed to grow up in. True, they had large appetites and tended to spoil as much food as they ate, but then so did a lot of the forest creatures. There was enough for everyone, and as long as human beings didn't get established here, there always would be. The púca had designed things that way himself, after all.

But he didn't want them here, in this precious place where all the young and delicate things were growing up. So, abandoning the batty cat thing, he climbed down to the forest floor and went to investigate.

Jenny smelled his goaty musk before she saw him. And there was another scent in that part of the forest as well, a more pleasant one that she hadn't come across since her own childhood.

'I can smell apples,' she said.

'You can smell what?' said the children. It was early in the morning and they hadn't yet gone their separate ways but were having breakfast together as they strolled along.

'Apples,' said Jenny. 'Look, there it is, see? That's an apple tree.'

The tree was covered in fruit and the children admired their shiny roundness.

'We used to have them in the old world,' Jenny went on, 'but this is the first one I've seen here. Apples are the best kind of fruit. You wait until you try one.'

The children stepped forward to do just that, but in a sudden rush of thundering hooves a huge white goat appeared from the undergrowth and barred their way. The children had never seen a goat before, but they were not afraid of anything, because nothing in the forest had ever threatened them before. But Jenny retreated, and they followed her example – because she had seen goats before, and she knew that this wasn't just any old goat. In fact she was fairly sure that she recognized him, and she wasn't at all surprised when he stood on his hind legs and grew tall like a man. She felt a pang of anxiety and regret. They had a history, these two, and for part of that history the púca had been Jenny's friend and teacher, and she had loved him very much.

But the ending hadn't turned out so well. By her trickery she had helped Mikey get to the beacon and thwarted the púca's scheme. She wondered if he would remember her. He did.

'Surely not,' said the púca. 'Is it Jenny?'

'It is,' said Jenny. 'Long time no see.'

'Long time indeed,' said the púca.

There was an awkward silence, during which Jenny mustered her powers, just in case. Apart from human ghosts, fairies were the only beings in existence that had power over a púca, but using it could be very dangerous, and Jenny hoped she wouldn't have to.

The púca was clearly weighing up the situation as well. To Jenny's relief, he opted for a peaceful approach.

'What lovely children you have. And I'm very happy to see they are almost grown.'

'Me, too,' said Jenny. 'You have no idea. But another year or two should do it.'

'Good, good,' said the púca. 'I'm sure it has been very trying for you, having to immerse yourself in time in this dreadful place.'

'No, no,' said Jenny. 'The place is beautiful, honestly. Fair play to you. A triumph of engineering.'

The púca was flattered. 'Well, make yourself at home until they are finished growing,' he said. 'But there is one thing. This part of the forest is out of bounds. That apple tree is the best one I have, you see? There are a few more in there among the trees but the fruit is ghastly. I don't seem to have the knack of this grafting business. The ploddies were a disaster, on the whole, but they did have their uses.'

'They certainly did,' said Jenny. 'I wouldn't have to be hanging around here like an eejit if there were ploddies around to do the child-rearing thing.'

'Hmm,' said the púca. 'On balance I think the place is better off without them. Anyway, if you lot could keep your nasty little sticky fingers off my apples, I'd appreciate it. Do you think you could manage that this time round?'

'No bother,' said Jenny. 'You hear that, lads? No one is to touch these apples.'

The teenagers nodded solemnly.

'Can I trust you on this, Jenny?' said the púca.

'Absolutely,' said Jenny. 'Why wouldn't you?'

'Because you deceived me once before, that's why.'

'I did,' said Jenny, 'that's true.'

'And look what a mess that caused everyone.'

'Well, I'm sorry about that,' said Jenny. 'But it's given you a chance to make a new start, hasn't it? And a lovely new start it is, too, fair dues to you.' The púca took a bow, and Jenny went on, 'So I promise not to touch your apples and I promise not to bring the children here again. Will that do?'

The púca knew better than to take a fairy at her word, and was trying to read between the lines. 'I suppose so,' he said at last.

'So we'll take ourselves off then, shall we? Get out of your hair?'

'Just so,' said the púca. 'You do that. So nice to see you again.'

5

Another year went by, and then another. Jenny saw less and less of the teenagers now because they didn't need her any more, and went off on their own adventures for days, sometimes weeks at a time. On more than one occasion she had been on the point of returning to Tír na n'Óg and leaving them to follow on when they were ready, but then someone would turn up with a broken finger or a belly-ache and she would realize they still needed her.

But the time did come, at last, when she saw that her work was finally done. She didn't know what exactly had changed, but one day she woke up and understood that the children were children no longer. They were adults, and ready to go home. So she took the ones she could find and returned with them to the rath, and sent them through to Tír na n'Óg to get on with their lives over there. Then she waited for the rest of them to return.

In ones and twos they drifted in, drawn by the fairy instinct that emerges in their young when they reach maturity. As they arrived, Jenny sent them on ahead. Some popped through the time skin as if they'd been doing it all their lives. Others were more cautious, and chose to crawl in the safe way, through the tunnel and the fluid wall. Soon they had all been sent home except for two, a girl and a boy. Jenny was growing more restless by the day now, and was dying to get home herself. She decided to give them just a few more days, and then go on without them.

6

Pup finally tracked down most of the parents at the quay. Some of them were playing and some of them were dancing, but he noticed Aengus sitting on his own at the side of the street, playing with a kitten.

'Hello, Pup,' he said. 'You've grown. Quite the strapping lad, so you are.'

It was true. He had. The wonderful food in the forest had produced a late growth spurt, and Pup had grown taller and filled out as well. But he wasn't in the mood to listen to Aengus's flattery.

'It's your turn to take care of the children,' he said.

'Oh, surely not,' said Aengus. 'I've only just got here.'

'I'm sure you have,' said Pup. 'But the children were ten years old when I left, and who knows how old they are now. It's not fair on Jenny, and—'

'Shh,' said Aengus. 'Can you hear that?'

The music was belting away in the background, but even so, Pup could hear the kitten purring away like a little generator.

'Yes, Aengus. But—'

'How do they do that?' said Aengus.

'I don't know, Aengus. But—'

'I can't make that noise. Can you?'

Pup started again. 'Look. It's your turn to go over and mind the kids. It's—'

'Oh, all right!' Aengus yelled, standing up so fast that the kitten stopped purring and dug its claws into his chest. He pried it off him and thrust it into Pup's arms.

'Mind that till I get back.'

And he was gone.

7

'Oh, brilliant timing,' said Jenny, when Aengus Óg appeared beside the rath. 'Just when all the work is done.'

'Really?' said Aengus, looking pleased. 'Are they all grown up already? No wonder you look so old. You must be nearly as old as me.'

Jenny gritted her teeth and was about to give him a piece of her mind, when a commotion among the trees caught her attention. The púca was striding towards them with the two missing youngsters, and he had one hairy hand around each of their necks.

'Aengus Óg,' he said. 'I might have known you'd turn up. You always do whenever there's trouble.'

'What's going on?' said Aengus.

The púca pushed downwards on the children's necks and they sank to their knees. 'I'll tell you what's going on,' he said. 'These foul offspring of yours have been stealing my apples.'

'Oh no,' said Jenny. 'Really, lads, what did you go and do a stupid thing like that for?'

'It was her fault,' said the boy, pointing at the girl. 'She put the idea into my head.'

'Wait a minute, wait a minute,' said Aengus. 'What's all this about apples?'

The púca's voice roared like a gale in the trees. 'Look what I've made here! There is food on every tree and every bush. There are nuts that taste like toasted cheese and puff-balls that taste like cinnamon buns. But it's so typical of you feckless people. The one thing that's forbidden to you acts like a magnet, doesn't it?'

'It wasn't my fault,' the girl whined. 'I was watching a snake going up the tree, and—'

'All right, all right,' said Aengus. Jenny saw a gleam enter his eye and knew that some kind of trickery was on the way. 'Stop panicking, goat-face. I'll sort it out. I'll punish them for taking your precious apples.'

'Oh really?' said the púca. 'And how do you intend to do that?'

'Well, it's like this,' said Aengus. 'We're badly in need of a few ploddies, you see? Jenny can confirm that, can't you, Jenny?'

'Well ... I just ... hang on a minute,' said Jenny, trying to see where this was leading.

'So that'll be their punishment. Do you hear that, you two? You did wrong to take the púca's apples, so you're not coming home.'

'You can't do that, Aengus!' said Jenny.

'Indeed you cannot!' said the púca furiously.

'I can and I will,' said Aengus. 'And if you touch one hair on their heads I'll be back to sort you out, have no doubt about it. I've got a new trick now. I'll shpigengog you. You won't know what hit you.'

Jenny watched the púca. He was swelling with rage, but she knew he would not challenge Aengus Óg. All the same, her nerves were on edge, and she was ready to jump back through the time skin at the slightest sign of trouble.

Aengus turned to the children, and went on, 'Now, you listen here, you two. If you're really good and have lots of children and grandchildren, then you might – just might – be allowed to come home. But not until you're old, you hear? Not until you reach death's door.'

'But this is outrageous!' said the púca. 'I don't want them here! I've started all over again. I don't want a new generation of human beings!'

'Don't worry so much,' said Aengus. 'You'll give yourself high blood pressure. We only need a few of them to mind our little ones while they grow up.'

'No, Aengus,' said the púca.

'And they're not dangerous,' said Aengus. 'I'm sure they haven't really got going with their magic yet, and in any case they'll soon forget they have it.'

'No, Aengus,' said the púca.

'And listen, you're the boss, all right? You hear that, lads? This white-haired fella gives the orders around here, understand?'

'No, Aengus!' said the púca.

'At least until I come back,' said Aengus. He gave a cheery little wave to the púca, then stepped sideways and vanished.

Jenny hesitated, but not for long. She had been locked out of Tír na n'Óg once before and she never wanted it to happen again. In the blink of an eye she, too, was gone, and the púca was left staring at empty space. He realized he still had a grip on the boy and the girl, and he whipped his hands away from them as if he had been burned.

'Go after them!' he yelled. 'Scoot! Scram!!'

But as the two young people reached the rath and the entrance to their own world, they felt the slightest of subtle jolts beneath their feet. They had never felt it before, but somehow, instinctively, they knew what it meant.

And so it was that a young man and a young woman stood alone, with nothing but fig leaves to cover their nakedness. They were locked out of paradise but they had their instructions. If they did their duty and obeyed the rules, they might be rewarded eventually, and allowed to go through to the land they had heard so much about when they were growing up. The place they had never seen but knew existed. The place where the sun never set, and where they would have eternal life.

Children and grandchildren, they understood that. They had no choice but to do as they had been told, and to start a new race of people in this huge and lonely world.

Creature of the Night
by Kate Thompson

'I'm not staying here. There's nothing to do.
No way to get out of your head.'

When Bobby's mother moves the family to the country,
Bobby's furious. All he wants to do is get back to Dublin
and resume his wild life there.

But that's not as easy as he'd planned.
An unexplained disappearance, whispers about a
murdered child and strange scrabblings at the dog flap
mean it isn't long before Bobby and his whole family
are involved with the eerie creature of the night.

Shortlisted for the Booktrust Teenage Prize.

Definitions: 978 0 370 32929 1